The Discovered

TRACY WINEGAR

OMNIFIC PUBLISHING
LOS ANGELES

Omnific Publishing
1901 Avenue of the Stars, 2nd floor
Los Angeles, CA 90067
www.omnificpublishing.com

First Omnific eBook edition, November 2015
First Omnific trade paperback edition, November 2015

The characters and events in this book are fictitious.
Any similarity to real persons, living or dead,
is coincidental and not intended by the author.

Library of Congress Cataloguing-in-Publication Data

Winegar, Tracy.
    The Discovered / Tracy Winegar – 1st ed.
    ISBN: 978-1-623422-22-6
    1. Civil War — Fiction. 2. Historical Romance — Fiction.
    3. Union Troops — Fiction. 4. Female Soldiers — Fiction. I. Title

10 9 8 7 6 5 4 3 2 1

Cover Design by Micha Stone and Amy Brokaw
Interior Book Design by Coreen Montagna

Printed in the United States of America

For Ben.

Chapter 1

When I looked at the man feverishly taking notes, I could detect the incredulity on his face, and I could understand why. He was probably not accustomed to hearing stories like mine. I myself was sometimes amazed by it. I waited for him to finish writing, and then his eyes met mine with the most concerned of expressions. I knew he was eager to find out what happened next.

"You were discovered?"

I smiled. I had him hooked, and I liked the feeling of it. "Yes. After that, Sam knew I was a woman."

"What did you do?"

"Well, Mr. Franklin, it was difficult to *know* what to do. The answers were not clear to me at the time. When you have woven such a tale and lived by it for so long, it feels as if your world has ended and the bottom has dropped out when someone finds out the truth. Back home in Richfield I knew who I was, I knew I was Serena. I was the daughter of Matthew and Rebecca Stark, the sister of Caleb Stark. I was to be a school teacher. I was to have my life play out in the small town known for its cheeses.

"Perhaps one day I would have married, maybe someone I might have been at least fond of. I don't know if I could have loved him as I love Sampson Barlow, the mill owner's son. But who's to say that I might not have been content—an ordinary life for an ordinary girl."

"An ordinary girl? You were no ordinary girl, ma'am," he argued.

"I felt perfectly ordinary. And should I have chosen to stay in Richfield, I'm sure things would have transpired as they should have.

I would've known nothing more than my small existence, and perhaps it would have suited me."

"Yes, but that didn't happen," he pointed out. "Should have, would have, all conjecture. I'm interested in finding out what really happened, not the guesswork."

"True. It wasn't the path I chose. I took a different route entirely."

"You intend to leave me in suspense?" he asked with a twinkle in his eye. He knew very well I wouldn't. He must have surmised if I'd told him the beginning of my story then surely I would share with him the end. After all, old people are sentimental fools who long to leave something behind, even if it is nothing more than their humble stories.

Once again, I thought about how it was my brother who had determined my future. If he'd lived, then perhaps I would have been home instead of in that cherry orchard the night Sam learned my secret. If I were home, Mrs. Dilly would be getting supper, the fire on the hearth warm and inviting, the evening calm and still there on the farm, as the katydids hummed in the darkness. I would never have known the hardships of army life, or the horrors of battle. And I would never have grown close to Sam or spent the last eight months with him. But then I realized it was something I wouldn't have traded for anything, despite my terrible predicament. Because my time spent with Sam was so precious to me.

If I had never gone to war, if I were with my father and mother over supper, Sam wouldn't have discovered I had deceived him and betrayed him, that was true. I wouldn't be wishing I'd never met him or fallen in love with him. I would've been in Richfield, and I'd have been safe from the dreadful emotions I was feeling. In exchange, I would have also given up the greatest adventure and the most meaningful relationship I'd ever experienced. What a high cost for peace of mind.

I thought it nothing short of a miracle I was not killed in that orchard. I couldn't pretend to understand why, but God preserved my life. Just the right angle, the way the bullet struck me, and the ball from the Reb boy's rifle bounced off of me like a rock skips over the water. It cut through my skin deep and terrible, making a trench big enough for my little finger to fit partially into, while it followed the route of my ribs, breaking a few of them as it ran its course.

Unfortunately I wanted nothing more than to die, and all it did was to cause me a great deal of discomfort. Had it pierced my heart, it would have done less damage. How would I go on humiliated and shamed as I was? If only it wasn't Sam. If only it was some stranger I would never have to face again who found me out. For just under a year I was able to somehow conceal my real identity, to hide the fact I was a girl, Serena Elizabeth Ann Stark of Richfield, New York.

Now the keeper of my secret was the very person I'd struggled so hard to hide it from. Sam. Oh, Sam. He sat there in shock, in disbelief, and I was too frightened and in too much pain to do much more than put my arms across my chest to cover my nakedness. I lay on the ground unable to move. For a time it was quiet. Sam acted as though he was in a trance, and I did not dare disturb him.

With my eyes welling up with tears and unable to keep the emotion from my voice, I finally managed to murmur, "Sam…" The trance was broken. He cleared his throat and shook his head as if to empty it. The forlorn expression changed to determination. Sam pulled himself together and drew himself up.

"We must get you back to camp," he said. Although his voice was a forced calm, there was a definite edge to it. He would not look at me. It was as if he were trying to appear unaffected by the revelation I was a girl, trying to behave as though he didn't know or didn't care. I attempted to move quickly to shut my shirt and hastily button it, but my body rebelled against me and I was forced to laboriously work at such a simple task through my pain.

He helped me up from the ground, but each movement was more excruciating than I thought possible. The pain radiated through me, spreading hot and insistent from my side and outward, taking my breath away. I cried out.

"Oh, oh! It hurts!" I groaned.

"I think you may have broken some ribs," he said.

It was an awkward silence between the two of us. I couldn't begin to imagine what he might be thinking, and I was in such pain and so troubled by what had just transpired I didn't know what to say. I wished he would just leave me behind. I didn't want to face what was to come.

Chapter 2

Getting back to camp was painfully slow progress. Each movement rendered such agony I thought I must be upon the threshold of death. Sam did not speak to me. He walked apart from me. It was suddenly as if we were strangers. The familiarity we'd had between us before was gone.

When we got back to camp, Reed Haney called out a hello to us, his face fully visible next to the fire, although his eyebrows seemed to arch menacingly in the shadows it cast upon him. Sam gave him a little wave without really looking his way.

"Good evening, Reed."

"What have you two been up to?" he asked.

"No good," Sam joked, his chuckle sounding nervous and forced. Was it as obvious to Mr. Haney as it was to me? I certainly hoped not. With such poor theater skills as Sam's, I would be found out for certain. I tried to keep moving, picking up my pace. This only brought on more unbearable pain.

"Is he all right?" Mr. Haney asked, motioning toward me with a nod of his head and looking me over with a suspicious eye. I was doing my best to act as normal as possible, although it hadn't fooled him. "He don't look good."

"No, he's not." I immediately grew alarmed. Was Sam going to tell? But then he said, "Got hold of some cherries that weren't ripe yet and ate a good lot of them before he realized it, so now he's feeling mighty poorly." At least it was something, a plausible excuse with only a moment's notice. I had to give him credit.

"Ya don't say," Mr. Haney replied. "Well, now that will certainly do it."

"I should get him back to his cabin," Sam said.

"Well, good night to you," Mr. Haney told us. "Hope you're on the mend in no time, Frank."

I couldn't manage to reply. My concentration was occupied elsewhere. I spotted our shabby little cabin and trained my eyes upon it. Almost there, and yet it seemed so far away. Why must Mr. Haney keep talking? But to be honest, I was only vaguely aware of his and Sam's conversation. It was difficult to keep my attention focused on anything but my pain and misery. My mind was racing.

"Good night," Sam said, answering for me.

Sam made a beeline, with me close behind. He ducked in and I followed him, moaning at the discomfort of stooping over to get through the door. Such a sense of dread consumed me that I thought for a moment I should run. I didn't want to be there, I didn't want to be anywhere. I wanted to dissolve completely and totally from existence, erase the day of my birth, strike my name from the family Bible, and dissipate like salt in water. None of these things being an option, I stayed quiet and tried to keep from bursting into tears.

"Is it your side?" he asked me. I nodded my head yes. I could feel the sweat wetting my face, making my hands slick and damp, trickling down my back, leaving me chilled and uncomfortable. I wiped my forehead with the sleeve of my coat.

"May I have a look at it?" he asked. It seemed peculiar how polite he became with me, all of a sudden very proper. He was asking permission this time, not fumbling and fighting me as he had before. I hesitated. I didn't feel it was proper at all for him to be examining me. But I really didn't have a choice. I reluctantly nodded again.

"Can you take off your jacket?"

I unbuttoned the brass buttons with some difficulty, and he helped me shrug my arms out of it. I winced and muttered beneath my breath, "Oh, it hurts."

As he pulled the jacket away, the chain on Caleb's watch pulled loose and it tumbled from my pocket. Sam bent to retrieve it, dangling it before my eyes for my inspection. The silver casing was bent and warped, resembling the jam cookies my mother made when I was a child. She always let me press my thumb into the unbaked cookies before she would dollop a bit of raspberry jam into the well my print left in the dough. Like the cookies, it looked as if someone had pressed a thumb into the metal. I shuddered once I realized what I was seeing. The watch in my breast pocket, Caleb's watch, had deflected the bullet. The injuries I sustained came after it collided with metal and ricocheted off. If it hadn't been for the watch, I would surely be dead.

"Saved your life," Sam commented. I took the watch from him and clutched it tightly in my fist, terrified anew by how closely I had come to my demise. I silently thanked God for sparing me.

I looked down at my side to the source of my pain. Where there should have been a growing and expanding stain of blood upon the white of my shirt, there was nothing but a small tear in the fabric and only a trace of red. He knelt down beside me, rolled my shirt up only enough to get a look at it, and pushed my suspenders out of the way. The cherries I'd stowed in my shirt tumbled to the ground.

It looked like someone had hit me, with a purple bruise the size of a man's fist, and directly in the center of the discoloration was a brownish-red mark where the bullet burned my skin. He touched it gingerly with his fingers, inspecting it with a furrowed brow. I reacted by crying out in pain.

"Right there?" he asked, looking up at me.

"Yes," I whispered, avoiding his eyes.

"Well, now, I still think it must be broken ribs," he said. "We'll have to wrap it." He fished around for the bandages we used when his arm was injured after Salem Church. He brought them back.

"Might hurt a little," he warned me. He slipped the suspenders off of my shoulders completely where they now hung slack from my waist, and I held up my shirt for him while he worked on me. His hands brushed against my skin as he held the bandage to my torso and then spun it around my rib cage, binding it good and tight.

"Ouch!" I cried. Sam winced, as though he felt the pain too.

"Sorry, but there's nothing more to be done for it," he said. "It's a miracle you aren't dead." He finished his work and then asked, "Does it feel all right?" I nodded again, even though it didn't. I wasn't about to complain.

"I keep wanting to call you Frank," he said cocking his head to the side and looking at me through narrowed eyes. "But that ain't your name, is it?"

"No," I admitted.

"You are Serena, aren't you?" he said, as if it had just dawned on him. I suppose it wasn't difficult to put it all together once he knew I was a girl. The cousin Frank no one knew about until the day we left Camp Schuyler, the letters to Serena from my father, Serena the sister of his good friend, the nurse he never crossed paths with. Perhaps he may have even had some vague recollection of me from before all of this, some glimmer of recognition that sparked a memory.

It took me by surprise he even knew my name at all. These many months I would have done anything to hear him call me by my given name. For once I wished he would forget who I was altogether. The thought of getting up and running away popped into my head again. If only I could get away from here and just keep going and never stop. I felt the walls closing in. I found it difficult to breathe, to expand my chest and fill my lungs. I began to panic.

"I can't breathe..." I whispered.

"Does it hurt to breathe?"

I nodded. The less I spoke the better.

"Just try to relax," he coaxed. "Perhaps I should fetch a doctor."

That's when the real alarm set in. I shook my head violently.

"No! No! You mustn't!" I begged. "No one else must know. If they should discover me, it will be the end of me!"

"All right," he tried to calm me. "All right."

"Please, Sam, you must promise me," I pleaded. "You mustn't tell anyone."

Chapter 3

I swallowed hard, watching him with wide eyes. If he knew, then he had a duty to report me. It was as simple as that. But I dared to hope it was not his intention to tell on me.

"It's you isn't it?" he asked. "Isn't it, Serena?"

"I suppose you are very cross with me," I managed to say.

"I am surprised," he replied. "I'm not sure what I think."

"Sam, you must not tell anyone," I began again.

"You shouldn't be here." He said it with a calm conviction that made me feel sick. All of the blood drained from my face, and I thought I might faint for a moment. If he felt that way about it, then I might not be able to talk him out of telling on me.

"But I am here. And if you tell anyone about me…Well, I should forever after live in disgrace. I would be sent home dishonored and everyone will know. That isn't something a girl could ever hope to live down. Do you see?"

"What have you done?" He was not only sober but seemed sad too. It made me feel terrible, knowing I was the cause of his problems. All this time I talked myself into believing I was doing him a service, I was making his life easier, and I had carried on as a boy *for him*. I suddenly realized I didn't do it for him at all. I did it for me, for myself. My motivation was completely selfish. I put him in a compromising position on account of what I'd done because I cared about me, about what I wanted.

"I'm sorry. I didn't mean for this to happen. I certainly didn't mean to put our friendship at risk. But you must swear to me you'll tell no one."

"I can't make such a promise."

What would I do? What would I do if he told on me? But he couldn't. He wouldn't. I would never have any kind of a life if he decided to report me. The future played out in my brain, and I could see no matter what was to become of me, it would not end well. It would be a tragedy, nothing less—forever after leaving a trail of gossips with their tongues wagging in my wake. I was positive I would never find a decent gentleman who would take me for a wife. What's worse is that my father and mother would pay for it too. They would not escape the repercussions of my poor decision.

"If you have any sort of loyalty to me as a friend at all, you will at least think it over before you do something rash," I said, my voice shaking with emotion. "If you cannot promise me you won't tell, then promise me you won't do it right away. That you'll think of the consequences before you do anything."

"How did you do it?" he asked, changing the topic of discussion completely. And he still didn't promise me anything.

"What do you mean?"

"All this time. I look back, and well, I noticed peculiar things, but I thought it was on account of your youth and your inexperience in the world, and because you had no father." I gave him a look I was sure was filled with chagrin. "The way you put on stockings..."

"I remember. I tried to do it differently when you pointed it out to me the day we waited to be taken to Fort Lincoln," I admitted.

"How you didn't need a shave," he went on. "And how private you were. I wonder how I didn't see it before now. How I allowed myself to be tricked. I was a fool."

"It was very difficult for me to keep it from you," I said.

"All this time we've shared the same tent." I could see his expression grow troubled, as if it had dawned on him what implications it might have for others. "It was so wrong."

"You didn't know," I consoled him.

His face changed. While we were talking it was a look of confusion, or trying to make sense of it, but then he suddenly became appalled. "No, but you...you did."

Those simple words brought on a whole new torture for me. I knowingly slept in the same tent with him for these many months, and he was angry I tricked him so grievously. I couldn't say I blamed him. If the shoe were on the other foot, I might have plenty to be mad about too. He felt used. He felt betrayed, which was all my doing.

Sam got up to leave. "Where are you going?" I asked desperately.

"I can't stay here," he said.

"Sam, you won't tell on me will you?" I begged.

He stopped and gazed at me. My only thought for my own self-interests made him angry, I suppose. "No. I'm not going to tell on you. But I can't say I won't sometime in the future. I must think this out." And then he left me alone.

My side ached, but I scarcely noticed it. My mind was in such turmoil I could do nothing but go over the events of the night again and again in my head. I shouldn't have gone to that cherry orchard. I should never have let him open my jacket and shirt. I should've just run away when I'd thought of it several months ago. It was as if I could somehow turn back the clock and change the events if I only concentrated hard enough.

I was in misery. I lay down upon my straw pallet and waited for sleep to come. But sleep eluded me. In the darkness, my eyes were wide open and my mind would not stop working furiously to come to a solution for my problems. I would tell myself to not dwell on it, to banish it from my head, but it was an impossible task. I would have given anything if the sun would decide to come up several hours early, and give me an excuse to get up. I have come to believe there is nothing worse than knowing exhaustion when sleep will not come, and enduring the long night wondering if you will ever see the day again. Because on such nights it seems the darkness might continue on forever.

Chapter 4

I don't know what I expected, but I suppose I was hoping for the best. Over coffee and hardtack the next morning, with a group of us sitting before our tents, Sam was decidedly absent. I dipped my hardtack into my cup, waited for the worms to begin floating, and fished them out, tossing them into the fire before I drank. There was little dialogue between us all. With Big Frank gone, conversation was more subdued. He was always the one to make funny comments to get the crowd laughing. Without him it hardly seemed right to be cheerful at all.

My sober mood got me a few sideways glances. Or perhaps it was because Sam and I were not together. After all, we were a team up to now, inevitably in one another's company. Seeing one without the other must have been an oddity. I didn't see Sam again until drill time. He avoided me then too, choosing to stand next to Vern Stapleton whom I knew he didn't care for, instead of me.

I tried to catch his attention, to speak to him when we were finished with drill, but he took off quickly, avoiding me all together. After his constant presence in my life since the beginning of our undertaking together, it was discouraging to be left alone. I felt abandoned and a gloom hung over me. He was everything to me, and I was nothing to him. Unrequited love is not nearly as romantic as they would have you believe in novels and plays. They could never adequately portray how painful it is to be rejected by the object of your affections. It is contemptible to think of the writer dipping quill in ink to then put it to paper in order to write otherwise.

I lingered in our little cabin, hoping he might turn up eventually and then I would be able to speak to him. But he never came. The day wore on, and I saw him here and there, but Sam didn't acknowledge me in any way. I can't say he was malicious about it. He just behaved as if I weren't there. Only it was abundantly clear to me, and everyone else who knew us, he was giving me the cold shoulder. If it wasn't obvious before, it certainly was now. He was doing all he could to stay away from me.

Several miserably long weeks wore on in the same manner. I felt the rejection sorely. It made time slow and nights drag on. I wondered where he was and what he was up to. I ruefully thought he was probably out having a good time with some of his other pals. Or maybe he was spreading the word, telling everyone about his cracked tent mate and what a laughingstock she was. If he told anyone about me, it was sure to spread like wildfire. I waited for Captain or Colonel to come collect me.

I was on edge, paranoid over every innocent remark, each insignificant exchange with the other men. But day after day, nothing happened. It got to the point I welcomed something, anything to happen. Then I would at least know where I stood. Why not just get it over with instead of suffering on in the same uncertainty?

"What's this about?" Reed Haney asked me after drill one afternoon. I knew he was referring to Sam and me, wondering why we weren't talking anymore.

"Just a falling out," I replied. I didn't know what more to say without giving myself away. He didn't fish any deeper. He let it go, and I was glad.

Sam didn't even return to our hut to sleep. I lay awake, listening, waiting night after night, but in vain. After loafing around for several agonizing weeks, I grew defiant. I came to the conclusion I should just face the situation head on. Instead of waiting for the axe to fall on me, I would take action first. If he wouldn't come to me then I would go to him. I must know where I stood with him. I couldn't bear the thought he might be so displeased with me that he wouldn't ever speak to me again. The unknown would drive me crazy. I couldn't leave things as they were for another second.

It was good and dark and all were asleep when I crept out of our little cabin in search of him. I wandered around camp without any idea where I might find him. The dying glow from the supper fires lit my way. There were plenty of vacant huts after the terrible fight in Fredericksburg. Perhaps he was holed up in one of them. I roamed aimlessly from hut to hut with no real plan, trying to surmise where he might be. But then it came to me. There was a spot he liked very much near the river, under a great oak, a place he liked to idle his time after drill or in the evening after supper.

I allowed my feet to guide me there, my boots quiet on the packed earth of the trail leading down to the river. As I drew near, sure enough I could make out Sam's profile in the gloom of the night, just hardly visible, sitting below the tree. He stirred when he heard me approach, grabbing for his pistol; he was guarded until he saw it was me. He eased the pistol back to the ground next to him and stood to meet me.

"What do you want?" he grumbled.

"I wanted to talk," I said softly, entreatingly.

"There's nothing to say."

"I can't leave it this way," I said, the desperation in my voice sounding pitiable. Couldn't he see I was remorseful, and feeling terrible over what happened between the two of us? That I was suffering?

"I don't know what you're talking about," he said, apparently not willing to discuss things.

"Sam, I am sorry. I am."

"I doubt that very much," he said.

"You must understand. I can't go back and change what I've done now, but if I could I would. I never intended to lie to you."

"Why, the things I told you. Thinking all the while you were some boy I was befriending," he declared. Again I felt a rush of guilt. "Some poor youngster with no father and mother in this world to look out for him. And you fooled me good. You made a right pretty dolt of me."

"Dim-witted as it sounds, I never thought of it that way."

"How did you think of it?" he asked.

How could I explain it to him? How could I tell him the reason I did what I did? It was as much of a secret as my identity had been. No one knew, no one but me, that I was in love with Sam Barlow. It was something I couldn't put into words and utter out loud. I remained still, hoping he would let his question go unanswered.

"Why did you do it?" he wanted to know. He wouldn't look at me when he asked it. Right away I thought *because I love you*. But I continued to not say anything.

"I'm talking to you," he said. His voice commanded attention, and now his eyes seemed to pierce through me. "I want to know why you did such a lunatic thing!"

"I…I don't want to talk about it," I stammered.

"Well, now you will. You came looking for me, remember? And I want to know why you done it."

"I don't know. I don't want to talk about it," I insisted.

"You can either tell me why, or I will report you and you can tell Colonel Upton why," he threatened. There was such loathing in his words, such hatred. I had never seen him like this. He was so angry. Usually he just laughed things off, made a joke to lighten the mood in a tough situation. But the disgust he was exhibiting now let me know he was serious with his threat.

"You wouldn't!" I cried. "You wouldn't report me!"

"Hell I wouldn't. You either talk to me now or you can talk to them."

"Sam, please leave me alone!" My mind was racing. Would he really report me? Would he really run and tell? He was mad enough and hurt enough that just maybe he would. I tried to walk away, seeing this was a bad idea. I should've just left him alone. He grabbed my elbow and swung me around to face him.

"I won't. You humiliated me, and I want you to tell me why," he insisted. His eyes were upon me, and they were filled with rage. He was glaring, resentful. I realized how betrayed he must have felt when he found out I'd deceived him from the very beginning. I couldn't really blame him. If it was me, if I were in his shoes, I might very well feel the same.

"You wouldn't understand," I snapped. "You could *never* understand."

"Whether I understand or not, I will know it. You tell me now, right now, or I will go immediately and speak with Colonel Upton. I'll wake him up if I must. Bust into his tent and tell him what I've discovered. But I will not continue on in this lie unless you at least give me the reason why you would do such a thing."

"No!"

"Tell me!" he persisted.

I remained silent. This seemed to infuriate him all the more. His lips formed into a menacing sneer, and he turned as if he might go, as if he might leave right now to tell on me. I pulled at the sleeve of his jacket, trying to stop him but he shook me off.

"Sam, please!" I begged, the panic making my voice quake.

"I am done with this," he said firmly.

"Sam, you can't!" I was jogging alongside of him, doing my best to dodge in front of him to get him to stop.

"Get out of my way!" he barked at me.

"Sam! I am *begging* you, please, you can't turn me in! It will ruin me. It will completely ruin my reputation. And my father…" I couldn't stand the thought of having to face him, of having him find out I'd lied to him for so long. What would he say? I was sure I didn't know, but I did know it would disgrace him. After Caleb's death, after my mother, and now this…I had no doubt it would hurt him deeply. He could not know. He could never know what I had done. I wouldn't allow it.

"Maybe you should have considered it before you done what you done," he said rather heartlessly. I'd never seen Sam like this. Not even when Big Frank got drunk and they fought. He forgave Big Frank right off and didn't hold it against him. Why was I any different? Weren't we friends? Hadn't we gotten through some hard times together? Wasn't that worth something?

I started to become hysterical. "You can't!" I wailed. "You can't!"

When he saw me in such distress, he hesitated for a moment. I imagine the gentleman in him felt responsible for my misery. But he would still not let up.

"You tell me why you did this. You tell me now."

"Because…" I began.

"Because why?" He saw me stalling, and then he grew impatient and acted as if he might leave again.

I stood in front of him and put my hands on his chest, pushing against him with the weight of my body, leaning into him to keep him from going. It caused a searing pain to run through my side where I was not healed yet. It was all I could do to maintain my stance, but I was not about to let him go anywhere. I was not going to step aside and allow him to go to the colonel and tell on me.

"I cannot say," I whispered.

"Why?" he pressed.

"I cannot say!" I cried out. He pushed my hands away.

"I've had enough." He meant it too. I could see. He really meant to go and tell on me. Nothing I was saying was holding him back or convincing him otherwise. He was so angry with me he was ready and willing to go right now, in the middle of the night, and report me. He didn't care what it would do to me. When I saw this I was fraught with nerves. Nothing I said was making a bit of difference to him.

"It was because of you, Sam!" I blurted out, the tears beginning to distort my vision. Once the words were out, there was no taking them back. I think it stunned us both equally. My revelation froze him where he was.

"What?" His face fell, and a look of pure confusion and surprise came over him.

"I came to follow you," I confessed with a groan. I didn't have the nerve to meet his eyes, nor did I think I could hold the tears back any longer if I did chance to look at him. I was so filled with humiliation I dared not let him see me any worse off than I already was.

"But I wish I never had now! I hate you!" I fumed. "I hate you!" I was so horrified by my admission I left him there and ran away.

Chapter 5

I t was my turn to avoid him now. It was my feeling that as angry as I was at Sam, it was not his fault I lied and misrepresented myself. I thought he shouldn't have to suffer for it any more. I was also very ashamed of my confession to him. How could he have made me disclose something so personal, so embarrassing? So wherever he was, I was not. If we should chance to find ourselves at the same fire, or with the same company, I averted my eyes from his, found a suitable reason to beg off, and disappeared.

With our numbers so depleted there were few who I called friend, fewer still whom I gravitated toward. Our company was so small it took a great effort on my part to stay away from him. Now with such a diminished regiment, Colonel Upton saw to it new men were brought in to the 121st. It seemed they cared very little for propriety or dignity when they went about recruiting the new men. But I didn't know the circumstances surrounding the replacements, only that they seemed to resent their new station very much.

They came as already seasoned soldiers from the 16th New York, with their haversacks and bedrolls and tents clearly worn and well used. They looked around, studying the camp and scouting out a place not already taken. There were plenty of empty cabins to choose from. So the men found one suited to them and took up living there. Most of them kept to themselves over supper and didn't seem to feel a need to be sociable or form new friendships. I knew how they must feel, outsiders uncertain of where they might belong in this new place. We'd all experienced similar feelings before. With only four of us left to the squad they filled the empty spaces with six new men from the 16th. Mr. Haney, whom I had grown to rely upon heavily with no one else to call friend now, and I were conversing over supper when two of them made an attempt at approaching us.

"Could we share your fire?" the one with blond hair asked. I can't say he was the dashing sort, but his looks were fine still. His face had a character, a quality to it that made him attractive, even if he was no dandy.

"Of course you may. I am Reed Haney, and this young fellow is called Frank Stark," he said. They took a seat with us, stretching out next to the fire.

"Felix Newburn," the blond said, but he didn't smile.

"Rowan Darby," the short dark one said. "But everyone calls me Darby."

"What a pleasant way you talk," I said. It sounded almost like he would break out in singing. "Where are you from?"

"I was born across the sea in Ireland," he told me with an amused grin. "But I call Ogdensburg, New York, home."

"We come from New York as well," Mr. Haney told them. "Richfield, New York."

"Would you like some coffee," I asked, trying to be amicable.

"I make it a habit never to say no to coffee," Felix Newburn said. I poured them each a cup full and handed it to them.

"You're a wee young thing to be fighting for ol' Uncle Sam, ain't ya now, boy?" Darby asked with what I took to be a good natured grin upon his face.

I shrugged. It seemed like I'd already gone through this same conversation more times than I cared to remember. What good did it do to explain it again? Thank heavens for Mr. Haney.

"He's proved himself a man in the worst of a brawl," he said with a chuckle.

"That so? You seen a bit of fightin' then?" Darby asked. It was something a soldier did, swapping stories over what battles they'd seen. There was an acute interest to hear where others had been, to share where you had been too.

"Lost over two hundred up near Fredericksburg in May. Nearly nothing left to us," Mr. Haney said, his tone growing somber. "We were part of Chancellorsville. Salem Church, you know."

"Old Lee refused to be outflanked," Darby said with a nod. He already knew our story. No need to fill him in.

"Well, it explains why they brung us in," Felix said to Darby. I could see by his expression he was neither pleased nor surprised by this bit of information.

"What do you mean?" I wanted to know.

"We've seen a bit of fighting ourselves. Been in it since the beginning," Darby explained. "So we do our time, and when it's time for re-enlistment, well…it don't go like it should. Lest you think us poor sports, I'll explain it to you." Darby was a nice enough man. Although somewhat of a spoilsport, I grew to like him. He certainly didn't mince words. No sir. He chewed at his mustache, which I learned was a particular habit of his, as he told us of their trials.

"The big men up top, they tell us we may choose where we go, you see. Do nothin' more than tell 'em and it be done on account of our brave service to this great country. And we can choose artillery battery from Massachusetts, we can choose a regular army battery, or now we can choose this here outfit, the 121st. So we put our bids in you see, only to find it don't matter one way or the other, we all get put with the 121st. All of us."

"You don't say?" Mr. Haney said, seeming genuinely sorry for their trouble.

"How can they do that?" I asked. It made no sense to me. Why give them a choice if they really didn't have one to begin with?

"They can do whatever they like." Felix laughed, a brittle, humorless sort of laugh. But it was clear he didn't find it amusing. "They are the government. They make the rules. And we poor saps must abide by them."

I simply couldn't believe it. They were done wrong; there was no way around it. After serving their country with honor for nearly three years now, they'd been cruelly betrayed. I realized I was nothing more than a naïve child. Every time I grew to think I understood the ways of the world, I was shocked anew by some weightier and more distressing truth.

"Someone must have a sympathetic ear in Washington for us to be here," Darby said, finishing off his coffee. "But Felix and me, we'll make the best of it. Only some didn't take it as well."

Felix tossed what was left of his coffee into the bushes. "Yes, we will make the best of it," he agreed.

The following day we discovered for ourselves just what Darby meant. Tempers flared and a dozen or more men from the 16th stood idle during drill in outright rebellion for having been forced into the 121st. They refused to comply with orders. Captain Kidder was furious with their dissension. His face colored up and his nostrils flared like a bad-tempered horse. I'd only seen him in such a state a few times and knew to be on guard for what was to follow.

"Mutinous dogs!" he screamed in their faces. "You've just earned yourselves picket duty!"

One of them yelled out, "I won't do it!" He was a mean looking cuss. Looking him in the eyes gave me a jolt. Then a few others joined in with him. "I won't neither!"

The man who began the protest, a man with a wild set of whiskers and some bad teeth from chewing tobacco, hollered, "We are expected to fight for the freedom of them darkies, while our freedoms are being trampled asunder! We won't have it!"

Captain Kidder was madder than a wet hen. His eyes fairly bulged out of his head, making him appear even more menacing if it was possible. He smiled in a malicious way.

"Oh, but you will!" he said. Then he called out names. "Privates Jepson, Barlow, Stapleton, and Hardy, Vanderbilt, Stark, and Walters step forward." We did as we were told, each of us eyeing the other in uncomfortable ignorance of what was to come next. We had no idea what Captain Kidder called us forward for.

"Your task will be to escort these soldiers to their posts this evening. If any man is derelict in his duties you will shoot him on the spot. No questions asked." He then turned to the men who caused the stir in the first place and gave them a scorching glance as he continued to address us. "We do not put up with deserters, and likewise, do not tolerate treasonous acts. Is that understood?"

We all at once said, "Yes, sir," with the utmost zeal. None of us was about to cross him, because there was something completely terrifying about his manner. Then he turned his attention back to the men who refused to do their duties.

"I don't know how you did it in the 16th, boys, but here in the 121st we have rules, and as with all rules, there are consequences for insubordination." He stalked off, throwing "Dismissed!" over his shoulder as he left.

If nothing else, they succeeded in putting the Captain in a very bad mood. The eight of us who were chosen were very reluctant to do as we were commanded, but we had little choice in the matter. It was a command, and none of us wanted to be punished like the others were now being punished.

When evening came, with our rifles at the ready, we escorted them, as instructed, to picket duty. There were two of them to every one of us. They most likely could have overpowered us if they wanted to. I was downright nervous with the strain of watching over my assigned two. It didn't help I somehow got the wild whiskered fellow under my charge. His chops were long and bushy, wiry and wavy, which gave him a fearsome and untamed appearance. I remembered with a sinking feeling it was he who started the whole rebellion among the newcomers during drills.

I tried to appear strong, with my rifle held defensively up in front of me, but he was a good head taller than I was, and I would guess he was enjoying the thought of toying with me. He waited until I was slightly more comfortable with my duty and then he sprang at me with a low and rough growl. I was so taken off guard and startled I jumped a mile. This brought on fits of laughter from him and many of the others. I glared, narrowing my eyes and frowning. He made a goose of me in front of everyone.

"Don't worry, little boy, I don't bite," he said, laughing again.

"Hey, you let him alone," Sam said gruffly. He seemed genuinely angry over my mistreatment, which surprised me. I would have thought it would make him glad, bring him satisfaction, and he would have been laughing with the others.

"You think you can take on a man like me?" he taunted, ignoring Sam completely and only concentrating on me. "You think you can shoot me 'fore I get a hold of you and snap that skinny little neck of yours? 'Cause I'd be willing to take bets on it."

I felt my throat ache from the thought of it. I didn't want to mess with him, but I knew I would lose my standing among the others if I didn't stand up to his challenge.

"I'm not so much afraid of your bite, Mister. You may resemble a dog, even bark like one too, but from the looks of those rotted teeth, your bark is worse than your bite. Pretty sure you'd accomplish nothing more than tickling me good with those pretty whiskers of yours. More likely to be your stench to kill me first," I blurted.

This got a good round of laughs from everyone too, even some of his friends from the 16th. But he didn't seem to appreciate my joke. He moved as if he might attack me, but Sam, his rifle ready, pushed the metal barrel to his whiskered cheek none too gently.

"You make everyone wonder as to whether you got a sense of humor," he said. "Now just you be a good sport and laugh it off."

"Oh, now, Sam, you gone and spoiled his fun," I taunted. "Let him go and just see how far he gets before I expire from his fumes. Put the rifle aside and let's have a good show out of it."

Old Whiskers didn't seem to care Sam's rifle was on him, he defiantly spat on my boots. I did what I could to hold myself steady, to not react. It took all of the will power I possessed to stand still and not turn and run. I could feel every muscle straining, every nerve tense.

"Looks like you made yourself a friend, Frank," Sam said. "He wants to polish your boots for you."

"Thanks just the same," I replied, "but I can take care to polish my own boots. Now what say you to cutting out this tomfoolery and getting back to the business at hand?"

Tensions were high, and having nothing else to do but escalate it, he decided to save face, turned back around, and minded his manners for the rest of picket duty. We broke up and spread out along the line, and I was left alone with the two men I was guardian over. They behaved, although I couldn't help but notice murder in Old Whisker's eyes every time he chanced a glance at me. I just smiled sweetly until he looked away. *I'll call your bluff*, I thought. *I won't back down from a bully.*

Already I had a strong and abiding hatred for him. And although I didn't know him at all, I was sure among all the enemy, in all the South, there was not a more despicable character than that man. I realized too I would have need to watch my back with him from here on out. I knew for certain I couldn't trust the lowlife. The second my guard was down, I had no doubt he would strike.

Chapter 6

What were we waiting for during all of this time at winter camp in Falmouth? It seemed the General was waiting for Lee to make a move. We stayed camped across from the enemy, the river being the only thing keeping us separate. And as we watched them, they watched us, an uneasy anticipation mounting between the two. We knew the informal truce could not last forever.

I heard one of the men say in passing, "It's getting about time for a Bull Run fight."

I was not there to experience Bull Run. But I knew enough of it to know it was a terrible scene. After having just been through Salem Church I felt great apprehension at the thought I would have to endure another battle. Every idle moment I tried to fill with chores or diversions just to spare myself the anxiety of dwelling on what was coming.

I was grateful to Mr. Haney for lending me a novel called *A Dark Night's Work*. Reading took my mind off of my worries. I enjoyed the premise of it very much, although it made me sad the main character, Ellinor, had to settle for anyone but her true love. I wrote to my father more frequently, describing life in camp, embellishing when needed, so he wouldn't worry over me. I foraged for food, which was an easier task now the weather was warmer.

Indeed, as cold and miserable as the winter was, it was now just as hot and dreadfully uncomfortable. Our sense of time became muddled in our minds. We received our news from papers days and weeks old. From this somewhat unsteady form of information we gathered that down south, Vicksburg was soon to fall. And each day we awaited confirmation of it.

On a hot June day, in the beginning of the month, we were baffled by what transpired next. We received orders to accompany Sedgwick and the 6th Corps across the river back to Fredericksburg. In quick order we packed up and abandoned our winter camp, following wherever we were led.

"What does this mean?" some of the men murmured. No one had a clear understanding of what was happening. Were we to join forces with another body of soldiers? Were we to engage in a similar offense to the one that left us broken and battered at Salem Church, acting as a decoy again?

Whatever the case, it was not for us to know, only for us to follow. Union artillery set up north of the river, making a way for us to cross undercover in the pontoons. If nothing else, we were certainly getting wear out of those pontoons of ours. There was some gunfire exchanged, but not anything to be alarmed over, just the usual skirmishing that often accompanied movement of any kind. The enemy pickets wanted us to know they were aware of us, and we wanted them to know we would put up a fight if need be. We made it safe to the other shore.

We watched as the last of the procession crossed over after us. The cannons, artillery guns, and wagons rumbled over the pontoons in a slow and winding column. I can't say for sure how it happened, perhaps the horses were spooked by something, but one of the wagons lurched forward and sideways just as it reached the bank. The wheels were at a side angle on the steep incline and the horses neighing and straining against the reins positioned in such a way that the whole thing tipped over, dashing the wagon cover and hoop to bits and breaking the axle as contents spilled out across the grass.

The driver attempted to jump clear, rolling along the ground and away from his rig. Just as I became aware of whom it was, a large group of soldiers surged forward and descended upon the wagon in a wave. Grabbing what they could get their hands on and then running away just as quickly as they had come they stripped the wagon clean. The driver of the wagon, Mr. Davies the hated sutler, was now standing and watching helplessly. He was yelling and screaming and carrying on, jumping up and down in an extreme and agitated state. He took his hat from his head and began waving it as if he were trying to shoo away flies.

Before long there was nothing left in his wagon. The soldiers took it all and retreated back to the line, shoving their loot into their pockets and haversacks with broad grins. Mr. Davies was left to the side of the river with only his busted up rig and the horses still chomping at their bits and prancing about in an obviously nervous state. Mr. Davies looked as though he were in shock and then he picked up a stick and began whipping the horses as though he held them accountable for what happened. I couldn't make out what he was saying but I could imagine he was cussing up a storm.

"Looks like the sutler got his," Darby said as he spit on the ground.

"Bad deeds and dishonest dealings have a way of catching up to a man," Mr. Haney added.

I thought of how mean and low down he was, and I thought maybe he deserved it until Mr. Haney said that. Then I thought I was no better than Mr. Davies. I was dishonest. I was a liar. Who was I to judge the sutler? I suddenly felt sick and couldn't stand to watch any longer, turning away from the scene in disgust.

The next several days we spent hard at work, digging and refortifying the rifle pits used in our earlier campaign against Fredericksburg. This was the place we stayed at Franklin's Crossing before the battle nearly two months ago. It was backbreaking work, leaving you thirsty and tired and ready for sleep at night. I welcomed this effort, because it took my mind off of things and helped me with my sleeplessness. Each time I put my shovel in and dumped the dirt to the side, my ribs would ache but I continued on.

Now we saw the Rebels and they saw us. We set up a short distance away and lingered by a mounted one-hundred-pound gun artillery set up to try to scare them off of causing trouble. Really it was no use to us. The gun would best serve for a siege, not field combat. I don't suppose the Rebs much liked the threat we posed. On an afternoon with nothing to fill our time and the idleness prompting us to behave childishly, the Rebel battery opposite us took aim (although not too carefully) and in sailed a cannon ball the size of a melon, bounced and then rolled a short distance from where we were sitting. It gave us a start, breaking the monotony of what was an otherwise uneventful day.

Vern got up and walked over to where it came to rest. He inspected it with his hands on his hips, as though he was quite put out by the nerve of them sending it our way.

"Damn Graybacks," he muttered, bending over to pick up the ball. His air was drawn in with a hiss as he promptly dropped it. "Hot!" He blew on his fingertips.

"We gonna let 'em get away with that?" Darby questioned. "Let's fire back, let 'em know we ain't afraid of the likes of them."

"We don't have anyone telling us to return it," Sam said. "Besides, they were just messing around, otherwise they would've blown us to pieces."

Felix walked over to the gun which was mounted on a wooden carriage, its cavernous mouth pointed at nothing in particular. He ran his hand along the cool metal. It was a big gun, the cylinder nearly twelve feet long and weighing ten thousand pounds. Those types of guns, as large and cumbersome as they were, were not as easy to move and maneuver as the smaller parrott guns we lugged around. It was an impressive size to say the least.

"I always wanted to see what it was like to fire one of these," he commented.

One of the new men, belonging to the pair of Carroll brothers, joined him with an eager grin. "Let's try her out and see what she'll do," he prodded.

"If you never fired one, it'd probably be best if you didn't try it now," I cautioned.

"What could it hurt?" Felix asked.

"Just one round, that's all," the Carroll brother begged, as if he were a small child pleading for candy.

I saw they weren't going to listen to me. I shrugged my shoulders and moved away from them, not wanting to be associated with their foolishness. I knew we weren't trained to fire that gun—it was artillery's duty—and I did not want to get in trouble for it. Yet I watched with interest to see what would happen.

"How does it work?" the Carroll brother asked.

At this point Old Whiskers joined up with them, acting very put out by it all and quite the authority on hundred pounders. "Bunch of pansies," he complained. "You take this here gun powder and put it in the barrel, tamp it down nice and tight. You load that there ball into it and let it go."

"How much you think?" The Carroll brother was hefting a bag of gun powder and weighing it in his arms.

"Ten pound ought to do it," Old Whiskers replied.

The Carroll brother emptied most of the bag down the barrel and took the large tamping rod from the ground, discovering it was not an easy thing for one man to lift.

"Come over here and give me a hand, Leonard," he called to his brother. Leonard grumbled as he got up from the ground and came over to help with the tamper stick. The younger brother gingerly ran it down the length of the cylinder with the help of Leonard. I'm not sure if he thought it would explode in his face or if he was just nervous about the whole process in general, but he took a great deal of care with it, which spurred on Jack Monroe's disapproval.

"You ain't making cake here, boy. Give it a good pounding."

"All right," Carroll brother (who must have been Alden if Leonard was his other half) said defensively. He gave it a couple of good thrusts and then stepped back.

"Now load the ball," Old Whiskers advised impatiently.

Felix and Alden picked the ball from a short row of them in the grass, struggled to lift it, and then sent it down the barrel. The heavy ball could be heard descending clumsily down the metal chamber and then came to rest with a thud at the bottom of the tube. I think we half expected it to blow up, our anticipation evident as we all kept our eyes glued to the gun, ready to run if need be, but it didn't blow up. It came to an anticlimactic rest and then all was quiet for a moment. The rest of us watched from a safe distance.

"Now let 'er go," Old Whiskers said with a laugh. Felix and Carroll's brother (Alden) gave a nervous chuckle too. They came back around to the tail end of the gun pausing for a moment, as though they were thinking twice about it. But it was too late. They knew, like I did, they would have to carry through with it to save face in front of the rest of us.

"You can go on and do it," the Carroll brother offered.

"I don't mean to take away your fun. If you want to do it that's all right with me," Felix Newburn said.

"No, no. You go on ahead."

Felix took the heavy lanyard which was attached to the friction primer in both hands, standing as far back and to the side of it as the rope would allow. Everyone else got clear back, huddled in a half moon shape near the trees, and waited. Felix gave the thick rope a strong tug to fire it.

The effects were nearly immediate. The sound was deafening, which made us all start and cover our ears as the ground shook thunderously beneath our feet. The ten thousand pound metal tube kicked back, the wooden undercarriage on wheels lurched forward, and to the dismay of us all, the gun ended up pointed toward the sky with its bottom end in the dirt. The cannon ball shot forward a good distance, directly into the fortifications the Rebels had set up. Luckily there were no Confederates in the vicinity, for it ripped the line to pieces.

We all remained dazed as we stared wide-eyed at the results. Felix looked as if he might wet himself, he was so distraught. How would he explain what just happened to his superiors?

"Standing right up on end!" the other Carroll brother Leonard remarked with a whistle. "That ain't gonna be easy to put right."

"Let's get out of here," Darby yelled. He took off toward the woods, and the rest of us were not far behind.

There was some talk in camp about how the heavy gun ended up off of its carriage. We remained silent on the matter, unable to meet eyes and unwilling to murmur a word on the subject. But justice was yet served. Captain Kidder addressed the 121st in a very candid manner. He was not happy and he let us know it, letting loose a string of foul words and name calling that could have curled our hair. Our company and a few others were chosen to put the gun back on its carriage. We were forced to work through the night in the rain like a bunch of mules pulling the gun back into place with heavy ropes.

We stayed there for over a week, still with no idea why. Then we got word there was fighting up at Brandy Station. Oh, the cogs began to turn and the inner workings began to come alive. Lee was on the move. The fox had outsmarted us. He left some of his men behind, just enough to make us believe he was staying put. But all the while he was taking most everybody else in his army on a trip up north, headed for Washington. If he should make his target, the results would prove disastrous for the Union. If he should attack Washington, all would be lost!

Chapter 7

General Hooker would be hard pressed to catch up to Lee and somehow make a barrier between the Confederates and the capital. There was clamor and chaos as we crossed over the river again, urgent in our mission to get to the Confederate forces before they got to Washington. Because we were across the river, we were some of the last to leave camp and ended up at the tail end of the great procession.

Our departure was heralded by the boom of thunder and the flash of lightning as the heavens opened and poured out upon us a strong and steady rain. The downpour made uniforms, bedrolls, and equipment heavy with water. We were traveling upon corduroy roads, slick with mud and rain, and finding it difficult to keep our footing as we marched. I had spoken very little to Sam, as he continued to sleep out beneath the oak tree while we were in camp and kept his distance when we were camped across the river too. I remained resolute in avoiding him when possible, yet we somehow managed to get thrown together in our march.

I would never have believed being around him could be difficult, because before our falling out we were the best of friends. Now I was uncomfortable with him, and I could tell he was uncomfortable with me too. At times he tried to make small talk, and I attempted to say something back when he did. But mostly it was awkward. I felt the loss of our companionship deeply. Although I didn't want to admit it, even to myself, I missed him.

As we marched, I nearly slipped and fell. Sam caught me by the arm and held me steady until I could get my feet under me again.

"Are you all right?" he asked, with something like concern in his voice. I was not happy I needed his help. I pulled my arm roughly away from his hand.

"Yes, fine," I said.

He didn't venture to make any more small talk. It was enough just to try to stay on our feet. We marched in this way all night long and into the morning. Finally the rain abated for a time, and we sat to rest in the scorching heat near the Potomac Creek Bridge. I got the feeling Sam wanted to say something to me, he stayed close and kept glancing over at me as if he might, but then he must have thought better of it, because he never did speak to me.

We stopped for a short rest, lying ourselves out upon the grass and propping ourselves up against our packs. When Mr. Haney got up to relieve himself near the tree line, Sam came and sat next to me, speaking to me in a low and confidential tone.

"I think it best if we remain jointly in a tent and keep to bunking together," he said, wiping the sweat dripping and wet from his forehead.

"What for?" I asked him.

"Well, so you won't be sleeping with any men," he reasoned.

"You are a man," I told him.

"Yes, but I mean a man who might take advantage of you should he find out…" Sam trailed off. "Besides, if we don't share a tent like we always done, it might arouse suspicions."

I shrugged. "I suppose." And even though I had told him I hated him, I knew then it wasn't true. It seemed like such a thoughtful thing for him to do, and I couldn't help but feel that familiar thrill run through me. I was angry at myself for feeling it and scowled.

"It's up to you of course. But I just thought I would offer." He got up to go.

"Sam…" I said.

He stopped and turned to me with an earnest expression. "Yes?"

"I never said thank you for helping me with old Jack Monroe," I said, for I'd learned since Old Whiskers was really named Jack Monroe. "It was decent of you."

He nodded. "Anybody would've." I knew it wasn't true. No one else was stepping up to assist me that night. No one but him. Still I didn't say anything more.

I suppose he had time to think things through, to get accustomed to the idea I was a girl, and maybe he regretted our falling out. I know I did. I missed him terribly. He was to me a sympathetic ear, a friend to lean on, someone who understood me and who cared about me. My life felt very empty without him. I tried to suppress a smile as I watched him leave.

We marched on, sleeping only a few hours upon the ground. The next day we came upon a sight that was horrific beyond belief. We passed the scene of the previous battle at Bull Run, and what we saw would have turned any man's stomach sour. It was such an eerie feeling it set us all on edge, making us mindful of our mortality. Thanks to the heavy rain, the shallow mass graves were washed away from the ground.

Rising to the surface of the muddy fields were the bones of the deceased in appalling jumbled heaps. Like crumbs of bread meant to mark the way, we saw teeth scattered in the dirt. Perhaps I should have been more offended by the decaying remains of a man, but it was the fabric from the clothes the bodies wore when they were laid to rest that upset me more. The thought that they were wearing those garments in their last moments of life, and they had then been buried in them, was more tangible to me than the fleshless vestiges of their bones. The wool of a coat, the splash of a calico with its varied patterns from a shirt or the homespun, painstakingly crafted by hands of loved ones, all fighting to be seen, all covered in the filth, refusing to be forgotten. The earthly apparel of dead men.

Most everyone just tried to keep their eyes forward, avoiding having to look at it. But I could not seem to pry my gaze away from the sight. It was as if my eyes were drawn to it unwillingly, and I was meant to record all of the particulars to convey to future generations so they might profit from our mistakes and avoid the same. It made me sick, but I couldn't turn away from it. I wondered if maybe there was something wrong with me, if perhaps there was some gross flaw in my constitution that made me suffer from such a morbid and sinful curiosity. I was certain my involuntary interest was not normal. I finally distracted myself from looking by fastening my gaze upon my boots and refusing myself the chance to look up again.

When we stopped for a brief rest and to have some food, I could not eat. My stomach pitched within my gut, and it was all I could do to have a drink of water. The mind is a funny thing. It remembers everything in detail, at times even embellishing the facts, or it stores some memory away in a place you cannot retrieve it at all. We do not remember the joy and pride of taking our first steps, or the specifics of some ordinary but pleasant day in the country, but the things we wish to forget the most are the very things which haunt us. Random and without order, they sit up in those heads of ours, the source of joy, pain, emotion, and torture. No matter how I tried, I could not erase the picture of those graves from my brain.

As I dwelt upon it, I had a fleeting notion that I didn't want to have children. I didn't want to bear a child who would grow to an adult and be forced to face such a cruel and bleak world. I didn't want to love a child so very much with my whole heart and soul only to have its spectacular body of bones, muscle, sinew, hands, feet, eyes, ears, mouth, nose, and mind—a glorious and miraculous creature created in God's image—to be disposed of so thoughtlessly. To be alive and breathing, feeling, and thinking and then to suffer such a malevolent end, to be tossed like so much trash into a pit of dirt without even last rights given, was unbearable to consider. Cherished flesh became nothing more than victuals for worms.

"Are you all right?" Sam asked me, standing over me as I sat with my head bowed down resting upon my fists.

"Fine," I mumbled.

"You look white as a sheet," he said. "Feeling kinda peaked?"

"I said I was fine," I told him, defensively. I didn't want to talk to him just then. I didn't want to tell him what I was thinking or have him know I was so deeply affected by what we saw. Why couldn't he just leave me alone?

They called for us to fall in. We scrambled to collect our things, then hustled to get into our neat rows and columns and again begin our march in earnest. I was close to tears, having done everything I could think of to expunge the terrible thoughts that plagued me. Try as I might, I couldn't calm my mind.

"It helps to count," Sam whispered.

"I don't know what you mean," I said with a frown.

"As I march, I count. One, two, three, four. One, two, three, four. It takes my mind away from things," he confessed.

"How can counting help?"

"I don't know, but it does."

So under my breath I began counting, and it did help some. After a while, I didn't even need to count. The business of marching made me so weary I didn't have to train my mind; it was already numbed beyond any coherent thought. We marched quick time, just under a trot, as we followed the road north. The discomfort was terrible. The rain was bad, but the sun beating down on you, and the dry dust choking your throat, and the dirt sticking to your perspiration and irritating your skin, was even less desirable.

I thought maybe I was able to forget because my brain was being fried within my skull from the heat, just as bacon fries in a skillet. Was it only my imagination, or did I hear it sizzle and pop in the cavity of my head? We stopped for the night to make camp, if that's what you could call it. Really it was just all of us scattered over the ground, sleeping under the stars. They woke us well before dawn so we might march without the heat and sun. But the darkness was no easier to bear. We stumbled over uneven ground, rocks, and roots. It was difficult to tell which direction we were even headed. I just knew to follow the fellow in front of me, as he followed the fellow in front of him.

The longer and farther we marched, the more men we saw lying by the wayside, sick and tired and weary and hopeless. There were moments when I thought I would like to just sit and rest, just for a moment. What could it hurt? I began to note it wasn't just soldiers littering the roads, when out of desperation the men began abandoning their belongings. Anything and everything that was weighing heavily upon their backs, the smallest and largest of items in all varieties, were carelessly left behind.

It says a lot about how those men were suffering. All the things dearest to them, all of the things they kept up to now, some vital to living such as canteens and knapsacks, deserted like so much rubbish. If this were desperation, surely we were beyond it. My side, not completely healed, throbbed with a deep and piercing ache. Sam could not carry his rifle and necessities as he should with his shoulder the way it was. He didn't say anything, but he began to drop things here and there too, trying to lighten his load. Everything else he shifted to his right arm to carry.

The battle was imminent, and all would be lost if we did not stop Lee before he made it to Washington. Every one of us knew what was at stake, and we did our best to push on. As we were amidst our meal one evening, word came we were to march to Gettysburg with all speed. Our new General, one General Meade, appointed only a few days before, needed reinforcements. A battle was underway. The excitement grew and was infectious as the particulars of it were spread from one man to another. As weary as we were, the seriousness of the situation compelled us on.

The band played as we marched. I did not recall ever having heard them play at a march before. It was Colonel Upton who requested it to cheer us onward. We marched all the long night, with no chance to stop and rest. I could hardly raise my feet from the ground to walk, I was so tired. Twice some fellow fell asleep while riding on his horse and tumbled to the ground.

Some of the men tried to get out of the march and the fighting altogether. Two men went so far as to shoot off one of their own fingers. I saw Captain Kidder threaten bodily harm to anyone who should think to try to get out of their duties using such tactics. One fellow started limping and tried to hold back and take up at the rear. Captain Kidder pulled his pistol from his belt and pointed it right at the man, right in his face.

"I shall not be troubled with cowards," he said. "If you'd like to trade your pantaloons for petticoats, well now, that can be arranged!"

The night seemed to drag on so. I wished for the comfort of a soft bed, and then I wished for the comfort of a hard bed. And then I wished just to sit, to sit and rest my limbs. There were long stretches of the march I could not recall, as if I were sleep walking and was not conscious for it.

Chapter 8

M orning came, and we were told we could stop and have ourselves a cup of coffee. I sat upon the ground, not caring for coffee, or anything else for that matter. My only thought was to rest. I took my boots from my feet, noting the holes in the bottoms of the soles. They were worn clear through. I peeled my stockings off, only to discover the terrible effect the march had upon me. My feet were covered in blisters, and on top of those blisters were more blisters.

"Looks as if you could use a new pair of boots," Felix Newburn observed as he sat down heavily next to me. He laid his sack and rifle out next to him and took a great breath, finding some relief, I suppose, in being rid of his burdens.

I noted Sam was in the midst of starting a fire so he might boil water for coffee, but he was watching us all the while. Not outright, just glancing our way on occasion, catching us out of the corner of his eye. And it seemed to me as if he were trying very hard to act as if he did not care one bit what I was up to. He only noticed me as much as he was noting his surroundings, and I was a part of them.

"Breaking boots in is more painful than wearing the old ones with holes. I suppose they'll do for now," I replied.

"True," he agreed with a chuckle. "With the rate we been walking everyone's feet probably all look about the same."

"Doesn't make it hurt any less," I told him.

"You aim to get yourself some coffee?"

I pulled my cap over my eyes. "I only wish to rest," I said.

"I will leave you to it," he said as he got up, collected his things, and left.

No sooner did I shut my eyes than they were yelling commands for us to get up, to get moving. Sam had only just got his fire going and hadn't even begun to make himself some coffee. I scrambled to get my stockings and boots on, while others were shoving their gear back into their packs. We knew whatever was transpiring up ahead of us was a dire fight, and we were needed right away.

The sun was beating down upon us, the heat more than we could bear. I began to think how wonderful it would feel if I could only take off my jacket. I could see men falling by the wayside, too tired, too hot, too sick to go on. I longed to be one of them — to say *I quit* and find a nice quiet place on the side of the road to throw myself down upon and sleep.

It was late afternoon when we arrived in Littlestown, Pennsylvania. In the distance we could hear the cannons, and the smoke hung like a great cloud ready to burst with rain on the horizon. The people of the town rushed forward with drink and food. One fine lady gave me a cider and some biscuits as I walked along the road. I took them up and ate and drank. The cider ran down my chin and wetted my chest, but I didn't care. I drank more. The lady looked as though she might cry.

"I'm sorry, it's all I have…" she said.

"Best cider I ever drunk," I told her.

"God bless you," she said. "God bless you."

We continued on the road, which they called the Baltimore Pike, marching at a speed that should not have been humanly possible in our current condition. The road was at least a good one, smooth and even. After close to an hour and a half upon the road, we began encountering the wounded.

They were a sore sight, trickling past in the opposite direction. I felt a familiar fear creep through me, making my heart beat fast and my stomach twist within me. You cannot help but be moved by the human condition when you see it so up close. Why is it witnessing human suffering and the cruel nature of mankind makes you cling to it and want to live all the more? I looked at Sam, and he looked at me with an easy to read expression.

"What kind of crazy must you be to head in the direction they are coming from?" I asked.

"A half-starved, half burned up, and dead tired kind of crazy," he said attempting a grim smile.

"Well, then I fit the bill. I will carry on," I said.

"You good pals with Newburn now?" Sam asked out of nowhere. He did not look at me but kept his eyes trained straight ahead.

"Who, Felix?" I asked. I checked his face from a sideways glance, but he wore no expression I could read.

"That's right, Felix."

"I find him a pleasant fellow," I replied. Felix was a good sort, although I sensed in him a vanity I didn't approve of. He liked to be liked, and he sought to be everyone's best friend. I figured you couldn't trust someone like that, who cared more for what others thought of him, than for what he thought of himself. But I agreed with Sam merely to make him envious. It was not kind, but I was still sore with him over our earlier quarrelling.

"Pleasant." He said the word as though he found it disagreeable. "Yes, I suppose he is…*pleasant.*" Then he didn't venture to say more.

We came upon a commanding officer, who appeared strained nearly to breaking. He was covered in sweat and grime, his eyes swollen and blood shot, bulging from his head. He was attempting to do a thousand things all at once. Upton approached him and they quietly conversed. The officer motioned with his hands several times, pointing to a map that was spread across a table before him, and then the Colonel came back and gave us our orders.

The battle was in full swing once we arrived. We marched down the main street of the town, Gettysburg, and it appeared the fighting had been here as well. There were bodies littering the lanes, damage to the homes and businesses, and not a civilian in sight. Word was the conflict has been fierce for nearly two days. At the end of the main street we climbed to a high bluff above the town. We were formed into two lines upon the ridge and told to wait.

It was a breathtaking sight. In the distance we saw mountains looming, rocky outcrops, and fog which hung thick and mysterious, giving it a dream-like quality. In the more immediate vicinity the land consisted of rolling hills, gently sloping inclines, and vast valleys. It was green with long grass and old massive trees, here and there densely forested areas. Before us were a peach orchard and a wheat field. To our right, but just out of view, was the town. Again I was struck by such beauty, and I knew it would soon be wiped clean by the destruction we brought with us.

You may think it callous and unnatural, but we lay down upon the ground, thoughts of death flung to the wayside, as we slept where we were. It was a marvel to me that we were capable of sleeping through the noise of the cannonade, but it proved to be no inconvenience at all. We slept with our weapons in our hands. Now I will tell you, there were no dreams in my head, no not a one. We slumbered in a dead sleep until nearly three in the morning, when we were awakened by the guns of the pickets from both sides. We couldn't see the fighting, but only heard it as the sound of gunfire cracked in rapid succession coming from the direction of Gettysburg, where there was constant skirmishing from the doors and windows of the town's homes.

In the dark we could hear the dying calling to us, begging, begging for aid, begging for their lives, begging for merciful death to come upon them all at the same moment. I thought I might go mad with it. When finally the sun came up, the battle unfolded before us. We were set upon what they called Cemetery Ridge, near Round Top Mountain to the far left.

It was a place meant for observing all there was to see. We waited and watched, not sure yet what our role would be. Colonel Upton, being a man who knew how to raise another man's spirits, spoke to us in very animated tones trying to prepare us for what might come.

"I have as much confidence in you at this moment as I do even in myself! For I can see your determination! I can see your patriotism! I can see the pride you take in your service to this great nation! There is not a man here I would not trust with my very life!"

At that moment we broke out in cheering which seemed to shake the ground beneath us. The noise was deafening. I could feel the blood running through my veins, my heart beating rapidly, a tingle in my scalp. If called upon, we would be ready to fight! We saw from our spot the battle raging, the sharpshooters firing upon one another, like tin soldiers lined up in a child's game. Colonel Upton would look into his field glasses and keep us abreast of what was transpiring elsewhere as the day wore on.

"It will be hot work," he told us. "Stay ready, lest they call upon us to join."

We were able to eat a little, and still greatly fatigued from our march, we also took to napping when possible. Colonel Upton and two others settled below a shade tree to rest when a round came sailing over them. That isn't such an uncommon thing to have happen in the midst of fighting. But the three of them got up and tried to figure out where the shot came from. No sooner did they clear out from the tree when it was hit by a shell and showered the place with splinters. Lucky they kept their heads, because if they had stayed put they would surely have been struck by the shell.

We got to talking with some of the other men, a regiment from Maine. They had seen some fierce fighting the day before and were now doing their best to recuperate.

"Didn't have a bullet to pass between us," one of them confided. "And they just kept coming at us and coming at us. Finally we was told to fix bayonets, 'cause there was nothing else could be done, and we charged down the hill at them, instead of waiting for them to come at us." He spoke with a peculiar accent, which Felix told me was particular to Maine. His tendency was to draw out the *A* and omit the *R* from his words.

I could see Sam was genuinely interested in this man's story. "And you lived to tell the tale?" he asked in disbelief.

"We let out such a yell they didn't know what was happening. Our boys caught them off guard and frightened 'em so, they up and surrendered!" he exclaimed.

Later, Sam said to me, "What kind of country is it that tells a man to hold the line at all cost and then don't give him sufficient bullets to defend it?"

"Sounds like us Yanks were hard pressed all around, Sam. I don't believe they were denying them. There was just none to give."

"Maybe so," he said with a shrug.

Now the cannonade began again, and the enemy let loose a steady stream. We were lucky not to be at the center of fire, but still received a portion of it, as the ground around us exploded in earth and debris. It was frightening, but did little more than give us a scare. Our boys fired back. The exchange went on for a short stretch, the noise deafening. Then it was just the Confederates firing, blast after blast with little effect. Our side hunkered down and chose to wait them out, saving what precious munitions we had for the real fighting. When it grew quiet, we knew trouble would be coming our way.

As we watched from our vantage point, we hardly trusted what we were seeing. The Rebs decide to make a charge across the front, right at the center of our defenses! I don't know if it was depriva-tion or stupidity that moved them forward, but a large body of the Confederates amassed at the edge of a vast field below. I could see them from an angle, so the entire picture was before me. There must have been tens of thousands of them, lined up in tight rows shoulder to shoulder.

"Madness," Sam murmured. "They'll never make it."

I was thinking the same thing. With a great blood curdling yell, they walked forward. Exposed for at least a mile or more of valley ground, they seemed to be on a suicide mission. They were easily picked off, large numbers of them falling as they vainly attempted to press forward. One would fall, and another would crowd in to take up the empty space. When they grew close enough, our boys in blue poured canister shot out upon them over the heads of our own infantry, who lay in cover behind a stone wall just below. Their flag would fall, someone would take it up, and they would press on, the line would falter as dozens fell, but then the line would reform and move forward again, trying to make for the stone wall that so nicely shielded our men from the brunt of the fighting.

It was a horrific scene, filled with slaughter. It must have seemed to last forever to them, but in reality it was over in less than an hour's time. Above the terrible disquiet of the guns, we could hear, faintly rising above it, the chant of the Federals. It was vicious, burning, zealous, insistent…"Fredericksburg!" Like a fever, like a fire, it spread through the ranks, gaining momentum until it was a crescendo of fiercely impassioned men's voices chanting, "Fredericksburg! Freder-icksburg!" The sound of it sent chills down my spine, made the fine hairs raise on my neck, on my arms.

Hundreds of them, those poorly clothed, practically defenseless Rebels, valiantly dying honorable deaths, were cut down before our very eyes. We saw our forces, which far outnumbered the meager few left to them, clash together, and when the two merged, for a brief moment it was difficult to tell which was ours and which was theirs, until there was nothing but the blue left. The dead lay where they fell, and the few men who made it to the hill were either wounded or taken prisoner.

From my perspective I could see the Confederates' folly. It was much of the same thing I was to see many times in this war, men of power sending lambs to slaughter as they sat upon their horses watching from a distance. Perhaps their job is the hardest of all, to have to live with all of those deaths upon their hands. There was no hope for those men, and yet they did as they were told, and facing great odds, charged into the fray. I understood then bravery is not only found in Federals, it is also found among Confederates. So much rested upon the results of the battle, and they surely gave their all.

The next day, as we surveyed the damage done while walking through a grove of peach trees, I could not help but feel some compassion for the blackened, bloated corpses wearing tattered gray uniforms, many without shoes on their feet. It rained all day, but it didn't wash away the rot and smell of them. The 121st were there to witness; we were not called upon to fight in the most infamous of battles. It seemed as though it was a pattern with us. There was relief we hadn't been among the dead and guilt because we'd been spared.

Chapter 9

Colonel Upton was on his horse riding back and forth before us. He was doing his best to encourage and inspire us. After sleeping and eating, and now that the battle was over, we were in a much better mood than we'd previously been.

"We may yet provide a service today," he said. "Lee's army is now in full retreat. We have been called upon to locate the Confederates' position and engage them in combat when possible to hinder their progress."

Selfishly, I was glad to be away from the battlefield and the duties of burying the dead. After Antietam I didn't want to have the chore again. Our new assignment was a legitimate excuse to wash my hands of the responsibility of tending to the remains of the dead in the aftermath.

"Seems as though we always have cleanup duties," Sam muttered. He appeared to be in poor spirits.

"Better than burying the dead," I said.

He smiled vaguely. "I suppose."

We marched down the Fairfield Road at a fair clip, making good time. Because we were not involved in fighting and able to rest some, we were better able to keep pace, but we were still tired out from our thirty-two mile march to get to Gettysburg. My feet were in bad shape and every step was agony. We cleared Gettysburg and were just shy of Fairfield when we came close to overtaking the retreating Rebels. We were ordered to take cover and fire upon them.

"We may see some action after all," Reed Haney said as he aimed his rifle and shot.

"Tough birds, they're firing back," Felix Newburn observed.

We fired and they fired, but nothing much came of it. They continued on their way, and we waited for orders. When they came, Upton seemed as put out as I ever saw him.

"They are headed through the mountain gap. Not wise to pursue that course. The gap is too easily defended and we would be at their mercy. But they are in bad shape, fairly crippled from Gettysburg. If we can catch up to them, we will certainly overtake them and defeat them for good," he said to Captain Kidder. "Could mean an end to all of it."

We took the road to Emmitsburg. There we rested briefly, ate a little, and filled our canteens. As the sun receded and the evening shade was upon us, we began a treacherous climb. In order to meet the enemy, we were required to hike South Mountain. It began to rain, a heavy and constant rain that made our gear heavy again and was a burden to endure. The trees were thick, the underbrush difficult to maneuver through. The incline was so steep we were hardly able to remain on our feet. I took a step and then slid backward, took a step and slid backward. The progress was painfully slow as we ascended. The way was dangerous, with a deep ravine to one side and only room enough for two men to march side by side on the trail. The darkness was complete — no moon or stars to light the way. We were shrouded by the storm.

I gave it my all, and yet I was too weak to continue on. After several hours of struggling, I fell upon my face, dismal and drenched, and didn't have the energy to get myself up again.

"I'm all used up. I can't go on," I cried.

"You'll be trampled underfoot if you don't move out of the way!" Sam scolded me.

"I don't care anymore!" I raged at him. Sam reached out to me.

"Take my hand," he said. I looked up at him but just lay there in misery, feeling as if I could not even lift my arm to grab hold of him. He didn't say anything more but reached down and helped me to my feet. He took me round the waist and dragged me out of the path. The rain rolled down my face, and the black night pressed in upon me. I knew I should try to go on, but I couldn't. I was too exhausted.

I allowed Sam to haul me over to the side of the path because I didn't have the strength to resist him. There was nowhere else to go but the ditch, a shallow channel where the runoff from the storm flowed. Sam took off his damp coat, lay down next to me, and spread the coat over our heads. There were no words exchanged between us. I was aware, for the briefest moment, of the smell of the soggy wool, the weak current of water beneath me, and Sam pressed close to me, before I fell off to sleep.

It was still raining when I became conscious of my surroundings again. The rain pattered upon Sam's coat. And while the coat was wet through, it kept the rain from hitting my face directly.

"Are you awake?" I whispered.

"Yes," Sam replied. "I'm afraid there'll be no hot coffee this morning. There can be no fire in this rain."

My body was wet all through. My fingertips were wrinkled and my joints stiff. I attempted to stretch and discovered quickly my whole body ached.

"Just as well. My rations ran out. I have no coffee to warm anyhow."

Sam peeled the wet coat from our heads, and the rain pelted against my skin, making me wince from the shock of it. I sat up and tugged the brim of my hat lower to cover my eyes. The ebony night was replaced by a lackluster gray morning.

"I haven't got much," he said. "But I do have a bit of salt pork and a biscuit to divide between the two of us." He rummaged through his pack and handed me half of what was left.

I thought I should protest but decided against it. I had shared plenty of times with him. And besides, I felt if I didn't have something to eat, I might not have the strength to finish climbing this cursed mountain. I would be stuck here rotting forever. I took my time chewing and swallowing, not to savor, but because I didn't have the strength even to eat. Each motion of my jaw seemed to take great effort. Sam put his wet coat back on and helped me up out of the ditch. I could see he was just as tired as I was. I suppose I should have felt some remorse for giving up last night. But I could not make myself feel anything but dread as I faced the mountain again.

Much like climbing a very steep set of stairs, we lifted our knees high and dug our feet in to make progress up the sharp vertical incline. As we struggled up the slope we encountered others who'd given up the night before, just as we had. After a short while the sole of my boot began flapping. Like a great gaping mouth, it yawned open each time I took a step forward to reveal my stockinged foot within. I sat down in the middle of the path, took both of my boots off, and flung them off of the side of the mountain into the ravine. I took off my stockings and shoved them into my haversack, and then continued on barefoot.

Once we made it to the summit it took several more hours for all of the other stragglers to filter in. We were able to rest for a while as we waited until all were accounted for. All the while Captain Kidder blustered and railed.

"Damn it. We're in the military. Did you think it would be tea and cakes? Be men and stop your grumbling," he complained.

When we were all congregated we began our descent. I might as well have sat on my backside and slid all the way down for as much as I was on it. I stumbled and fell many times, each time wishing I did not have to get up again. Once we came to the base of the mountain, we took up on the road to Middletown. I felt the pangs of hunger in my belly and tried to think of something to take my mind from it. There was nothing, and so I gave into my despair.

My feet were raw, blistered, cut up, and swollen. They gave me a great deal of pain, each footstep accompanied by a terrible ache. There was no point in complaining. There were others who suffered likewise. That was just how it was. My duty was to carry on.

The town of Middletown was our salvation. Fresh bread and meat were provided for us there. We acquired much needed supplies, spent the night, and then headed out the next morning. Sam was somehow able to find me a pair of boots. They were too large for my feet but better than having none at all.

He brought them to me with a casual, "Try these on," as he held them out to me.

I narrowed my gaze. "Where did you get them?"

"Does it matter? I traded for them in town," he said.

"I don't need them," I told him. "I can take care of myself." After my weak moment on the mountain, I didn't want to owe Sam any more than I already did. I knew he probably thought I was pathetic and needy.

"You do need them. You are hardly able to walk on those bloody hooves of yours. You wanna continue going around barefoot like that?"

"I can get boots on my own, Sam," I told him rather stand-offishly.

"Well, now you don't have to," he said in annoyance. "Take 'em or leave 'em. I have no use for them." He sat them down before me and walked away. There was nothing to do but try them on. No point in throwing away a perfectly good pair of boots.

When Sam saw me wearing them over dinner he wore such a look of satisfaction I considered tugging them off and tossing them in the fire. I was already beholden to him far more than I would have liked. The fact he was keeping my secret caused no end of torment for me. As wicked a thing as it was to think, I would have liked to have had something over him to balance our association.

Over the next several days we passed from one town to another. From Middletown to Hamburg; to Boonsborough, then Hagerstown, and on to Williamsport; and then on to Funkstown, Maryland, we marched. Every day we were told to be on the ready, the Rebels had been spotted, and there was skirmishing. I didn't take much stock in it. I sometimes thought the constant threat they held over our heads was merely to keep us on our toes. It began to feel like the story of the boy who cried wolf. And yet I was driven by the promise that if we should catch up with them, perhaps the war would be over and I wouldn't have to suffer any longer.

Upon the shores of the Potomac River, the very river we had traversed across so many times, we discovered we were too late. The Rebs had beat us and crossed over.

"Lost them by only two hours," Darby confided. "I chanced to hear the uppers talking on it, and they said as much."

I looked over the vast waters, seeing nothing but wilderness, and like everyone else present, felt my heart sink. Lee was gone, and the advantage we had went with him. The speed at which we pursued Lee's army, at the cost of our physical health and great mental strain, were all for nothing. I sat down upon the bank and allowed the weight to slide from my shoulders. I breathed deeply, looked upon the striking landscape before me, the vibrant purples and reds of the setting sun melting together in reflections upon the water, the forested scene beyond in deep shades of green, and I felt some peace for a short moment.

Chapter 10

Our company was to camp near New Baltimore, Virginia until further notice. It was a pleasant looking place, with numerous trees and fertile green hills, a quaint country scene dotted with modest cottages. And like a sore thumb our white tents were peculiarly out of place. The locals didn't care much for us. Most were Confederate sympathizers. To be among the enemy was a sore thing for us, especially after the death and destruction we witnessed at the hands of those who represented them. The men railed bitterly against the locals and all Southerners in general because we couldn't help but think on Salem Church and Gettysburg too. We had grown to become a jaded and hardened lot.

The most vocal about his hatred was Old Whiskers—Jack Monroe. He blustered and carried on to anyone who might give an ear.

"They deserve no mercy!" he railed. "What they count as theirs would go to support the very army we fight against. Whatever would benefit them, let it benefit us instead."

"I heard what them savages done on their way up north. They helped themselves to whatever they took a liking to," Vern Stapleton chimed in. "Women not excluded." He let his meaning sink in with a strange smile upon his lips. It was as if he enjoyed thinking on the implications. There were all sorts of rumors of pillaging and rape going around. Whatever the Rebs took a liking to, they helped themselves to it. Where these wild claims originated from was not clear to me. Who knew if there was any validity to any of it? Certainly some of it was probably accurate, but how much? There was no way of knowing for sure what was rumor and what was real.

The truth was, we were all in such a state we would have believed anything. I was horrified by what they were saying. Sam spoke up.

"Anyone that would harm a woman is the worst sort of coward. Nothing better than an animal," he said.

"Well, I say we take what we might as a reckoning to them, for what they took from us," Vern said.

"We get close to no pay, an' they nearly starve us, while these people sit in their homes, in comfort and without a care," Darby complained.

Looting grew to grand magnitudes. Nothing was safe at our hands. I still maintained I should take only what I must to survive. I didn't see the harm in taking food, although I vowed to myself I'd stop there. But not all shared the same sentiment. The commanding offers insisted we respect private property while encouraging us to take all we liked at the same time. They spoke in riddles which left them void of responsibility for the troubling things happening at the hands of our soldiers.

As upsetting as much of it was, I was not exempt from witnessing things that bothered me. When it was possible, I chose to look the other way—until I was put right in the middle of it and there was no choice but to take a stand.

"Me and some of the boys are going to get us some dinner," Darby told me after drills one morning.

I thought Darby was a decent fellow. I saw no harm in it. I agreed to go before I knew what company he was keeping. It was Darby and Felix, with Old Whiskers tagging along. I felt apprehension at seeing he would go too. He had a way of looking at me that made me feel as if I were a goose at Christmas dinner. I could vaguely picture him with a napkin tucked into his collar, pointy teeth meant for tearing flesh bared as he smiled, and a knife in one hand with a fork in the other, ready to devour me up and spit out my bones. I think he derived great pleasure from seeing me squirm. I always tried to look him in the eyes and never back down, because I did not like for him to think I was feeling cowed by him.

"Him too?" I murmured to Darby when I caught sight of Old Whiskers standing by waiting for us. Darby didn't answer, just gave me a shrug. For a moment I thought I should back out, but I didn't like the notion of conceding to Jack Monroe, letting him know he scared me. So against my better judgment I went with them.

I thought perhaps I should go and ask Sam to come along too. But I knew he was sleeping. He was up late and I knew how tired he must be, because I had felt the same after being up the whole night on other occasions. Besides, I could take care of myself. I didn't always need him to back me up. He was another I didn't wish to show any weakness to.

So we struck out upon the road, walking at a lazy pace. I stuck with Felix mostly, while Darby and Old Whiskers talked among themselves. After a time we came upon a small stand of apple trees. I took out my sack and began to pick a few to take with me. From our spot on the sloping hill, just below, we could see a small farm which consisted of a white house with black shutters and a modest barn, the pastures penned in with split rail fencing and a small garden just out back. It reminded me of home, although this home was more refined than my own. Darby and Old Whiskers decided to go on to the house to see what they might find, while Felix and I stayed to pick.

I took a bite of an unblemished apple, crisp and ripe to perfection. When a thing is rare, even if it is as commonplace as an apple, it seems so infinitely beautiful, so pleasant to behold.

"Good," I said to Felix with a nod. He too picked some of the full grown fruit, stuffing them in his haversack until it was full. I reasoned we were not taking enough to hurt the owner too sorely. My conscience always pricked when I dwelt too long upon what I was really doing. For whether I was hurting the owner or not, I was taking something that did not belong to me.

"I have a notion to cook them over the fire. Haven't had stewed apples since forever ago," Felix said.

Just as we finished helping ourselves to the apples we heard a gunshot ring harsh and clear from the direction of the house. I nearly jumped right out of my boots from the surprise of it. Felix and I looked at one another with dread. I am sure we were thinking the same thing. *What sort of trouble have they gotten themselves into?* We readied our rifles and took off down the hill to investigate. When we reached the yard, Darby was there before the barn, a dead pig at his feet.

"What have you done?" I asked.

"Bacon, ham…good meat," he said. "It will make a fine dinner."

"And how do you intend on getting it back?" I yelled.

"We can each carry a portion."

"You know nothing of slaughtering pigs," I complained. "By the time we get it back, the meat will be spoiled. What a waste."

"It should still be good," he said, sheepishly.

"He is telling you the truth, Darby." Felix agreed. He was put out. I could only guess that, like me, the scare of hearing the gunshot put him into a bad mood. "Have you never killed a pig before, you fool?"

Darby shrugged and acted as if he didn't care.

"Matters not to me," he said. "At least it will not be useful to any of that Southern trash." He turned back toward the barn and motioned with a nod of his head. "There is a cow we can take back with us at any rate."

We followed him into the barn where it was dark and smelled of hay and manure. In the gloom we heard the quiet whimper of a child.

"What is it?" Felix asked. I followed the noise until I found three little ones hiding in one of the empty stalls, cowering there together in fear and misery. They looked like little mice cornered by a cat. The gunshot must have frightened them just as much as it did Felix and me.

The oldest of the three was no more than ten, and she drew her arms over the others as if she might shield them, brave girl. She did her best to keep the others quiet, but they continued to moan pathetically. How could you not feel sorry for the poor little mites?

"It's all right," I said softly, not wishing to frighten them further. "We don't aim on hurting you."

"Mother!" one of them wailed.

"Well?" Felix wondered.

"Three little ones," I said. "The noise of Darby's rifle must have frightened them." I spoke to the oldest. "Where is your mother?"

She looked at me as if she weren't sure if she should speak to me.

"She told us to hide," she said quietly.

I turned back to Darby and saw him tying a rope around the cow's throat with the intent to lead it from the stall.

"Darby, we cannot take that cow." He seemed confused by what I said. He didn't let go of the rope or act like he would leave the cow.

"And why not?" he huffed.

"They will have nothing left," I told him.

"They'll make do," he said.

I became insistent. "Leave the cow, Darby. It will be winter soon. They must have it to survive."

Darby paused in tying the rope to meet my eyes. I gave him a look like I meant it. This made him angry.

"You'd have pity on them, when they don't have no pity on us," he blustered, taking the rope from the cow's throat. "Fine soldier you are!"

I ignored his anger. It didn't matter to me if he was mad, just so long as I got my way. At that point, I realized Old Whiskers was nowhere to be seen. Right away I got a sinking feeling. If he was not with us, then where was he and what mischief was he up to?

"Where's Jack?" I asked.

Darby shrugged. "I ain't no mammie to him. He's around somewhere."

I took off at a run toward the house. I burst through the door, not waiting for the others to follow. There in the parlor was Old Whiskers with the woman of the house. She was a pretty girl, I think not many years older than myself. And that skunk was upon her, touching her with his dirty hands, kissing her with his foul smelling mouth as she struggled beneath him.

The two became still when I entered. She looked at me with tear filled eyes, too terrified, I suppose, to make a sound, and I felt the rage surge through my body.

"Get off of her!" I hollered.

Jack did not move away from her; she remained pinned beneath him. He smiled at me, a slow crafty smile.

"You can have your turn with her when I'm done," he said with a wink. "Make a man out of you yet."

I pulled my rifle up to my shoulder and aimed it very carefully at his head.

"By God, if you don't get out of this house now, I will shoot you dead, Jack Monroe!" I yelled through gritted teeth.

He paused for a moment, trying to determine if I was true in my intent. I did not blink an eye and I did not breathe as I held my rifle steady. He got up begrudgingly from the settee, giving me the most hateful look I'd ever seen. The woman moved too, quickly pulling her skirts down. She shot up and away from us to the far corner of the room, whimpering with her arms crossed tight against her chest. She was no threat to me. He was. I didn't take my eyes from him for a second. I kept my bead on him as I followed his movement toward the door. He picked up his haversack, heavy with loot, and slung it over his shoulder. The contents of his sack clanked as he did this. I realized he must have taken far more than food.

"Put the silver back," I ordered.

Again he looked at me as if he might kill me. I'm sure he was working out how he could get to me and disarm me before I could get a shot off. He reached his hand into the sack, pulled the spoons and forks and knives from it, and flung them across the room. They clanged loudly and then came to rest in varied positions all over the hard wood flooring. It was about this time I noted Felix and Darby standing in the doorway, watching the whole thing, neither of them willing to help in the matter. Felix looked to be in shock, and Darby was evaluating the situation up to see what role he should play in it.

When Old Whiskers emptied the silverware from his sack, he stooped to pick up his rifle as it leaned against the wall.

"Leave it," I said. "I'll see to it you get it back later."

He turned on me, and with a voice filled with ill intent, he hissed, "You gone too far!" As he stormed out he mumbled, "Just you watch your back, sonny boy. No telling what may happen in the chaos of battle."

Old Whiskers was plenty mad, this I could see. But I figured his blusterings were nothing more than empty threats. I had crossed him twice now. And really what could he do when we were surrounded by so many men? My strength was in numbers. I would make certain I was never in his company alone. If I were to judge him, I would judge him to be a coward, not having the fortitude to do anything outright, preying upon the weak. He shoved past Felix and Darby at the door.

I looked over at the woman, still and silent. I was ashamed for us all. What must she think of us?

"I'm sorry," I said. I took the apples from my haversack one by one and left them in a pile upon a chair. Without saying another word, I bent and picked up Old Whiskers' rifle. At that moment, through the parlor window sailed a rock, raining glass over the room as it broke through the thin visage of pane. The woman completely lost her composure, falling to a heap and screaming hysterically. I was perhaps as terrified as she, but I managed to keep my wits. Instinct took over, and I squatted to the ground, drawing my rifle up in a quick jerk, trying to make sense of what was happening and looking for a target. Then the window to my left burst into shattered fragments, as another rock was thrown at it. Likewise, I could hear the windows upstairs breaking and the dull thud of the rocks as they rolled across the floor above me.

Old Whiskers was out upon the lawn ranting and railing, stooping to pick up a rock and then making a mark of another window before letting it loose. I suppose he didn't want to go quietly. There must be some retribution for his humiliation.

I handed Darby the rifle and said, "Give it to him when we get back to camp."

Darby seemed reluctant to have stewardship over it, but he took it from me. We filed out into the yard and saw Old Whiskers was finished with his task and already walking briskly toward the road. I turned around and saw the pleasant little farmhouse with all of its windows busted out and felt relieved something worse hadn't happened. On our way back to camp, I hung behind and kept my distance, making sure I kept Jack in my sights the entire way. He seemed to want no company for he stayed ahead and acted as if we weren't even there.

Chapter 11

We returned to camp late afternoon. Perhaps we looked as wretched as we all felt, unwilling to meet eyes, with hangdog expressions upon our faces. Sam spotted us, and without waiting, came right up to me, giving Felix and Darby a suspicious glance as he did.

"Where have you been?" he asked.

"He doesn't need to report all his doings to you," Felix said. I was certain Felix was being so standoffish because he didn't want Sam to know what transpired while we were away.

"I wasn't talking to you," Sam replied coolly.

Felix shrugged as if he didn't care, although it was obvious he was unhappy with Sam, and then he turned toward his tent and walked away. Darby, with Old Whiskers' rifle still in hand, dropped his gaze in a most self-incriminating manner and headed off in another direction. I slowed my pace and came to a stop so Felix and Darby would put some distance between us and leave me to some privacy with Sam.

"Well?" he prodded.

"I went to get food," I informed him.

"With Old Whiskers?"

"I didn't know he'd be coming along until I already agreed to it," I said, fidgeting with a button on my coat.

"And?" he persisted. He was looking at me in exasperation.

I wasn't sure if I should tell him. I did not wish to cause trouble for him, and there was always the possibility he might go after Jack

Monroe and either get in trouble for fighting or get in over his head with Jack. The man scared me. I didn't put anything past him, including killing Sam if given a reason.

"I took care of myself," I said. It was everything I could do not to blurt it all out, tell him everything. My nerves were raw from what I just experienced, and it would have been wonderful to break down and cry to him about it, but what good would it do?

"So you mean to keep it from me, then?" Sam seemed offended.

His displeasure was more than I could bear. "We found a farm, not far from here," I began.

"Yes?"

"Felix and me were getting some apples."

"Alone with Felix?" His mind began to formulate stories revolving around Felix and me and the two of us being alone. Sam's eyes told me he was jumping to all sorts of conclusions in fast order.

"What did Felix do?" he fumed.

"Felix? Nothing. He didn't do anything."

"What then?"

"Let me tell it, Sam," I complained. He didn't say anything but nodded and let me continue. "Felix and me picked the apples. And Darby and Old Whiskers decided to go down to the house and see what they might find there. When we came down later, I mean Felix and me, when we came down from the orchard, we find out Darby and Old Whiskers have been causing trouble."

"What kind of trouble?" Sam wanted to know.

"I...well, it was awful. I see Darby has killed a pig and then means to take the cow. She was alone there, Sam. With three little ones..."

"*What happened?*"

"I told Darby we must leave the cow for them. All alone, without a man to care for them and winter coming on shortly. It was the only honest thing to do. And then I notice Old Whiskers, he isn't anywhere to be seen." My palms began to sweat, and I felt a revulsion roll over me at the thought of him, at the thought of what he planned to do to that poor woman. "So I went up to the house."

He looked about, as if he were making sure no one else could hear our conversation.

"Serena," he whispered. "What did he do?"

"He was upon her, Sam. He had wicked intentions, that was certain. She was doing her best to fight him off. Well, so…I told him to get off of her. I told him to leave her be. What kind of man would do such a thing?" My voice broke with emotion, but I did not cry.

"Oh, Lord," he mumbled.

"He wouldn't. There was no remorse! Not a bit. So I put my rifle on him and I told him I would kill him if he didn't. Oh, that made him plenty mad, Sam, plenty mad."

"What did the others do?" he questioned. He took a deep breath with his eyes closed and ran both of his hands through his hair. I could tell he was very upset.

"Nothing. They just stood there and watched the whole thing."

"Cowards!" He paused, waiting for me to continue. When I didn't, he grew impatient. "And then?"

I jumped a little.

"Then Old Whiskers went outside and took up rocks from the ground and busted out every one of the windows on the front of the house. Every one of them."

Sam looked as though he could barely control his rage. He pursed his lips and shook his head as I told it to him. He was pacing back and forth in front of me, unable to keep himself still.

"That swag-bellied pansy! I'm gonna have a talk with him! I'm gonna go have a talk with all of them!" he barked.

I stepped in front of him, to keep him from going anywhere.

"No, Sam. You must not say a thing. Please! It will only cause problems. And I don't want to be the reason for it. You know and I know there is much at stake here. Please do not cause trouble for me."

"He's capable of anything," Sam said. "And what if he should discover…" He shook his head violently. "You are not safe here."

"He won't do anything. He's all bluff," I argued.

"Like hell he won't! I trust the man as far as I could throw him. And that ain't far." He wagged his finger at me. "You knock down a hornet's nest, you gotta assume you're gonna get stung."

"What can he do?"

"No telling. You shamed him in front of others. He's not gonna let it go."

"What should I have done, let him have his way with her?" I raged.

"No, that isn't what I'm saying. Anybody with any bit of decency would've done the same. Just wish it hadn't been you." He stopped in his pacing and looked at me hard. "You stay clear of him, Serena. I don't trust him. Have you noticed how he always has more rations than everyone else, and how he always seems to have his hands in all of the shady dealings? He's trouble. You stay as far from him as you can manage."

"That's just what I planned on doing. You'll have no argument from me. You can rely on it."

"For now, you must never be alone. You must always make sure you are in the company of others. Always."

"You know that's not possible," I pointed out. I could not take care of my needs or bathe myself in the company of others. Out of necessity I must be alone at times. There was no getting around it.

"I mean to say whenever you can. If you tell me when you must be alone, I could keep watch for you," he offered.

I felt a deep flush color my face. "I don't think that's necessary," I said. "I will be fine without your watch."

"For heaven sakes, Serena, take it seriously, will you! You must guard yourself and give him no opportunity to ambush you."

"Can't be any worse than what Vern Stapleton and Rueben Morrell did to me."

He gave me a confused look. "What are you talking about? You mean Vern's teasing and giving you a hard time?"

I sighed. "That was only part of it," I admitted.

"You never told me of it," he complained.

"I didn't want to get you involved," I confessed. "But what I am trying to say is he and Vern are much the same. Notice how they enjoy one another's company, just as Vern and Rueben did."

"That may be true. But, well, now, don't confuse Vern with Old Whiskers, Serena. They are two different sorts of animals. Vern is a pup compared to Jack Monroe. A pup and a wolf. Be on the guard."

"I will do my best," I promised.

Chapter 12

The weather was not near as hot anymore, which helped some with our comfort. You may think there was plenty of idle time in camp. But that wasn't the case. Upton kept us drilling endlessly. He required perfection, to the degree we drilled all morning, parted long enough to eat, and then returned for more drilling. He also required an inspection of our rifles, gear, and uniforms. It was difficult to try to meet all of his expectations. But somehow Sam managed it easily.

He got a promotion. With our losses being so great after Salem Church, there were many vacancies in the chain of command. He was now a second lieutenant. He told Reed Haney and me about it one evening, after he came from speaking with Upton regarding it.

"Means an increase in pay," he said with an overly confident grin.

"Yes, and also it means you are accountable for the squad," I reminded him. Really I was very proud of him.

Besides me and Sam and Vern and Reed, there was now Alden and Leonard Carroll, these two being brothers, Bostwick Tanner, who went by the name of Boss, Felix Newburn, Rowan Darby, and of course, Jack Monroe.

The brothers were, in general, pleasant enough, but kept to themselves. I suppose they had a trust and friendship that satisfied their needs and didn't need anyone else. I could understand. I stuck with Sam mostly. He and Reed Haney were the two I trusted most. These were the men I knew to be my true friends.

Boss Tanner's name made it sound as though he ought to be a large man with bad manners. But he was neither of those things. He was only slightly taller than me, thin and quiet. He mostly didn't speak unless spoken to. I knew very little about his life outside of his service in the military. He never shared personal information.

There was Darby, who came from Ireland to America when he was ten. His father was a farmer in the old country. When he died, Darby's mother had five small children and no way of supporting herself. She agreed to serve as a maid to a wealthy family in New York for passage upon a ship, and she made agreements for her children as well. Darby earned his keep serving as a stable boy, living the life of an indentured servant until his master's name was chosen in the draft. Rather than serve himself, he offered Darby as a substitute. "Old Abe don't care who it is as long as the boots are filled. A rich man can barter for his life, while a poor man's life ain't worth spit," Darby drolly observed.

Now Darby was on the whole a good fellow, but he also harbored an anger which wasn't difficult to see. He railed against any injustice, whether to him or anyone else. He saw all things as an affront, took most things as an insult. You always took care what you said and did around him, because he was so easily offended. His cynicism suffused everything he did and said. He was a somewhat miserable fellow, in an irritable mood and looking for a cause to take up much of the time.

Felix Newburn was an apprentice to a man of law before his service. He freely shared his opinion on all topics of conversation. Felix told fascinating stories of people and events he'd had dealings with in court. Some were difficult to believe and seemed outrageous, but he swore up and down it was all true. Sam tended to roll his eyes and openly acknowledged he doubted much of what Felix said. Felix seemed confident enough not to care what Sam thought and mostly ignored his disapproval.

Then there was Old Whiskers. He was a tavern owner in his former life. I don't know what it was over, but he got himself into legal trouble, and in order to get out of it he opted to serve as a soldier instead of serve time in prison. I had never yet met anyone but Old Whiskers that was a convict, which made me very frightened by him. There was no problem imagining him in vile dealings, doing the sorts of things which would bring the law down on him. So you see he really was the lowest sort.

And now Sam was to be in charge of us all. When I pointed this out he gave me a peculiar grin. His eyes narrowed and he seemed to get great satisfaction from it.

"That means you must do as I tell you, Frank," he said. "I'm your superior now."

Mr. Haney was amused. "It gives you no pleasure we see, Sam." He chuckled. "Don't go getting too big for your britches, son."

"Your well-intended advice has come too late, Mr. Haney. The look of glee he wears as he asserts his power over us only proves it," I joked.

Vern Stapleton and Jack Monroe were not far off from us and must have overheard the particulars of our discussion. They came over, wanting to be included in the talk. I became immediately uncomfortable, as I always did with those two around.

"What is this about?" Vern questioned.

Mr. Haney spoke up, giving Sam a slap on the back as he announced, "Sam here has been promoted to Second Lieutenant."

"Why Sam?" Vern asked. But I suppose he was really asking, *why not me?*

"Because he was the best man for the job," I told him.

"We all have served the same," he argued.

"It is not for you to say," I pointed out.

"He's a sassy little fellow," Old Whiskers said to Vern with a mocking laugh, as he referred to me. "Uppity gal-boy."

"Lay off," Sam injected. "Haven't you got anything better to do with yourselves?"

"What are you, his wet nurse?" Old Whiskers said to Sam.

Vern ignored the rest and focused in on me. "Come on, Frank. I thought we was good friends now," he teased.

Normally I would have done what I could to get out of a confrontation, but it burned me the way he was patronizing me and enjoying it with his new pal Jack Monroe. I looked him right in the eyes with a sneer.

"Some friend! Do you nearly drown all your good friends like you did me?" I said coolly.

"Frank! I told you I was only helping you to take a bath. How was I to know you don't swim none?"

At this Old Whiskers burst out in loud hooting. I suppose my inadequacy was the best sort of amusement for them. I felt my face burn, and I was too angry to think of any retort. I was completely tongue tied. I found being in their company was too much to stand at the moment, so I turned on my heels and left them there. Sam tried to call after me, but I ignored him and kept on going. I did not look back.

Sam must have gotten himself out of talking with the group and came jogging after me.

"Frank!" he said. He caught up with me and began walking next to me.

"What do you want?" I spat, in a rank mood.

"You shouldn't let them get to you like that," he told me.

"What do you care anyway?" I complained.

"You only give them fuel for the fire, you know. Show them where your soft spots are and they will know where to strike. Your best defense is indifference."

"I'll keep it in mind."

"What is the matter with you?" He seemed genuinely perplexed.

"Do you think they would treat me the same if they knew I was a girl? No, sir! The hypocrisy of it makes me sick…rotten, foul men. It makes me boiling mad. Every lady from here to Kalamazoo ought to know what they really are! Be on the alert in case those men should try to snare one of them."

"We are all of us dogs," he replied. "Only there are some better trained than others. But it don't change the fact we are all dogs."

"You're no dog," I argued.

"Just one of the better trained," he said with a smirk. And then he left me.

"What a curious thing to say," I yelled after him.

We patrolled nearly every day, looking for the enemy. There was in those parts a certain group which called themselves Mosby's Raiders. They did all they could to cause trouble for us. Their raiders stole supplies and munitions, anything they could do to be a thorn in our sides. The locals were loyal to Mosby and would do all within their power to shelter him and protect him.

Upton did not like it, but he also didn't want to have egg on his face. If he made a fuss over it and concentrated all of his energy on bringing Mosby in, well, if he failed, it would make him look awfully bad. So he sent us out regularly to see what information we could gather, and to see if we could find him, without saying too much about it.

"If he becomes impertinent he may get chastised. But I don't think there will be much trouble," the Colonel said.

That was until it touched him personally. One day a woman showed up. I saw her come into camp, with such airs you would think she was the queen of England. This woman came to speak directly to the colonel and refused an audience with anyone else. After someone went and informed the colonel what was transpiring, Upton came from his tent and used his most polite manners with her, even bending to kiss her hand. She took his arm and walked with him as they spoke.

She had rich black hair and a waist the size of a teacup. She seemed so harmless, so fragile. It made me envious and hateful all at once. She wasn't even very beautiful, but all of the men drank her up with their eyes. It was a rare thing to have dealings with a woman. We saw them in town sometimes, or while scaring up food, but these men were sore for lady companionship, which could only be found if one was willing to pay. Many of them longed for affection, for a meaningful intimacy that could not be bought. Someone to love. Someone who would love them in return. After so long without such attentions from a female, any woman, even one without looks, seemed like Aphrodite. They were men after all. And in the absence of attractiveness, a set of breasts would do. I watched Sam to see if he was paying her attention, but he acted as though he didn't see her.

"What do you suppose that's about?" I asked Sam, watching with the same interest as everyone else.

"Couldn't say," he answered, as if he were uninterested. But how could he not be?

When she finished speaking with the Colonel he motioned for his own personal aide de camp to come to him.

"This good lady has requested someone to attend her as she travels through to Warrenton. I would like you to accompany her and see to it she comes to no harm," Upton informed his aide.

The aide nodded. "Yes, sir," he said.

She climbed daintily back into her carriage, taking the reins in her delicate, gloved hand. All of the men fairly salivated over her as she waited there. I suppose it's not saying much because, as I have told you before, they salivated over anything wearing a skirt, if it promised female attention. Finally the aide came around, now on horseback, to be her personal escort. She led the way and he took up the rear, giving a wink to the boys as he left, as if he might say, *Look at what fun I'll have. Lucky me!* He spurred his horse on and was gone.

The poor fellow never returned. She was only a clever ruse to draw someone away from the fold. Mosby must have been waiting on down the road somewhere in ambush. The next day we discovered the aide's body dancing merrily upon the breeze as it swung from a thick limb upon the sycamore tree he was hanged from. He was missing his hat and boots. His eyes were bulging, his tongue hanging limp from his mouth so he hardly looked human. Under the warm sun, he had begun to smell. Upton was in the saddle and reined his horse in, looking up at the unfortunate aide thoughtfully. He took his handkerchief from his pocket, pressing it to his nose to block the rank odor. He wore a most unpleasant expression upon his face as though he were both horrified and angry all at once.

"Cut him down!" he roared.

Boss Tanner climbed the sycamore and used his knife to cut the body down. No one spoke. It was a hushed silence as the body fell to the ground, limp and heavy.

Chapter 13

This was something Colonel Upton could not take sitting down. That it was his personal aide waylaid by Mosby's men only added insult to injury. It gave him the motivation to go after Mosby after all. Our directives changed. He wanted Mosby hunted down and brought to justice.

"We'll smoke them out!" he vowed. He organized several groups into search parties of three hundred men and sent us in pursuit of Mosby and his guerillas, each group sent in a different direction.

Our company headed out under the command of Lieutenant-Colonel Egbert Olcott. Now, he knew what he was doing, I cannot deny it. But he was also a reckless sort, who liked the drink and loved the ladies. In my opinion, it was difficult to feel loyalty for a man who behaved like a school boy. But he was my superior and therefore, I did as he said.

"Olcott has a negro in his services that says he can tell him where Mosby's home is," Sam told me.

"What good would it do to know where his home is?" I said. "He certainly won't be there."

"I don't think that is the Lieutenant-Colonel's intent. I think he means to harass, not capture."

Reed Haney good spiritedly said, "Gives us an excuse to stretch our legs, anyway."

"Notice it ain't Upton himself leading us. No he must stay and attend to things more important," Darby grumbled.

Several hours later we came upon Salem, Virginia. It wasn't much to speak of, a hole in the wall sort of place. There were no more than six hundred or so townsfolk who called it home. Olcott ordered us to surround the place in a picket line, while some of the others swept the town looking for Mosby.

"You have permission to take all the forage you can carry," Olcott said. "I don't want none of you grumbling for want of rations. But remember, we are gentleman of New York. I'll have no pillaging. Take only what you may eat or what may be useful to us." He smiled rakishly.

"Any horseflesh you may find is yours for the taking, boys. And if you find yourselves any male old enough to fight, you are to arrest him on the spot! If he should attempt to run, you have permission to shoot him. You catch yourself one of those Raiders I don't want them as prisoners. Take care of them then and there. Shoot them down. Understand?"

Three hundred shouts of "Yes, sir!" in unison ascended up to him.

"Don't go getting any ideas, mind you, about the womenfolk," he continued. "They are not to be abused in any way. Lest you think me not serious in the matter, I will personally take care of any man that should attempt to molest innocent women and children in any way. Understand?"

Again three hundred replied, "Yes, sir!"

Vern snickered at this comment and whispered, "If they are asking for it, is it still considered molestation?"

I gave him a look of contempt.

"Ah, come on, Frank. Ain't you never met a woman that was askin' for it? Once when I was visiting Albany, there was this gal, real pretty, and she had some big ones." And Vern used his hands to indicate he was talking about the size of her bosom. "Battin' her eyelashes and makin' advances to me—"

"Vern, shut it!" Sam growled. I noted his ears were bright red but wasn't sure if it was because he was mad or embarrassed.

"I was just saying—"

"I said shut it! There isn't any cause for crude talk like that," he insisted. I knew this was for my benefit. Vern was known to say worse about women in my presence, but that was before Sam knew I was a woman. The idea of someone speaking so crassly in front of me never offended his senses before now. I didn't want to hear what Vern would say, but I also didn't want anyone to become suspicious as to why Sam was being so sensitive about it. I chose to ignore the whole thing and walked away from both of them.

I remained in the picket line while a good portion of the group fell upon the town in a riotous clamor. They kicked in front doors, tore back curtains, ransacked barns and chicken coops, while the women and children screamed and cried and carried on. I was glad to stay behind. Harassing civilians was not my idea of fun. I didn't want to be involved in any of that business. Once they were gone, Olcott then addressed the men who held up the picket line.

"Should anyone attempt to run through this line, shoot 'em dead!" he said. Then he joined the others as they turned the town upside down looking for Mosby and any of his men, searching each building thoroughly and taking what they liked as they went. "Take what's useful" was very loosely interpreted by the men. Yet, Olcott didn't seem to notice.

Not a single Confederate soldier was found among them. They did, however, arrest all of the men of the town. Not a one was left, not even the preacher. They rounded them all up like livestock under guard and forced them to come along with us as prisoners. The women stood in the doorways weeping and moaning piteously as we left with their men.

Some of our boys rode out upon horses they'd confiscated, while others marched with prisoners in tow. Olcott rallied our detachment and ordered us on.

We left Salem, Virginia with prisoners, horses, and plenty of booty, burning the suspected house of Mosby as we went. We spent the night without our tents, sleeping upon the ground. The night was warm enough, and I was comfortable in my coat with no need for a blanket. While I slept, others in the detachment took turns keeping watch over the prisoners.

A clear cool morning came, leaving us damp with dew, and we began our march again. On the road in the distance some ways along we spotted a great sprawling estate. The master of the home was brutally interrogated, but insisted he knew no information to aid us in finding Mosby.

"I don't know anything!" he squealed. "I swear it! I swear it!" Finally Olcott gave up on him.

"Round up the horseflesh," Olcott commanded. We confiscated the man's horses, and now a great many of the men rode instead of walked. We made it nearly forty miles from Salem when Olcott let the prisoners go, directing them to go ahead and walk on back home.

"It will certainly put them out some," Felix observed.

"At least they get to go back home. How is that a punishment?" Darby asked.

We returned to our regiment with much food and provisions, as well as horses. Now the Negro who was giving them information told Upton that Mosby often hid in Middleburg. We pulled out and hastily headed for Middleburg, hoping we would catch him there. It was nearly two in the morning when we arrived just outside of the town. Again no tents, as we slept for an hour or so and then were ordered to prepare to take the town.

There was no resistance. The town's people made no attempt at defending themselves against us. They all put flags of truce on their doors to show they didn't have any intention of fighting against us.

"They don't wish for us to make any mistake about how they feel," Sam observed. On each door hung the bottom end of their under garments meant to represent the white flag.

I chuckled. "They are all showing us their rear ends!"

"Yes, indeed."

Captain John Mosby was nowhere to be found. But we collected a bounty of food from the town too. We came back to camp laden with poultry, produce, fresh milk in our canteens, and canned goods. The town's people stood by with tight lips and angry eyes as we took every last bit of food we could find. Let them show us the seats of their britches! They would suffer all winter long for it.

The following evening, after drills and a most generous supper, Sam pulled his chess board out.

"Would you be up to a game?" he asked me.

I nodded. "I suppose." He set the pieces up with the board between the two of us, then sat down opposite me and made himself comfortable.

"You may go first," he offered. Our two heads were bent nearly touching over the center of the checkered board as we observed the pieces and plotted our strategies.

I moved one of my pawns forward with slow deliberation, trailing it along the squares casually, no particular plan in mind. It was his turn now. With a look of concentration, he moved one of his pieces then caught my gaze and gave me a small smile. My mind was not clear. I was having a difficult time concentrating on the game. It dragged on in a leisurely fashion, as we lazily move our pieces about the board, in my mind the game secondary to the banter between the two of us as our hands brushed one another's now and then. At one point I went to move my piece and he put his hand over mine to stop me.

"Are you sure you want to do that?" he asked me with a raised eyebrow. His hand continued to linger over mine.

"It can't hurt," I said, meeting his eyes demurely. I reluctantly pulled my hand from his and finished my move.

"I've captured your queen," he said, snatching it up.

"Yes, you have," I assented.

"And now I have your king," he informed me, taking his piece and knocking mine over. He looked at me with a playful grin on his lips. "Checkmate."

"Then it seems you have won," I said with a casual shrug.

"And you don't seem to care one bit."

"Not such a bad way for a queen to go, is it? In defense of her king?" I inquired with a cocked eyebrow. I was flirting with him, something I was fully and painfully aware of. What made me do a thing so brazen, I couldn't say. I was nothing but a desperate and shameless muttonhead, and I knew it. Heaven help me, I knew it. And he must have known it too. How could he not? What sort of person was I to behave in such a way?

He seemed taken aback, blinking a few times with his brow furrowed. Perhaps it was because he never saw this side of me. Or he was appalled by my brazen disregard for decorum. I couldn't say for sure. I just got that feeling that maybe I had gone too far. Maybe I had crossed a line. I began to second guess myself, wondering why I would have done such a fool thing.

"No, I suppose not," he conceded.

"Shall I make some coffee?" I asked, working to draw attention away from my earlier moment of weakness.

"That would be nice," he agreed. "Or perhaps I should make it for you?"

"To the victor goes the spoils," I teased. And I got up to get the coffee pot and water to boil. A short while later I brought him his cup of coffee.

"You will always be better at chess than I," I told him. "I see no point in pretending I may someday surpass your skills."

"You shouldn't give up so easily," he said.

"Caleb used to play at checkers with me, and never was content with me as a partner, because I was no competition for him either. He wished for a real opponent and he got only me."

"Knowing Caleb as I did, I am sure he was not too sore over it," Sam said.

"I think it vexed him something awful that he must endure me for a sister." I laughed. "I relied heavily upon him."

"That so?"

"Yes. I'm surprised you don't remember it. Me always hanging around and plaguing the two of you," I reminded him.

"I don't recall," he said. "It seems so long ago now."

"Well, I never expected you to. I have always been utterly forgettable," I admitted taking a sip of my coffee.

"I don't suppose I paid much attention to you then," he confessed. "But it doesn't mean you are forgettable." He grinned broadly as a thought came to him.

"Although I do remember when you were just a little weed," he said, holding his hand up to show how short I had been. "And you lost your bonnet in the water." He took a sip of his coffee before he went on. "You were sitting on the bank, great big tears rolling down your face. Oh, and a terrible pout. When I came upon you, you couldn't even speak to me. You looked so forlorn, so lost...such a serious little thing."

"You knew it was me?"

"You were my best friend's little sister," he pointed out.

"But you called me little girl. That day, you didn't call me by my name," I said.

"I knew you were his little sister. I never said I remembered your name."

"Yes, well, I remembered yours. Sam. You swam out and brought my bonnet back to me. And I was very grateful to you for it," I acknowledged. "My mother would have tanned my hide good if I'd lost my bonnet."

"Glad to have saved you from a tanning." He grew sober. "How is your mother anyway?"

I could feel the smile fade from my lips. "She was not well when I left. But father said in his letter to me that she is slowly growing better."

"She must miss you very much," he said.

I shook my head. "I don't think she recognizes I've even left. With Caleb gone…well, she was not the same."

"I'm sorry for it. She was always a kind and generous woman to me. And your father too."

"Yes, Father…" I cleared my throat, trying to keep from being emotional. "Father is one of the best of men. I feel remorse over how I left him. At least I spared him the truth."

"Why? Because he thinks you are a nurse?"

"Yes."

"He would not like it if he knew what you were really up to," Sam said.

"I know it well," I agreed. "I would rather die than have him find out I've lied to him as I have. I never should have done that to him."

"Maybe it's time you went home," he suggested.

"Maybe," I replied.

"You were raised to be a gentle lady. This life must be a burden to you," he observed.

"Don't try to flatter me, Sam. I was not born a gentle lady. I was born a farmer's daughter. You and I both know there's a difference. I don't possess the soft white hands of a woman who has never known manual labor. My hands are coarse and rough from hard work. How's that any different from what I'm doing now?" He chose to ignore this. He was set to make a point, and I was interfering with it.

"The things you've seen…It is something I wish you hadn't. I wish I could've kept you from all of that ugliness."

"I have borne it well, haven't I?" I said, defensively.

"Admirably. I was in no way implying you haven't done your share. I didn't mean to insult you. I only meant to say you deserve better. You deserve a good life, the life of a respectable woman."

I gave a short, cynical laugh. "Huh, I think I'm beyond respectable at this point, don't you? Take a hard look, Sam. I'm scarcely what you could call proper."

"I've made you angry. I didn't mean to. You must understand I'm only trying to think of what's best."

"For whom?"

I didn't know what to say. He was trying to get rid of me. He wanted me to go home and be out of his hair. I felt the bitter pangs of rejection at the thought of it. A moment ago I'd thought there was something between us, something in his eyes, something in our touch, something…

I threw the rest of my coffee out and got up, doing my best to hide my disappointment at his wish for me to go home.

"I am tired. I think I might turn in," I said in a neutral voice. It was my way of saying the subject was closed. I didn't want to talk about it anymore.

"Thank you for the coffee," he said, lifting his cup in my direction to salute me.

"It was nothing," I said, and then I turned away and left him there.

Chapter 14

Colonel Upton was now in Washington. He took ill and was sent there to recuperate in a proper hospital. In his stead we were led by Olcott. Now I have told you what a rascal he was. I suppose it would be a difficult thing to be as dashing as he, with his fine mustache and dark looks, and not be somewhat imprudent. In Upton's absence, Olcott, while strict with the men and diligent in executing his duties, indulged in questionable behaviors elsewhere.

We continued to scour the countryside looking for Mosby, but with no luck. We all believed the townsfolk we interrogated not only harbored him, but possibly rode with him as well. What better disguise? Shopkeeper by day, guerrilla by night. It would explain how they so easily disappeared and evaded capture. Who would think to look in plain sight?

On one of our excursions looking for the devil, we came upon a fine plantation, grand in every way. The property was vast, with fields that were once planted in cotton, and orchards upon several acres just beyond the main house. The slave quarters were like a small village a stone's throw away, although it looked fairly abandoned now. An informant led us to this place in the late afternoon, telling us the master of this fine home rode with Mosby's Raiders, as did the man's sons.

Olcott ordered a group of the men to wait back on the lane leading up to the main house and took only a handful of us with him in his investigation. Mr. Haney and I were among those who accompanied him. We mounted the steps and knocked on the door intent upon questioning the occupants. A servant girl drew the door open, her brown eyes filled with fear when she discovered it was a swarm of Yankee soldiers upon the veranda. She abruptly shut the great door when she saw us, and we could hear her feet running on the floorboards as she went to fetch the mistress. Shortly the door opened again. This time a white woman greeted us.

"May I help you?" she asked. Her voice was soft and her accent charming. She was middle aged but handsome nonetheless with vivid blue eyes and a perfectly pale complexion. She wore fine clothing, and her posture was straight and dignified. She didn't seem at all frightened or put off by our presence.

Olcott's attention was immediately piqued, as was the case when any female was in his company. He put on his most pleasant smile. Where before he was ready to give somebody the what for, he was now his most charming self.

"I don't know that you can," he said. "But perhaps. Perhaps. By chance are you Mrs. Marie Sturbridge?"

"I am she," the woman confirmed.

"I am Lieutenant-Colonel Egbert Olcott. Might we talk further inside?"

"It is only me and my daughters here, sir. Do I have your word you all will behave like gentlemen?"

"You certainly do, Madame," Olcott solemnly assured her.

She opened wide the door, and we all filed in to the spacious front room. Olcott took the seat offered him, while the rest of us stood at attention.

"Could I offer you some tea, Lieutenant-Colonel?"

"That would surely be most welcome," Olcott said.

The pretty little negro girl who opened the door to us was sent off to prepare the tea. And Mrs. Marie Sturbridge sat primly at the edge of her tufted chair, her hands folded upon her lap, with her full attention upon the Lieutenant-Colonel. Olcott's face was most pleasant as he leaned back in his chair, crossing his leg, making himself comfortable. He was confident in the presence of the woman. After watching him at work, I presumed he must have experienced only success in his pursuit of the fairer gender.

"How may I help you, sir?" the Southern woman asked, her face appearing guileless, with her eyes wide and inquiring.

"You perhaps are aware, Madame, of a most dangerous character who is said to ride in the vicinity, a Captain John Singleton Mosby?"

Her face didn't change one bit. She maintained her calm composure, betraying nothing. I admired her for that. She was just as good as Olcott, cool and collected.

"I have heard of Captain Mosby, sir. Although I have no personal knowledge of him wandering these parts," she replied.

"Now, I don't wish to alarm you, dear lady, but we have it on good authority this charlatan is indeed somewhere close by, stirring up trouble where he may."

There was a slight sound, the rustle of skirts as then entered the breathtakingly beautiful daughter carrying a tray of teacups and such. Her skin was like fresh milk, her hair a deep and rich auburn red. She glided into the room as though her feet did not touch the ground, a vision of loveliness even I could appreciate, and certainly envied. Mr. Haney and I exchanged a glance. A most fine-looking woman such as she was not a thing Olcott could pass up easily. It begged his attention. You could almost see the cogs of his brain spinning furiously, as you might imagine the innards of a clock that has been wound too tightly.

As she entered, Olcott jumped from his chair as if his hind end were pressed to hot coals, and gave his assistance in carrying her tray to a small side table next to Mrs. Sturbridge.

"Let me help you with that, Miss," he practically begged.

"Thank you, sir," she said sweetly.

"Catharine, this is Lieutenant-Colonel Olcott," Mrs. Sturbridge said as she poured tea into the china cups. "Lieutenant-Colonel, this is my eldest daughter, Miss Catharine Sturbridge."

Olcott bent low and kissed the back of her hand. "Miss Sturbridge, a pleasure," he said.

The young Miss Sturbridge responded with adequate modesty, lowering her eyes with just the slightest of smiles, although it was obvious to me she was sure of her effect upon him. These things are difficult to conceal from other women I suppose, because they know the games females play, but easy enough to deceive a man when he does not want to see the cunning devices a woman is capable of employing.

Her voice was soft and low as she said, "It would be good to meet you too, Lieutenant-Colonel, if you were not wearing that uniform. Blue does not become you." He seemed shocked for a moment and then burst out laughing.

"Well, I say…I believe I like a woman who speaks her mind."

"Unless she has a horsey face or an unsightly figure," I whispered to Mr. Haney. "Then she should abstain from speaking all together." He suppressed a laugh.

"Hold your tongue, Frank," he shushed. "Before you get us both into trouble."

Olcott waited for the young lady to sit before he resumed his own seat.

"I was just speaking to your mother, Miss Sturbridge, on matters of local security. We have it on good authority that a fugitive seeks sanctuary in these parts, a fugitive who poses a threat to the military and private citizens alike."

Catharine Sturbridge cocked her head to the side. "And who is this dangerous character you speak of?" she asked with just the slightest hint of sarcasm.

"I speak of Captain John Mosby and his infamous band of Rebels," he informed her.

"Captain Mosby? Here?" She laughed. "I don't believe it."

"I don't want to frighten you," Olcott continued. "Lord knows what such a man may be capable of. And you ladies alone without the protection of a man—"

"Why should we have fear of him, sir? His aim is not upon molesting Southerners," she pointed out. "He hunts Yank trash such as yourself." It was fascinating to watch her work, throwing him away with insulting comments, and then reeling him back in with her shameless flirting, a master of her skill.

Olcott shifted uneasily. "You may perhaps think that. But I believe him capable of anything. He is a notorious robber and murderer, Miss Sturbridge, which is what brings me to your doorstep, I am sorry to say. I am here to reassure you we will do all in our power to make sure no harm comes to you from this impertinent fellow. I am at your disposal, here to defend and protect."

"How very generous of you, Lieutenant-Colonel. But really, very unnecessary. We have been here alone for quite some time, with no serious threat to our safety," Marie Sturbridge said.

"Why doesn't he ask about her father?" I whispered to Mr. Haney.

"Think nothing of it," Olcott replied. "I count it my duty and will act accordingly. My men and I will set up camp out back, in the orchard there, and do our best to keep the rascal from afflicting you in any way."

Mother looked to daughter with raised eyebrows and then back to Olcott. "Perhaps you would join us for dinner?" Mrs. Sturbridge offered.

"I would be most pleased to partake of your hospitality," the Lieutenant-Colonel consented.

Chapter 15

The peach trees were bare of fruit, it now being autumn. But the leaves were still upon their limbs, not yet having fallen. They'd just began to turn orange — rows and rows of green trees, speckled with vivid orange patches.

We pitched our tents in the empty spaces, making fast work of it. We set up our fires for cooking and made ourselves comfortable for the evening. Some of the men played at a game of cards or smoked their pipes, whatever they preferred to pass the time. Sam was full of questions, having been left in the lane when Mr. Haney and I went with Olcott and were privy to the conversation within.

"What in thunder are we doing here?" he asked.

"The Lieutenant-Colonel has set his sights upon a prize. A very lovely girl named Catharine Sturbridge," I told him.

"What?" he said incredulously.

"Yes. She batted her eyes and insulted him sorely, and he ate it up," I replied. "Imagine the stupidity of it!"

"What was said?"

"Olcott said he wished to protect them from Mosby's molestations."

"Protect them? Their men are the ones riding with him," Sam groaned.

"You needn't remind me. He didn't even question them about the father or the brothers. It all makes me very irritated indeed," I complained. "May I ask you something, Sam?"

"Certainly," he said.

"Why is it that boys are so easily swayed by a pretty face?" I asked.

"It is the nature of man." He shrugged. "It is what we eat, sleep, and breathe for. Our very existence in this world is to find a woman who will have us. I suppose some are more prone to be ruled by this weakness than others."

"Well, I see these women, endowed with the gifts of beauty and grace, betraying themselves for their own purposes, and it makes me feel scornful of them," I disclosed. "I wonder at what sort of lady would behave so unspeakably for the attentions of a man. They make objects of themselves, worth no more than a piece of furniture or candlesticks, or…or ear bobbles. They sell their souls for a mess of pottage. They make women look weak and shallow and unworthy of being taken seriously. And I wonder too how any man could look upon them with any degree of respect."

Sam smiled. "It is not with respect they look upon them. It is something more base than you could understand, I'm sure. Mostly they have no affection for them — after all lust is not love."

"If that is so, then why is it these women are the sorts who seem to draw a man's eye and get all of the attention?"

"Because until a man is ready to settle down, he wants the milk for free, and so, why buy the whole blessed cow? When a man goes to marry, those don't tend to be the women he chooses for a wife. Not the smart men anyway. The smart ones know better."

"So you're not taken in by a beautiful woman?"

Sam cleared his throat, probably feeling put on the spot by my question.

"I do not care for women who play games, toy with a man's affections. A fast trick don't suit me. But it don't mean I can't appreciate their looks," he said frankly.

"I see," I said, feeling dispirited.

"But God created beauty in many varied forms. What one considers run of the mill may be a sight to behold through someone else's eyes. It's all comparative."

"What a kind way of making the *run of the mill* feel less unexceptional," I told him with a sad smile.

"There is nothing unexceptional about you, Miss Stark. If that was your understanding of my speech you were mistaken."

"As always, Sam, you remain the boy who rescued my bonnet."

Lieutenant-Colonel Olcott walked past, headed for the main house for his supper, straightening his coat and tugging at his cuffs as he went.

"Oh, for heaven's sake, there he goes," I grumbled.

"Poor fellow," Sam said.

"Poor in what way? He must suspect what those women are."

"And yet, he cannot help himself."

"I'm sure he could if he wanted to," I argued.

The Carroll brothers came by, whistling a tune. They carried a large burlap sack between them. When they spotted us, they stopped.

"Found a right good treat," one said. The other took a generous handful of goober peas from the sack, handed it to Sam, and then did the same for me.

I always forgot which was which so I said, "Thank you, brother Carroll."

They went on, distributing more to the others. I saw them give some to Jack Monroe, and I couldn't help but scowl. Sam was right when he said Jack always seemed to have more than everyone else. I wondered how he managed it.

"You know, I think you were right about Old Whiskers. He never seems to run out of rations. Do you think he steals from the other men? Or perhaps he uses blackmail to get extras?"

Sam cracked a shell and tossed the oddly shaped nuts into his mouth. "I have kept my eye on him. But I can't seem to figure it out. Whatever he's up to it is shady. You can be sure of it," Sam said.

Sam and I spent the rest of the evening cracking shells and tossing them away as we ate. Gradually the night came on and we crawled into our tent. It was the blackest part of night, while we were in the deepest of sleep, when a blast rang out clear and shrill. And then a barrage of others followed. I started, disoriented and frightened. In the darkness, Sam sprang from his bedroll and made for the tent door.

I got up and went to follow him. Horses whined, tramping through the trees and tents, pistols discharged, in a chaotic scene. When we reached the door of our tent we saw men on horseback forcing their way through tent doors and firing upon the occupants inside. The scene was one of frenzied confusion with Olcott in nothing but his short underwear, a pistol in each hand, swearing and firing randomly upon the intruders as they came. The men were running to and fro in the confusion, in various stages of dress, groggy from sleep, many without a weapon. They were sitting ducks for the attackers who were firing upon them.

"Get back!" Sam yelled. He backed up through the tent door, jerking me in with him. Sam scrambled for the tent pole, ripped it out of its place, and let the canvas tent fall in on us. Still clutching the tent pole in his hand, he tackled me to the ground, the back of my head bumping abrasively into the packed earth. Then I felt the heavy weight of his body as he lay on top of me in an effort to protect me. I was utterly taken aback. Everything was moving too quickly for my brain to even process it all.

"Sam, what are you doing?" I loudly protested.

He put his finger to my mouth. "Ssh!"

Outside the crisis raged on. Men were yelling, guns were being fired, and the beat of horse hooves was all around. I lay perfectly still under Sam's weight, secure in the knowledge he would defend me if it should come to that. We were in a cocoon, safe and apart from the commotion outside. I was aware of it all, but it seemed somehow separate from us. My heart beat wildly, yet I was unsure if it was from fear or from having Sam so close to me.

While the turmoil of the raid seemed to go on forever, in reality it lasted only ten to fifteen minutes. The sounds of horses receding, and our men scrambling to take chase, let us know the danger was over, but we remained where we were on the dirt floor of our collapsed tent for a time, motionless and silent, neither of us able to move. Strange how aware I was of everything happening, yet still unable to understand any of it. My brain was empty of all thought, of all reasoning.

"Are you all right?" Sam finally whispered. It took me a moment to determine whether I really was or not.

"Yes," I finally replied.

"You're shaking," he said. I was not conscious of it until he pointed it out to me. Indeed my limbs were trembling uncontrollably. I couldn't tell if it was the shock or the fear that caused it.

"I'm all right," I insisted, angry at myself for being so fragile.

Sam got up and then gave me his hand and helped me to my feet. We felt our way around the tent until we found the opening and stumbled out. Everyone was running around in a general state of confusion and shock. Olcott, still in his underwear with his pistols slack at his sides now, was wandering about camp with a muddled look on his face, stunned by the turn of events. After taking stock of the situation, we discovered the sentry who was assigned to keep watch at the road had attempted to stop the Raiders. He asked for identification and was shot in the face for his trouble, as the raiders moved past him and descended upon us. Mosby managed to make halfwits of us yet again.

Chapter 16

Humiliated and in a sad, sorry state, we went back to camp in New Baltimore. Olcott attempted to make it look as if what happened was of little consequence. It only made the men angrier than ever. It is a difficult thing to have someone you so admire do something of such weak character. Everyone involved simply wished to forget it. I think we were all of a like mind when Colonel Upton returned from Washington — relieved and pleased.

The doldrums of camp life wore on us all, as did Mosby's persistent raids to harass and cause turmoil. A year was gone now. A year since we'd left our homes in New York. There seemed to be no end to the war in sight. What would it take to end it? To see home and family once again?

Sam seemed intent on me going home. He pestered me regularly with suggestions of it. Really there was nothing keeping me. My whole purpose in enlisting was to aid him in any way I might. If he didn't want me there, I should seriously question why I remained. There was no reason for me to act this part any longer. Why hang around, seeking the affections of a man who didn't want me? Was I some pariah that I should continually thrust myself, unwanted, upon Sam? It seemed downright ridiculous that I couldn't take a hint and move on. With each passing day, the idea of leaving became more appealing.

One day Sam and Boss Tanner and I were given horses and told to go investigate the claim of a farmer who resided a day's ride away and was said to have information regarding Mosby's Raiders. We accordingly packed our provisions for several days and headed out southeast of camp toward the residence in question. There were many such claims and none amounted to anything. Mosby remained at large.

With all of the horses we stole there were plenty to go around. We selected our mounts and headed out. Luck was with us when at midday we found an inn along the way where we stopped and ate some fine food, fresh and hot. We were counting ourselves pretty fortunate to have gotten the assignment after such a meal.

When we arrived at the farm in late evening, it looked much like what I should think the witch's cottage from *Hansel and Gretel* might appear, only without the candy. It was a sweet little house surrounded by trees turned red, yellow, and orange, picket fencing, and finials decorating the porch railings and posts giving it a charm most appealing. A woman who appeared to be in her forties or fifties met us out front, although it was difficult to tell for certain how old she really was because she'd seen hard times. That much was evident, with her worn out face and gray hair falling dirty and limp from the bun she tried to secure it in. She greeted us on the porch with a wary sort of smile.

I noted right away she was not expecting us. She seemed flighty and agitated when she saw us, as though she hadn't seen another human being in quite some time and was taken aback by our arrival. Indeed she appeared not to know what to do with our company. The three of us exchanged skeptical and fleeting looks; a sense of something not being right with her hit us all from the start. What made us carry on I couldn't say. I think it was the thought of being rude or inhospitable toward her which perhaps led us onward.

"We were told you have a complaint and may have information about a John S. Mosby," Boss Tanner said to the woman from his mount.

She looked quite mad to me. Her smile seemed suspiciously wicked as she nodded slowly. "I have?" she said with a laugh. "Yes, yes. That's right."

We dismounted and tethered the horses to the posts of the porch, standing awkwardly in the yard and waiting for her to invite us in. She acted as though she didn't know how to proceed, trying to straighten her hair and looking about for some cue from us. It gave me an uncomfortable feeling. It wasn't so much that she was a woman who had lost her wits, it was more a combination of that fact and also being in enemy territory and not knowing who could be trusted and who would wait until your back was turned so they might put a ball in it. Seeing as how she was behaving so erratically, the latter seemed the most likely.

"Should we come in?" Sam asked with a kind prodding.

"Come in?" she repeated. "Oh, yes. Yes, come in."

We followed her into the house, where the light of the fire on the hearth was the only light illuminating the dark interior of the room. The smell immediately assaulted me, like mildew and over-ripe fish. There was a frightening compilation of rotting food, piled up newspapers, unclean canning jars, piles of filthy rags, and worse crammed into the small space, stacked against the walls and upon the furniture. The table was scattered with dirty dishes, a bowl piled with dried and wrinkling peels shaved from fruit, a glass bottle filled with some sort of dark brown greasy substance (meat drippings perhaps?), and cornbread half eaten, now molding, still in its cast iron pan. The woman horded all sorts of strange things, a human magpie who found any small and useless item a treasure to claim and be used to pad her nest with, so there was nary a place to step without encountering a pile of something.

My eyes found it difficult to focus on any one thing, until I noted soon after entering the room a picture of a gentlemen in uniform upon the mantle seemed to have its own peculiarly clean place. Strangely enough it was the only item in the room residing in an uncluttered space, which made it stand out from all else. Either a husband or a son, I couldn't be sure, but it was obvious he was a Confederate from the colors he wore.

"Sam…" I whispered urgently.

He turned to me in a fog of confusion, not sure what to make of this woman's living conditions or her odd behaviors. Distracted, he looked at me with his eyebrows drawn together, pondering the poor woman's circumstances, no doubt. Once I got his attention I motioned as discreetly as I might with a bob of my head in the direction of the mantel so he should see the picture as well. What with all of the rubbish to distract him, he looked back at me with a shrug. He didn't know what I was talking about. He hadn't seen it.

"What?" he hissed.

I didn't want to arouse the woman's suspicions, so I looked from him and pointed with my eyes to the picture. He attempted to seem casual as he walked toward the mantel, tripping over a pile of newspapers as he went. He drew near enough to the picture to see what it was, and his drawn eyebrows changed expression quickly, raising in distress while his face fell as it registered with him. He understood now why I directed him there. We were in the home of a Confederate. This was no Northern sympathizer wanting to share information.

This woman knew absolutely nothing of Mosby. She knew absolutely nothing of anything. She hadn't summoned us. Whoever sent us to this place had ill intent on their minds, this was certain. It was a snare. A trap. We'd been drawn away from the fold.

Boss was trying his best to converse with the woman, who was mumbling madly, with not a coherent thought in her brain. He didn't have any idea what Sam and I saw. Without consideration of being rude or impertinent, I interrupted Boss.

"Where is your man?" I interjected rather forcefully. I thought my voice had a fraught quality to it which betrayed my distress.

"What?" she asked, her face confused.

I strode over to the mantel and plucked the frame from its place, holding it up toward her. "Where is your man?" This time I displayed more control. I worked hard to sound more authoritative, instead of like a scared silly child.

"Hartley?" she whispered. Her eyes grew far off as her thin and fragile hand with bulging veins floated slowly to her breast and rested softly there. I must have made some connection with her, something she at last understood.

"Yes, Hartley," I encouraged. "Where is he? Does he ride with the Rangers?" I was referring of course to the Mosby Rangers.

"He…he is gone," she murmured, as though she herself were surprised by that bit of news. Her eyes were wide and she looked from me to Sam and then to Boss with an expression like puzzlement. Or perhaps it was an entreaty. It is difficult to read a crazy person because there is no logic or reason to them.

Now the three of us knew right then there would be trouble. Although it was not evident exactly what was soon to transpire, we knew some ill intent was planned for us. We had been hoodwinked. I lay the framed picture on the table, and we collectively backed up toward the door, eager to exit the place and be on our way. She seemed startled by our actions, moving after us to the threshold, as though she didn't wish for us to leave and meant to keep us there but didn't have the power to do so.

"Where are you going?" she wanted to know. "Won't you stay? Don't…don't leave me."

"We have others we are to meet up with," I lied. "A whole passel of them, just up the road a-ways, and we mustn't be late or they will come looking for us. We don't want any trouble."

"Thank you for your time," Sam offered, taking his hat off to her. I felt sorry for her when we left, so forlorn and pitiful, but not so sorry that I was willing to be strung up over it.

We hastened to the horses and tore out of there like the devil himself was at our heels. Once we got a safe distance from the house we paused in the road, our horses prancing nervously after the push we gave them.

"What did you make of it?" Sam asked.

"Was she working for Mosby?" Boss wanted to know.

"I don't know if she was capable," Sam answered.

"I don't feel good about it," I said. "There is some villainy at work here."

"That picture…" Boss began.

"A Confederate. Likely some kin of hers. I don't think she had any idea what was going on. Someone has set us up," Sam replied. "Someone sent us there in hopes she would keep us until they could come along and gather us up."

"If that's so, they are not far off then."

"We'd do best to get as far away from here, as fast as we might," I agreed.

"Stay off the road," Sam cautioned.

We guided the horses off of the road, staying in a close knot as we traveled north. When dark came on we made camp, not daring to start a fire. If we hadn't feared for the horses we would have pushed on, for there was no sleep for us during the night. The enemy was about, we had no doubt. We sat miserably huddled together, our blankets the only warmth on the cool night, as we ate cold jerky.

"It must be Mosby," Sam ventured. "This is the sort of hoax he'd plan."

"He's growing worse by the day," Boss said.

"Darby says he hung seven of our men. Strung them up right on the edge of Custer's camp, as bold as you please. He has no fear," I informed them.

"No fear and no mercy," Sam added.

We were not far from the road, and a short time later we heard horses on the path. Boss crept quietly through the woods to try to learn who it was. We lost sight of him for a time. Sam was looking at me in alarm while we waited together apprehensively.

"If anything should happen…" he whispered.

"Nothing will happen," I insisted, although I wondered where his train of thought was leading him.

Boss came silently back. He held up his fingers to indicate their numbers. "Seven," he breathed.

"Pack up," Sam directed. "Be ready to move."

"They are tracking us," Boss said. "I heard a bit of what they was saying. They know we must have left the road. They are going back to try to discover where."

"We haven't got a chance," I squeaked. "Not against seven."

"Pack up," Sam said again, more insistently this time. "I don't aim on making it easy for them, staying here like sitting ducks."

We rolled up our blankets and provisions, piling them in the saddlebags. Sam took a branch from the ground and went behind, sweeping the ground where we trod, trying to cover our tracks. Then we walked the horses, as quietly as was possible, through the woods.

Chapter 17

They were close on our heels and we knew it. Just before dawn, we came to a place where the forest thinned out and the road curved due to a change in landscape. The ground dropped away to form a deep valley on the left and right, leaving only a narrow path on which to traverse across. Sam and Boss and I stopped where we still had cover left and stewed over what we should do.

"If we get out in the open there's no telling what will happen. They for certain will overcome us," Boss said. We could easily read the fear on each other's faces. None of us even bothered hiding it. Doom was upon our doorstep. We would be lucky if we ate another meal.

Sam looked at me nervously, and then looked away, unable to meet my eyes. Finally he addressed Boss as though I wasn't even there, as though it were just the two of them.

"Boss, you and me are the adults here," he said. "I would sure hate to see this boy suffer on account of our stupidity, letting ourselves be baited as we have. The best thing to do is let the boy go and you and me give ourselves up. At least one of us will get away."

"What?" I cried. "You aren't giving yourselves up. Not on my account!"

Boss was older than both of us and knew a thing or two I suppose. He was reluctantly nodding his agreement. "There seems to be no way out of it. Maybe they will only take us prisoner if we surrender and make it easy for them. There are worse fates," he said.

"The two of you must be full on crazy if you think I will let you do such a thing!" I turned to Sam, who avoided my gaze. "You don't know me at all if you think I'll go along with this."

"Frank, you don't have a say in it. You're too young to know what's good for you," Sam replied, still not meeting my eyes. "Besides, we need someone who can report back…let them know what's happened."

"It won't be me!" I insisted.

"You'll do what you're told," Sam said. He was mad. I could tell. That's how he was when he was under pressure and saw no way out. I remembered him behaving similarly when we found the old woman in her cellar back in Fredericksburg.

"There's gotta be some way," I fumed. My brain was working furiously to come up with a solution. In desperation I latched on to an idea and hastily mulled it over.

"You got your pistol?" I asked.

"Certainly I have my pistol," Sam answered.

"Listen, maybe there is yet a way," I told them urgently. "You two head back toward Mosby's men, find a good spot to hold up where you've got plenty of cover, guns loaded, ready to fire, and wait for them to come to you."

"We're outnumbered, Frank, more than two to one!" Sam grumbled.

"Maybe so, but they don't know it," I reasoned.

"Even if they don't know how many of us there are, if we engage, there's too many of them, they'll beat us for sure," Boss pointed out.

"They don't expect us to come at them, do they? They expect us to run. We have surprise on our side. I will wait up here, just out of their shooting range, and when they get to where you are, I will give my horse a good smack, send it across the road. It's still mostly dark. They won't see who or what it is. They open fire, and you've got a few moments before they can reload.

"That is when you let them have it. We have three rifles and Sam's pistol. Take aim on the man in front, take him down, and then just keep shooting."

"I don't know…" Sam said. "If it doesn't work, there'll be hell to pay. It doesn't work and we're all dead men, strung from the nearest tree, you included. If you got away, it would be at least one of us."

"It will work," I pleaded. "They won't know what's hit them. They'll scatter! I know it, they will scatter!" The two of them looked at me skeptically, but I could see Boss was coming around.

"Come on, Boss. It's better than just giving up. You don't want to go without a fight, do you?"

"I'm willing to try it," Boss finally said. I saw I'd swayed him and pressed on, talking in an excited and quick manner, trying to gain momentum.

"You remember the story of the battle of Jericho? You make as much noise as you can and you shoot off the guns, take a few of them out, and they'll run. They aren't expecting us to stand against them. They won't know what's hit them. I'm telling you it will scare the dickens out of them and they'll run." I was sure what I was saying was true, even adamant, but Sam looked doubtful.

"I don't want to risk it," Sam said. I knew what he was trying to say without coming right out and saying it in front of Boss Tanner. *I don't want to risk you getting captured.*

"Well, I won't go along with hiding like a coward and letting you two give yourselves up," I maintained.

"He has a plan, unless you can come up with something better," Boss said. "But we need to decide quickly or it will be too late and we won't have time to prepare."

Sam sighed heavily. "You stay put," he told me, pointing his finger at my face with his jaw clenched and his eyes hard. "You stay put and out of the way once it all starts. You hear? And no matter what should happen, you don't come out for anything!"

I nodded my head in reply, just to get him to agree to what I'd proposed. Boss was watching the two of us interact in confusion, as if he were trying to figure us out.

"We haven't got time for this bull," he complained.

Sam shrugged his shoulders, trying to come off as if he didn't care so much. "Let's go," he said to Boss. "We'll double back, situate ourselves fifty yards or so from here. I'll give a whistle when it's time, and that's your cue to let the horse go."

The two of them trudged off and left me alone with all of the horses. Boss carried his rifle and mine in each of his hands. Sam carried his rifle and revolver. Eventually the shadows engulfed them, and I couldn't see or hear them any longer. It was deathly quiet as I stood waiting, my knees quaking, and my heart thumping. I was afraid. It terrified me to think we might fail and just what that would mean for all of us.

The light of morning began to creep up, a soft glow which hadn't become a full sunrise yet, when I heard Sam's whistle. Every muscle taut, waiting for the sound, I reacted instantly, giving my horse a brutal slap on his backside and letting loose a loud holler at the same time. The horse bolted forward, running headlong through the trees and out onto the road. It vanished almost instantly into the woods on the other side.

At the same time I heard Mosby's men fire. The fools had no idea what they were even firing upon, but they were so startled their instinct was to shoot, regardless of what it was they were shooting at. Once they all discharged their weapons there was a brief moment of quiet, and then the real noise began. Sam and Boss opened fire upon them at close range, and they let out a whoop that could be heard from here to the Mason-Dixon Line. I joined in with them. Between the bullets flying and the noise, the lot of them became disoriented, finding it difficult to stay mounted with their horses rearing back in alarm. After two fell to the ground, the rest turned tail and hastily galloped off to where it was they'd come from.

When Boss and Sam returned to me a moment later, they were breathless and triumphant. Sam's eyes met mine, and he tried to conceal a smile. This did not escape my attention. I had been right. He knew it, and I knew it. I couldn't help but feel a smug satisfaction over it. But it was Boss Tanner who voiced it.

"You done good, kid."

"Yes," Sam agreed. That was all he said.

"Now let's get the blazes out of here!" Boss said.

Between the three of us there were only two horses left now, what with mine being long gone, and we still had a good four hours or more back to camp. I rode on the back of Sam's horse for the remainder of the journey. Not a bad way to travel, in my estimation. I did my best not to seem pleased about it, which was a hard thing to accomplish, even more so with Boss there. I could not rest my cheek against his shoulder, or pull myself too closely for fear it might seem odd. I let my arms hang loose at my side for the most part, unless we came to rough terrain, then I was lucky enough to have to put my arms around Sam's middle. I looked forward with anticipation to every bump in the road.

Chapter 18

Things were quiet for a spell. Camp life fell into a sweet monotony as we whiled away our time. Mosby was always a threat, but we were far more careful after our frightening experience at the mad woman's cottage. Mosby and his men did all they could to harass and pester, it was true, but we managed to give it back every now and again, which brought some satisfaction. In truth, it probably made our lives a little less dull, although I'm sure any one of us would have done what we could to bring him in to justice and put an end to the whole cat and mouse game.

Then, on the night of November sixth, we were told tomorrow we would be moving out early. They issued hardtack and pork to each of us, eight days' worth. Our haversacks were overflowing with food. It was obvious something was coming down the pike. Upton was assigned command of the whole brigade. In his stead, Major Mather would be in charge of the 121st.

"Won't see fighting for several days or more I should think," he told us.

The following morning we were up before the dawn, taking down tents and packing gear. The mood was cheerful, the excitement apparent as the men assembled and followed commands to head out on a march.

Sam leaned in toward me and said, "The thought of a scrape certainly makes a man jovial, don't it?" as he observed those around us and their enthusiasm for our march.

"It's either bored to tears or facing the terror of death. No in-betweens," I replied.

We headed out before the sun came up, marching along the Orange and Alexandria rail lines. The Rebs were never far off, usually just across the river. I figured wherever we were headed, it wouldn't be too far a stretch to meet them. The men all seemed in good spirits, joking and speculating on our movements, discussing politics, and things they read in the paper. I was of a mood to listen to it all and not talk. Not knowing what was to come always put me on edge in a way that stopped my mouth up. My father always said I was the brooding type, like an old hen stuck fast to her nest.

The railroad tracks led to Rappahannock Station. But the station itself was no longer standing. The town of Remington, where it was located, saw some fighting early on in the war and the station, along with a bridge spanning the river, were burned down. Now only their charred frames remained. The Rebels compensated for the loss of the bridge by straddling the water with pontoons. Five miles from the skeleton of the burned down station was Kelly's Ford, a place where one of the pontoons was positioned. As we approached this place, our left column, commanded by Major General French, broke away from the main body. The rest of us continued on. This was the first sign to alert us whatever we were here for would be soon to follow.

The 121st continued on toward Rappahannock Station. As we approached the old station, we were kept in the shadow of the tree line and told to stay put. From where we were positioned I could see clear to the river where the Rebels had done a good job of fortifying their position. It gave me a sick sort of feeling because I could see the fighting wouldn't be easy on us. My eyes wondered along the bank, where there were several well-guarded buildings made of roughly hewn timber. These were constructed on some of the higher ground. Connecting each to the other was a series of deep pits the enemy had carved out, which provided a safe shelter for the rifleman concealed within. All areas of approach were easily defended.

Just past all of these defenses lay the river and their pontoon bridge. Beyond these there was a piece of ground angling up to a hill. On the hill they placed their artillery, so should we attempt to attack the pits, we could be blown to bits by cannon. Should we make it to the pits themselves, after somehow managing not to be blown to bits, the men waiting in the pits had sufficient time to shoot us down without risking any exposure to our fire.

"Impossible!" I whispered to Sam.

"Come now, Frank. Nothing is impossible," he said with a smirk. "Take heart. Whatever is to happen will be over quickly."

It was roughly noon when the fighting began.

"*A few days before fighting,* my hat!" Darby said with a grimace. "Don't believe a word they should utter. No sir! They will lie to your face if it should suit 'em."

The report of parrott rifles coming from Kelly's Ford, where we earlier left Major General French and his men, was our first inclination the battle was soon to come our way. Yet, we still held back and waited, hidden behind a veil of trees. We watched a ragtag group of skirmishers exchange fire with our skirmishers with little effect. It was more noise than anything.

It wore on much the same throughout the afternoon. The rifles made a tremendous noise, the Rebs stood ready, but there seemed no progress. We began to wonder what purpose we would serve, because it seemed as though we were standing idle and doing nothing for quite some time.

"Suppose we'll sleep on it," Mr. Haney commented. "Expect it is getting too late to do much now."

But Mr. Haney was wrong. Now the men who were on the front line would soon need to be relieved. Out of all of us, they were the only ones to see fighting that day. So Upton devised a cunning plan. He called upon our company and several others to move forward, as if to give the tired skirmishers a chance to switch out, so they might get rest and we might take over for them. Clever and sneaky all in one, Upton would use the opportunity to advance our position unbeknownst to the enemy who would think we were merely changing out men.

"Those skirmishers will be our way in," he told us all. "You will act as if you are there to relieve them. The Rebels will pay little attention, thinking you are not a threat, it's nearly dark and they won't believe we will make our move now. Once you are up to the first line of skirmishers, you and the skirmishers will jointly move forward to attack. Our objective is capturing the fort and those breastworks. We want that pontoon to be in our hands before morning."

It seemed a risk to me, but I never was one to understand strategy very well, as was evident from my chess game losses. Upton pointed to the six companies amassed to the left.

"Once your line advances in what looks like picket relief, the picket line will advance with you. And moving forward as one, we will drive the enemy off of that crest! Understand?"

He got a flood of *Yes, sir!* from the men.

"The success of this operation lies solely with you," he continued. "You must make it seem as though you are there to relieve them of duty, and it must seem convincingly so to the enemy. Do not — I will say it again — *do not* fire unless fired upon. The element of surprise is what will make this endeavor a success."

We formed a line and waited for the signal. At which time we slowly and casually moved forward. The silence was unbearable as we closed the gap upon open ground, without a thing for cover if they should decide to fire upon us. Just short of the skirmish lines, the mayhem began. We took up with the old line as instructed and pressed forward jointly, and then our companies to the left joined in. Where there was silence before, the air was now filled with reports from rifles, guns firing in quick order.

We did our best to return fire, as thousands upon thousands joined in the action. Now when the Confederate skirmishers saw what we were up to, they didn't have a choice but to turn and run for their lives because they were so outnumbered. They ran in full gallop to the breastworks and began to throw themselves into the rifle pits for cover. Without a thought for ourselves, we blindly pursued.

Chapter 19

Once the Rebs got to the rifle pits, they opened fire on us. We ducked down and sheltered ourselves in a ditch stretching between the two roads running horizontal on the sloping hillside. I immediately began reloading, as we waited in the brief interval, while they wasted their ammunition firing. Not one of us was hit by their bullets.

"Stay close!" Sam was yelling above the noise. I nodded to him with what I was sure was a grim face.

The order came down, "Fix bayonets!" and we scrambled to do as we were told. Upton, pacing back and forth, was visibly excited as his voice carried above the din.

"Boys, I am with you again! Our friends at home and your country expect every man to do his duty! Some of us have got to die. That's an unfortunate truth. If you die, I tell you now, you are going to heaven!" He was prepared to move and us with him, but he continued, "When I give the command to charge, move forward. Don't fire a shot until you're told to. If they fire upon you and take you down, I will move six lines of battle over you and bayonet every one of them down to the last man! I swear it!"

"That's supposed to inspire confidence?" Darby muttered.

Maybe Darby was right. Maybe speaking to us about dying was not the thing to do in such a situation, but no one else seemed to notice. His speech roused us all. We were ready to follow him anywhere, even if it meant giving up our lives.

When they spent their rounds we rose up in a great wall of blue, our rifles at the ready, and pressed forward upon them. As a unified whole we took up yelling with a deafening roar that must certainly have struck terror into the hearts of our enemy. It frightened even me, although I too was screaming with everything I had in me. My ears rang, and I was finding it nearly impossible to have a coherent thought in my brain. This is what happens when you know you must kill or be killed, all reason flies out the window and you are left a simpleton, reverting back to the most base of human instincts. It is a wonder anyone comes out of war alive.

What few Confederates were left to hold the line crumbled before us, turned tail and ran for it. We took chase, driving them back and back until we too were at the trenches. I couldn't say who was more surprised, them or us. We looked down upon them in their pits, close enough to see the details of the features on each of their faces. Mostly they seemed completely taken off guard.

It was like a bunch of rabbits caught in their burrow. The Graybacks all looked up from their hole in astonishment, wondering, I suppose, how such a thing could have transpired. It all happened so fast, they scarcely knew what to make of it. Some, with a strong sense of self preservation, had the wherewithal to try to fire their rifles. Most either surrendered on the spot or tried to escape by scampering up the back side of the pits and making for the river.

We secured the pits in five minutes' work. Upton was strutting like a prize cock, shouting out orders and routing our prisoners to the back lines.

"You," he said pointing to Sam. "I need you to carry a message back to Major General French, Second Lieutenant Barlow."

Sam was pleased the Colonel knew him by name. He was giddy with excitement. He was about to leave when he brushed past me. He stopped only briefly to check with me.

"Will you be all right?" I could see he was torn between ensuring my safety and the thrilling time he might have while delivering the important message Upton entrusted him with. I didn't want to be the reason he missed out on his fun.

"I'm fine, Sam. You go on," I told him with a reassuring smile. So Sam eagerly went over to Upton, took the message, and disappeared at a trot into the chaos and clamber of the riotous scene.

Colonel Upton then ordered the 121st and the 5th Maine, under Major Mather's command, to secure the bridge and the river where the Confederates were attempting retreat. We headed posthaste to the pontoon spanning the river and began right off preventing the Confederates from crossing. Now some of them did not like the idea of being taken prisoner, and in desperation they began to jump into the freezing waters trying to swim to the other side to escape. The water was so intensely cold that those poor Confederates were crying out in agony.

Felix Newburn caught a mess of them trying to cross the pontoon bridge and hollered out to them. "Surrender or I'll run every damn one of you through!" I'd never heard him curse like that before, so he must have been in a state. The Confederates knew they were caught and gave up without any trouble. Felix led them off to the rear, where the other prisoners were being kept. Major Mather called over to the Carroll brothers and me and Jack Monroe. We obediently came to him.

"I need you boys to go downriver and detain those men trying to swim to the other side. Bring 'em on in," he said. "They won't escape so easily."

We tramped across the bridge and headed downriver. Now my apprehension began to grow, because of course the Carroll brothers were going to stick together. Which left me to Jack Monroe. Oh, if Sam were there I knew he would be very mad at me for getting myself into such a situation. But I didn't have a choice. As we searched along the bank of the river the unsettled feeling grew to a full on stomachache. My head told me again and again to get out of there. I must not be left alone with him. I must not! The Carroll brothers moved off in a different direction from us. I called out to them.

"Shouldn't we stick together?"

"Cover more ground this a-way," one of them replied. As I said before, I never could tell them apart.

A terrible foreboding spread through me. Old Whiskers and I were alone. In my worst nightmares, this was the sort of thing that would frighten me most. To say I was wary of him would be to say too little. I was downright distrustful and watched him suspiciously. I kept my gun up in front of me defensively, thinking I would run if I needed to, all the while trying to behave as though I was not terrified of him. He simply led the way and ignored me, as if I weren't even there. I tagged along behind, keeping him fully in my vision, aware of every move he made.

We got up near the river and began searching for anyone who may have swum across. The water was littered with the bodies of men who had drowned, their corpses looking disturbingly serene as they bobbed along with the current, collecting along the edge of the river. Old Whiskers poked at them with the barrel of his gun, watching them go down and then spring back up again.

"Awful way to go," he said.

"I guess any way would be an awful way to go."

"Not compared to going in your sleep, or having your heart give out of a sudden. It would be over right quick then. No this way is slow and terrible. Endeavoring to get breath in your lungs as they burn, fighting to make it to shore, trying to get air as you go under…And the shore right there where you can see it but too far away to get there."

I got the idea he was trying to scare me. And while it was working, I was not about to show it to him, doing my best to be indifferent to him. I chose to ignore what he was saying and continued to look for survivors.

"Don't you think?" he asked.

"What?" I said with intentional ignorance.

"Don't you think it would be a bad way to go?"

I didn't answer him. I didn't have a chance. In the distance we could hear someone crying out for help. "Help," he called out weakly. "It's bitter cold. God have mercy…"

And then the poor wretch came drifting into view. He was still in full uniform, struggling to keep his head above the water. At times he would thrash about wildly and then he would grow tired and still, until he became desperate for a breath of air and would begin to struggle again.

"There is one, there." I pointed. "We must pull him out," I told Old Whiskers.

"What for? He will surely die anyway. And it would be one less prisoner to have to be accountable for," Jack said indifferently.

"Maybe so, but can you watch a man die like that? I can't." I chastised him self-righteously. "I won't."

"I have no misgiving over it," Jack said with a hateful sort of smile, as if he were getting pleasure out of riling me up. Indeed, I do believe that is exactly what he was doing.

I disregarded him, thinking I would not give him the satisfaction of a reaction. What sort of a man would say such a thing, anyhow? I took off my belt and threw one end to the man while holding fast to the other. He grabbed at it frantically. The poor Reb missed and went under. He batted about in the water for a brief moment and then came back up, more desperate than before. I tossed the end of my belt to him again. This time he managed to take hold of it. I did my best to keep myself anchored by squatting down low to the ground and leaning back.

Just as I nearly got him to the shoreline, Jack came up behind me and put his boot into my back, sending me catapulting forward. When I hit the water, the shock of the cold sucked the air right from my lungs. I went under and then desperately struggled to come up again. I gasped for air, inhaled water and began coughing violently. There was a brief moment of understanding. Jack pushed me into the water knowing full well I couldn't swim. And yet the only thing for me to do was call upon him for mercy.

"Jack!" My head went under the water, and I struggled with my arms and legs flailing to pull myself back up. "Jack! Please!" I screamed, before I went under again. Jack continued to walk away without even a second glance. Not a care in the world. He left me there to die. Now the Rebel man I intended to rescue was fighting hard to keep above water as was I, and shamefully, in my terror, I latched on to him. We struggled together for a time, until his head went beneath the water and didn't come back up again.

I knew I must surely drown too. My head went under, until I could fight my way to the surface just long enough to catch a frantic breath, and then I was dragged beneath again. There wasn't even a thought in my head. Perhaps I had the fleeting notion I would die. But nothing more, as I struggled to survive. I kicked and floundered about, my head going under, then resurfacing as I gulped air, and swallowed water, coughing violently, my hands searching for something solid to hold on to, until finally I grabbed hold of a floating body. He was only one of many grouping together and collecting in the current like apples in a barrel.

Once I got hold of him, I hoisted myself from one body to another, using them to help me stay afloat. I thrashed desperately in the water until I managed to get close enough to shore so I could tow myself to safety. I had been pulled with the current and didn't have any idea where I was or on which shore I landed. I crawled across the freezing mud, dragging myself by sheer willpower away from the water. I began to vomit up river water and then I collapsed, without the ability to do anything more for myself.

I don't have any recollection as to how long I lay there. I must have lost consciousness. I woke to the nudging of someone's rifle. My eyes fluttered open, and right off I felt a coldness penetrating my skin and sink deep into my bones. I was shaking uncontrollably, frozen all the way through. My coat and pants were stiff with frost, my hat gone completely. I abruptly sat up, looking about me in full hysteria, surrounded on all sides by men wearing gray. Not a friendly face in sight. It was still dark, but I could see there was a faint glow on the horizon, a soft blush lending a little light.

"Get up!" one of them ordered.

I was frightened half to death, but I had the wherewithal to do as he said. I stumbled to my feet, my vision growing blurry around the edges. They waited for me to get my bearings, until my brain was no longer foggy. I could see I was nowhere near my earlier location, the only familiar thing being the river I managed to fight my way out of. I thought briefly to run. But I knew I shouldn't do that. Either they would shoot me in the back or easily catch me again. There was no way out of it.

"What are you doing out here?" another asked.

"I fell into the river," I stammered.

"Awful luck, friend," a third said, with an ironic grin. "Come along then."

So I walked along with them, until they took me to a larger group of Confederates. When I saw their numbers, I was aware I'd been captured and there was nothing to do but whatever I was told to. I was too worn out and in too much shock to think of anything but doing as I was told. They were on the run, these men, and I, out of default, would go along with them. In my head I cursed Jack Monroe.

Chapter 20

Given my predicament there was nothing more I could do but stay to myself and do as I was directed. It gives a person a great deal of time to think. I wondered what Sam was doing, and if he missed me at all. So many times he prodded me to go home. I bet he was thinking *I told her so*. I bet he was thinking *serves her right*. And although his burden was removed with my absence, mine grew heavy with his.

It dawned on me that my only hope of salvation was escape. And so I then determined I would observe everything, most especially my surroundings to try to figure a way out of it. I was the only prisoner I could see. The Rebels moved out so quickly from Rappahannock Station they left many behind in the hasty retreat, having little or no time to worry over captives, I supposed. I knew I wouldn't be here myself if it wasn't for that snake Jack Monroe.

They had no food to give me. They had no food for themselves even, much less an enemy captive. When they stopped to rest, they would eat their meager portion and observe me suspiciously; as if they were afraid I might spring up and snatch it away from them. I watched with hungry eyes, saliva wetting my mouth in anticipation of something to eat. Each meal I went without made my stomach feel sore and empty.

I tried to drink as little water as possible because I didn't want to have to relieve myself, but then I still had to urinate, whether I wanted to or not. The first day, I waited until it was dark, tried to hide myself behind a tree for some privacy while the guard stood close by with his rifle at the ready. I nearly couldn't go I was so nervous about it.

As we walked, I couldn't help but think I was headed further and further into enemy territory, further away from Sam, and my chances of being discovered for what I really was grew with each passing moment. They would take me to a prison, and I would languish there, with no hope of ever seeing my home or those I loved again. Perhaps they would discover I was a girl, in which case I might be sent home. But if I were sent home, everyone would know what I had done. There would be no concealing my double life.

Oh, how vexing a lie becomes. It was my own stupidity which had brought me to this. I was bound by the game I played. My mind worked furiously, to the point of mental exhaustion, to figure a way out of the situation. My head hurt, my stomach ached, I was exhausted, and yet I was forced to press on.

Maybe I should just tell them, and finally own up to the truth. But then I recalled all of the tales they told of women being taken advantage of by the Rebs. I saw for myself what Old Whiskers was capable of and I was sure there were others of the same make as he. I didn't have any idea who I could trust. So I carried on with the ragtag lot as they marched on and on. I was near the back of the procession, under the guard of about four or so men, who would rotate in the responsibility of watching over me. I became certain if I couldn't beg mercy as a woman, I must try to get away.

This notion ran round and round my head. The first day I thought of it and nothing else. If I should try to get away, it must be for once and for all. I could not let them catch me again. What would be the best way to go about it? When would it be an optimal time to make my move?

My captors said very little to me. I suppose they were feeling sore over their recent loss. I knew what it was like, how hard it was to accept a terrible defeat. The only things I could derive from them were things I was able to observe by watching and taking note. I could not tell much by looking at them. They were lean and hungry and tired. It becomes difficult to even tell the age of a man so worn by his circumstances. They looked collectively old in their sagging skins. I knew their names from when they addressed one another. Perry, Phillip, Donavan, and Curtis. As I observed them, I came to realize if I was to try to escape, it must be on Perry's watch. Out of all of them he was the most polite and seemed to be the least threatening toward me.

He offered me drink. He turned his back and allowed me privacy when I must do my business. He wore a soft and kind look about his eyes. The others looked upon me with nothing but scorn. They allowed for no favors on my behalf. They touched me with rough hands and eyed me with contemptuous glances.

I somehow managed to make it through the first day. When night fell, they made camp. I sat next to the fire, saying nothing, trying to remain inconspicuous. One of them approached me, stood before me as if to observe. I kept my eyes down and remained still. He bent down and took hold of my feet and began tugging at my boots.

"No!" I cried, as I tried to move away from him, near panicked because I didn't know what he was going to do, but he held my foot firm and wouldn't let me go.

"What are you doing?" one of them asked him.

"I could use some boots," he responded.

"Leave the boy alone, Phillip," the one called Curtis said.

Phillip did not listen. He continued to pull the boot from my foot and then went to work on the other. When he was finished he sat down and tried them on for size.

"How's that?" Donavan asked.

"They are small, but better than going without," Phillip replied.

I scuttled backward into the shadows, clamping my hands onto my feet, feeling violated, feeling frightened beyond belief. I thought the worst. I thought he meant to hurt me. When his purpose became clear, I was relieved, but I was also sorry to lose my boots. The nights were very cold now and without those boots, I knew I would suffer, and to have them wrenched from my feet in such a manner upset me terribly.

Everyone settled in to sleep except for the one called Donavan, whose turn it was to watch over me. I lay awake in misery, turning once to get more comfortable. I chanced a glance at him and he scowled at me.

"Don't get any ideas," he said. I didn't answer. I did not move a muscle again. I lay in a ball upon my side and cried silent tears, hoping no one would know.

Sometime before dawn, I struck upon an idea. If I was to escape it must be soon. I must be ready to act at the next possible opportunity.

In the darkness, I reached out my hand tentatively and dragged it upon the ground, sweeping it along the loose soil, feeling deliriously for the object of my desire with my extended fingers. Cautiously and almost unperceptively I widened my arc, fingertips stretching and searching in the dirt and darkness until I encountered what I was looking for. I inched it back toward me, doing my best to make as little noise and motion as I could. With no reaction from my guard, I was confident my work went undetected. Once my hand was back at my side and no one was the wiser, I clutched my prize with a feeling of elation. Then slowly, slowly I slipped the palm sized rock into the depths of my pocket and waited.

In the morning after, they banked the fire and cleared camp. We continued on, at times close to the river, other times, seeming to move away from it. It was just after midday when I informed one of them I needed to stop.

"I must relieve myself," I told the one called Perry.

"I'll take him," Phillip said to Perry. He grabbed me roughly by the arm and led me off into a wooded area. I was right away very alarmed he was ruining my plans. I intended upon Perry taking me. Instead it was Phillip, the one who wore my boots. Just the sight of those boots on his feet seemed to crush my morale. We walked a short distance, and as we did so I took in my surroundings, working out in my head any possible hiding places that might harbor me.

"Get on with it," he said, with a disapproving tone. He held his rifle, ready to use it.

I turned as if I might empty my bladder, but really I was working the rock from my pocket. I clutched it firmly in my hand. A feeling of dread coursed through me, making my knees feel week.

"Might I have some privacy?" I requested.

He sighed as though he were very much put out by me, but turned his back to me in honor of my request. The second he wasn't looking, I spun around, lunging toward him. I threw myself upon his back, using the rock to beat him upon the head. He began to cry out and I put my free hand over his mouth and knocked him hard again. Out of surprise he dropped his rifle, grabbing franticly at his head as I gave him another good blow.

The blood ran down his forehead and into his eyes as he tried to fight me off, his mouth attempting a yell with my fingers clumsily working to suppress the noise. He stumbled and fell to the ground and I with him. I nearly got the wind knocked out of me and lost my grip on the rock, dropping it. He was clutching at his head, trying to rouse himself from the ground. Strangely enough, he made very little noise, just an odd sort of groan as he cradled his skull in his hands. My best defense was his bewilderment. Before he could do more, I rolled away from him and sprang to my feet. I took off at a sprint through the trees, my eyes darting this way and that in hopes of finding some shelter to conceal me. I heard him then, calling out to the others.

"He's got away! Damn it! He's got away!" he was bellowing.

Chapter 21

I ran on, deeper into the woods, thick with underbrush. I came upon a massive hedge, overgrown with limbs of thorn, and thick with leaves. Without any hesitation, I dove toward the base of the briar patch and worked my way in, feeling the barbs ruthlessly tear at my flesh, yet pressing myself deeper still despite the terrible pain.

My breath came at a quick, heavy pace. And I did my best to calm myself, to regulate it, so no one could detect me. I was so thick in the tangled brambles that I didn't think they would follow after me, even if they knew I was there. I lay with my belly flat upon the ground and waited.

"Do you see him?" One asked to the other. They must have been within a stone's throw of me, because I could hear their voices distinctly.

"Neither hide nor hair," the other replied. They continued to explore the area round about me as I could hear their foot falls all about. I braced myself, fearful they might detect me, and force me out of my hiding place.

"Did you check over that a-way?" I heard one ask. I could perceive them as they investigated the vegetation growing thick in the forest, poking with their rifles, testing with the toes of their boots. I waited until the sound of them became more distant. Eventually they must have given up and moved on. I still didn't budge, too frightened to chance being seen. The afternoon wore on into evening, and then progressed into a dark and chilly night. Yet I remained. At some point I dozed off and slept. When I woke, it was midday again.

Tentatively, I crawled from my hiding place among the thicket of thorny limbs and sat on my bottom, listening. I didn't hear a sound for some time, but I knew I must be careful and guarded. I took stock of my situation, trying to decide what my next move should be. My uniform was ripped to shreds, as was the exposed flesh upon my hands and face and feet from the prickly bramble I sought refuge in. I hadn't had food in over two days and water in at least twenty-four hours. I wasn't in the best condition.

I could hear the river in the distance. I was no good with direction, this I knew. Sam did his best to teach me ways of acquainting myself to where I was. When I was captured they'd mostly followed the river as we traveled south. I knew if I was able to reach the river, I could ascertain which course I must take to try to find my way back. I thought I should simply follow it back in the other direction. There I could get a drink too. But I was hesitant. I didn't want to be out in the open.

Under the cover of trees I made my way toward the water, stopping every so often to listen and observe. There didn't seem to be any sign of my earlier captors, but I remained alert for them. Upon reaching the river, I was sorely tempted to dart out and get myself some water, but I managed to hold myself back, waiting until it was dark again.

I belly crawled all the way to the river bank, cupping my hand and drinking again and again, until I thought I might burst. I washed my hands and face, feeling the sting in the many places where I was scratched up. I crawled back to the trees and took note of the position of the stars and the direction of the river before I started out at a slow pace, listening to the water slosh in my belly as I went. I soon became tired, but I pressed on, knowing the night would shroud me from the enemy. As it grew light out, I searched out a proper place to hole up.

A dry creek bed was just the thing for it. I recalled how at home, there were many such creek beds which ran fast and steady in the spring and connected to the lake, but lay dormant in autumn and winter. I worked fast to gather branches to make a loose bundle and then covered it with a sufficient pile of leaves to conceal myself, and then burrowed in. By this time my energy was fast leaving me. I was walking all night and still nothing to eat. Even if I had my rifle in my possession, I couldn't have gone hunting, for fear someone might be in close enough proximity to hear it discharge.

Lying in the creek bed with the leaves for protection, my mind began working over my dilemma. It being fall there were no berries or fruit growing wild. Without some sort of a weapon, I didn't have any hope of catching meat, and I couldn't light a fire for fear of being detected. Before I could come up with any solid solutions, I fell off to sleep.

Now as I slept, I dreamed of Antietam again. It was not the same old dream I usually dreamed, of me lying dead in the cornfield. Very different this time. An officer stood over me and gave me a shovel and told me, "Dig!" I undertook to do as he commanded. I scooped out the dirt and tossed it aside. Yet no matter how hard I worked to dig a trench, it was as if I'd done nothing. There was no progress made. The futility of it discouraged me, but also drove me to try harder.

I was determined to make the hole bigger. With unwavering zeal I plowed the shovel head deeper, frantically tossing soil to the side. Still it remained as it was. Despite my fatigue and hard work, it was nothing more than a diminutive gash in the earth. There was naught to show for my struggle.

Evening was just setting in when I awoke with a start, and for a moment I became disoriented. I did not recall where I was or what I was doing there. My stomach lurched within my gut. I staggered up and looked about in a panic. But slowly it dawned on me I was on the run. I remembered what Old Whiskers had done to me, how he had sorely betrayed me. I felt such hunger and such emotional distress that I threw myself to the ground and I cried.

I thought perhaps I should just lay there and give up. Would it be such a bad thing to give in and just let death find me? As much as I wanted to, I also wanted very much to see Sam again. And dare I say, revenge drove me to collect myself, get up, and move on? What would Old Whiskers say for himself if I were to show up back at camp again, the old devil? So I walked on, putting one step in front of the other.

Just as it got good and dark, I came upon a small farm in the middle of nowhere. The lights from within glowed like bright stars on the horizon, and I followed those beckoning lights, as a moth to flame. In this place, one could not be certain whether you were encountering friend or foe. I couldn't chance asking for help. I would not go to their door looking for compassion.

Erring on the side of caution, I crept closer, waiting and watching at the boundaries of the farm's cleared land. After a while, I saw the man of the house come out onto the porch and then he scraped the supper plates into a bucket. He took the bucket up in his hand and started to whistle as he headed out to a pen near the barn. I heard the pigs running for the fence, grunting with glee, for it was their meal time. The man lifted the bucket over the fence and dumped its contents into the trough. He checked the barn to see it was latched proper. I could hardly hold myself back. *Why doesn't he go back to the house?* And then finally he headed back.

In desperation, I took off at a run toward the pen. I dropped to my knees, and reached through the fence, pushing snouts aside as I grabbed what I might from the trough. A crust of bread, the remains of a stew with generous chunks of meat, an apple core with enough left on it for a few precious nibbles from its flesh. I wasn't concerned over what it was, just pleased it was something to eat. I shoved it in my mouth and hardly chewed before I swallowed. I reached through the fence again, my fingers grasping for more as I fought the animals over the food, but the pigs had already devoured the rest by the time I got to it.

Having exhausted my means of getting food, I crawled on hands and knees to the barn. The door creaked loud upon its hinges, and I paused for a moment to see if it would garner any reaction from the occupants of the house. There was nothing, and so I slipped in and shut the door behind me, my bare feet shuffling against the cool dirt floor.

The cow was quiet in her stall, chomping contentedly on her hay. I opened the stall door and slipped in. She mooed in protest, spooked by the stranger in her pen. I tried to soothe her by rubbing her sides and shushing her. Then I crouched down to help myself to her milk. With nothing else to drink it from, I shot it straight into my open mouth in even, steady streams. It was warm, and tasted better than I remembered milk ever tasting. The heat from the cow made me feel a comfortable drowsiness leaving my limbs languid and slow to react.

Once I got my fill, I ventured over to where the chickens roosted. Now a chicken and her eggs aren't easily parted. They began squawking when I reached beneath their feathered bottoms and procured an egg or two, pecking at my hands all the while. I tried to shush them like I did the cow, as I shoved the tawny eggs into my pockets, but they continued to voice their disapproval. I got one for each pocket, and thought to leave, when the door burst open and the man of the house came charging in, rifle in hand. He must have heard the chickens. He must have realized something was amiss. I realized, with a deep sense of dread, I was trapped.

Chapter 22

I froze where I was, thinking perhaps if the farmer didn't see me right off, he might leave. I pressed myself into the shadows, hardly chancing a breath. He swung his lantern this way and that, his other hand gripping his rifle. Surely it was how a quail must feel when it knows it is being hunted, but flies from the shelter of a bush anyhow, to become exposed to the danger. The waiting became too great. The suspense drove me to motion. I lit out for the back door of the barn, the door they let the animals through in the mornings to pasture. I unlatched it, without looking back and I ran.

The farmer was taken off guard for a moment, but then he composed himself, dropping his lantern to the ground, he pulled his rifle up, and he got a few shots off in my general direction before taking chase. I didn't hesitate for a moment. I continued running with all haste as he yelled after me, "Stinking thief, stop I say!"

Perhaps he may have overcome me, for I was tired and hadn't eaten in many days, but for the cow dung he come upon in the pasture. In the darkness he didn't see it. He ran into a patch of it, slipped, tried to catch his balance, but failed, and tumbled to the ground. Struggling back to his feet with a great effort, he began to curse—a word, in my estimation, which was most appropriate considering the poor man's current predicament. This gave me the time I needed to successfully elude him.

My heart beat nearly out of my chest, as I hid among the trees. He was not in the best of shape, and after making it halfway through the pasture he stopped, bent over, putting a hand to a knee, to try to recover. Poor fellow, I suppose he saw it was a lost cause and gave up. I felt some remorse for having intruded upon him as I did, but I didn't have a choice in the matter. My hunger drove me to it.

Now, I did not have to run any longer, but I continued to jog along, wanting to put some distance between me and the farm. My hands were in my pockets, my fingers wrapped around the two eggs I stole. There was security in the knowledge I possessed another meal. I would eat them raw if I must.

I came to a shallow bend in the river, and decided this was as good a place as any to try to cross. I didn't want to get in the water. As a matter of fact, I was downright loathe to do it. I thought of nearly drowning just a few days previously and I shuddered, taking trembling breaths, trying to work up my courage. The water was cold, so cold I was nearly paralyzed by it. Eventually I forced myself to move forward. The current tugged at me, trying to force me downstream. I leaned into it as I walked along the river bottom, my already battered feet smarting from the jagged rocks on the river bed. At the deepest point, I was forced to stand on tip toe with my head tilted up so I was not engulfed by the water. It took everything within me to squelch the panic I was experiencing.

Cold and wet, another long night of walking passed by. In the morning I chanced a small fire. I discovered a large flat rock and dug it up with a stick. The rock was put up close to my measly fire where it grew hot. While I waited, I collected pine cones and picked the pine seeds out of them. With my back teeth I cracked the seeds opened and ate the nuts within.

Once I deemed the rock of a sufficient temperature to cook upon, I cracked my eggs onto it and waited until the translucent outer edges became white, and the yolks were firm. I burned my fingers peeling them off to eat them. But it surely tasted good and was worth the effort.

It is true I was very tired after having walked the whole night through, but I felt I must be close now to our camp. I decided to press on. It was mid-morning when I was forced to stop again. Although I knew I was close to camp, I physically could not continue on. I found a place in a dilapidated outbuilding, ducked in and slept for several hours. I was still tired when I awoke but I forced myself to keep going.

In the late evening I spotted the campfires bright and inviting. I staggered around, looking for a familiar face. A man I didn't know approached me and said, "You look lost, where have you come from?"

"The 121st," I croaked. "I am looking for the 121st."

"Wrong side of camp, son. They are on the other side."

So I continued on. And when I made it to the other side of camp, I saw Felix Newburn by his fire. He seemed surprised when he recognized me. "Frank?"

"That is me," I said. My voice sounded tired and weak.

"Why, Jack told us you was most likely dead. Said you was waylaid by a sorry Reb," he said.

"He would've said such a lie!" I raged.

"What has become of you?" he asked.

"I was captured. Managed to escape."

"How in the name of blue blazes did that happen?"

"Do you know where Sam is?" I wondered, without answering his question. He seemed thoroughly confused. But I realized I must not be making much sense to him. I did not care. I wasn't going to stand around trying to explain myself to him. I needed to find Sam. I could trust him. He would help me.

"His tent is that one over there," he replied, pointing it out to me.

"Thank you," I said, and left him there.

When I went over to the tent, pulled the flap back and looked in, it was empty. No one inside. I thought perhaps I should wait there, maybe try to get some rest. But I had to see Sam. There was no way around it. Only I was afraid I might also see Old Whiskers if I was not careful. He was here somewhere in this same camp too, carefree and not wasting a second thought over what he did to me.

Mr. Haney was cleaning up his supper when I came upon him. He seemed just as astonished as Felix was to see me in the flesh, alive and well. When he wanted to know what happened to me, I explained to him, as I explained to Felix, I was a prisoner and somehow managed to escape. I wanted to tell him everything, to tell him about what Jack Monroe did to me, but something held me back. He didn't know my history with Jack and if I stopped to tell him everything it would take time. Time was something I didn't feel I had just then.

"Do you know where Sam is?" I asked him too.

"Well, now I believe he has picket duty," Mr. Haney informed me.

This was good. We would have a measure of privacy so I might speak to him alone. I struck out, looking to find him, careful as I went so I didn't run into anyone else. Out of all of the people I knew he was the one I could trust. He was the one I could go to with anything. He was the only one who knew my secrets.

Chapter 23

The darkness of the night was accentuated by the distant glow of campfires behind me. I was careful not to be seen, wandering along the picket line, observing without interacting with anyone until I should find Sam of course. With Mosby's Raiders a constant threat, everyone in camp was on edge, especially those on picket duty. Rightfully so, for who knew where they might strike and when? After our success at Rappahannock Station I was sure the men on picket duty would be on high alert, waiting for retaliation. Since I was coming up from the direction of camp I didn't think I would cause too much alarm, but you could never be too careful. It would be a shame to escape the enemy, only to be shot by a friend. When I found him, I made no attempt at being stealthy because I didn't want to frighten him.

My best attempt at being transparent was a failure. I caught Sam off guard. He heard my footsteps in the darkness before he saw me. He spun toward me with a start, drew his rifle and called, "Halt!"

I raised my hands up in front of me so he could see I was unarmed, but continued to walk slowly toward him. "I mean no harm," I said urgently. When I got up close enough for Sam to see who I was, his face registered recognition and then complete shock. I suppose Sam must have been reminded of the ghost of Hamlet's father who appeared at the morning watch, when I drifted into his view. He was told I was dead and gone. And here I was come to haunt him. I can't imagine the surprise he must have felt upon seeing me.

"Sam, it is me," I whispered.

"Serena?"

Sam bore the most peculiar look upon his face, as he stared at me fixedly. I must have been a sight. Dirty, scratched to pieces, my uniform much worse for wear, and barefoot, I was a pathetic scene and ashamed I didn't think to clean up a bit before presenting myself to him.

"I'm sure I must be a wretched sight," I said. He didn't seem to have anything to say. It was as if he didn't have the ability to form words. He just stared at me with his lips puckered and his eyebrows drawn together, as though he was having difficulty registering I was actually there in one piece and not dead in a ditch somewhere. Finally he spoke.

"Not to me you aren't," he replied soberly. "To me, you've never looked better!"

If I could have, I would have laughed, because his words seemed so outrageously silly, but I was too worn out and dog-tired to find it humorous. He always had a comical quip, even at the most difficult moments. Generally I found it endearing, but now hardly seemed the time to be making jokes.

"You haven't been hitting the bottle have you, Sam?" I responded sarcastically. He did not laugh. No, he remained perfectly serious. I grew concerned. What was wrong with him? Was it too much to ask for a warm welcome? An enthusiastic reception to a friend he thought dead? Finally he spoke.

"I thought I might never see you again, Serena," he replied. "The things I imagined might have befallen you..." His voice was tortured, emotional even. He dropped his rifle to the ground and came to me, taking my face in his hands and gazing into my eyes with strong sentiment playing upon his expression. I was surprised by this. I knew he probably felt guilty over our recent falling outs, but I certainly didn't know the depths of his fondness for me until this moment. And then he kissed me!

At first it was soft and tender, his lips warm and easy. I was so dumbfounded, I didn't respond. Although, I felt the heat spread through my body and I experienced the strangest sort of joy rushing through me all at once, I just stood there like a fool, frozen where I was. I must have worn a look of astonishment. He pulled away and seemed ashamed.

"I'm sorry," he murmured.

"Why?"

Sam cleared his throat. "For a moment I forgot myself."

"I liked it very much," I admitted, shyly, unable to bring my eyes to his. "I wish you would forget yourself more often."

It seemed that was all he needed to hear. He moved in purposefully toward me, tilting his head at an angle he paused and studied my lips, as if they were the most fascinating thing he had ever seen. Then he put his mouth to mine again. This time it was not so chaste. It was more like being in water and desperately coming up for air and then plunging back into the water again, as it was when I thought I was drowning in the Rappahannock. A kiss, a breath, a kiss. I felt a certain sense of desperation for it, aching to not have to breathe at all.

I let the pleasure of it run over me in flushed exhilaration. Sensations and emotions I'd never experienced played over my body, through my brain, as I touched his face with my fingertips, and he held me fast with the pressure of his palm on my lower back and his other hand cradling the back of my neck. I was hungry for more but I abruptly pulled away. He meant to kiss me again, and I stopped him.

"We must take care," I said a little breathlessly, leaning in to him for support. "We must not do something we may regret later."

"I do not regret it one bit," he said. He seemed somewhat hurt by my refusal.

"That's not what I meant, Sam," I told him. "I like it very much too. But we must exercise temperance."

He sighed deeply. "Yes, I suppose."

"I am somewhat surprised by it all."

"Why?"

"I didn't think you cared for me."

"I tried to be angry with you, Serena. But it was far more taxing than it was worth. Honestly, when you were gone, I nearly went mad with worry. I couldn't think of anything else. I knew I couldn't be angry with you anymore."

"And all that talk about me leaving...you weren't trying to be done with me?"

"Silly girl." He laughed and kissed me again. "I would selfishly have you stay. But I am in constant fear for your safety here."

"I thought you were sick of me. I thought you wanted to be rid of me." And I can't say why, whether it was the kiss, or the relief of hearing him say such a thing, or just exhaustion perhaps, but I began to cry. He didn't say anything. He just held me.

"It will be all right," he said. "It will be all right. You are here now, safe and sound with me. I will never let anything happen to you."

Chapter 24

I went back to our tent alone, because Sam needed to finish picket duty. I lay down upon his bedroll and fell fast asleep. When I awoke, Sam was there. He gave me breakfast, which I seemed to devour in one bite. Being alone in our tent and with some measure of seclusion, he began to question me.

"Where are your boots?" he first asked.

"They took them from me," I told him. "I never knew how precious boots were upon a person's feet before all of this! What a struggle it has been to find and keep a pair of them."

"We will have to find you another pair," he told me taking my feet into his hands and inspecting them. He shook his head and winced on my behalf. He busied himself with inspecting the soles of my feet while he continued with his line of interrogation.

"Now, tell me what happened to you," he said.

"What did Jack Monroe tell you?" I countered.

"He told us all you were shot by a Reb who was trying to avoid capture," Sam told me. "That he was forced to leave you behind in order to save his own life. He didn't know if you were dead or alive. He thought most likely dead, but if not dead then surely captured."

"The old liar!" I raged. "None of it's true!"

"What happened?"

"Mather told Jack and me and the Carroll brothers to go downriver and stop the Confederates from escaping by swimming across," I explained. "A whole slew of Graybacks tried to swim for it, if you can believe it. And the water so cold…So we went," I said. "The whole time I was thinking I should not be alone with him, Sam. I knew it but I couldn't do anything about it! I couldn't disobey Mather. The Carroll brothers stuck together, as I knew they would, and that left me with Jack." I noted Sam was listening intently and did not take his eyes away from me, my feet now forgotten.

"I told you to watch out for him, didn't I?"

"I know it. I know it. So, the Carroll brothers took off and left me alone with him. I tried to act like I wasn't afraid of him and I went on about my business. Started looking for prisoners as I was told to. Most of the bodies we found were already dead. But then there was someone in the water. Some Confederate begging for help. He managed to survive the cold somehow and he came floating by us. I could hear him asking for help. I said to Jack we should fish him out. But Jack didn't care. He didn't want to help the man. What was I to do? I tried to save him on my own. I threw him my belt. I meant to pull him out with it. And that's when Jack comes up behind me and put his boot to my back, and in I went. He tossed me right into the freezing river!"

"What?"

Sam's reaction was one of shocked disbelief. I suppose it was hard for him to accept anyone would do such a despicable thing.

"It's true. I had my back turned to him and he threw me in. I didn't know what to do. I called out to him. I begged him to help me, and he didn't even turn back once. He just walked away and left me for dead. He knew I couldn't swim!"

"I'll kill him!" Sam roared. His nosed flared, his lips formed into a grimace, as his face turned a deep red with indignant rage.

"Sam—" I began in surprise. I didn't expect such an instantaneous and volatile reaction from him. It frightened me a little.

"I'll kill him for what he's done!"

"Stop," I moaned.

"*I am going to kill that son of a bitch!*"

I started when he cursed. He rarely used bad language. It wasn't like him at all. His rage caused me a great deal of distress, my insides all in a turmoil. I felt sick. I felt pushed to the edge. My nerves went to jelly.

"Please, Sam, don't! Think it through. You know what'll happen if you cause trouble. If you kill him they'll hang you or put you up in front of a firing squad," I reasoned.

"You think that would stop me from making sure the sorry cuss couldn't ever hurt you again? You think I would stand by and do nothing if I felt you were in danger? Hang me from the nearest tree, put me in front of a firing squad, I'll rot in the stocks if I have to if it means getting rid of him. I swear to you now, I will take care of that man. Wait and see if I don't!"

"Please! I can't stand it. I don't want to talk about it anymore. I have been through hell and back and I just want to forget it all." I began to get emotional. It was all too much. If anything happened to Sam because of me I would never forgive myself. I should never have told him what Jack did, because now I had put him at risk too.

When he saw how upset I was he gave up on threatening Jack and tried to comfort me. "There's no need for you to worry over it anymore. I will see to it you're safe," he promised.

"I'm telling you now, Sam, I don't want you to get into trouble because of me. If anything should happen to you, I don't know what I'd do! Please don't do anything crazy."

"I'm sorry. I didn't mean to upset you. Don't think about it anymore. I don't want you to have another moment's trouble over it. You've surely been through enough," he consoled. I let him calm my nerves and began to relax a bit. I knew I didn't need taking care of, but I wanted to be. I'm sure it says nothing of my character that my desire was to be weak, to do as he said and let him take care of it. I looked at him curiously.

"I feel confused over what's happened between us, Sam. What does it mean?"

"I don't know if I understand the question?"

"Well, you kissed me last night," I replied sheepishly. The thought of it brought color to my cheeks. "Have you forgotten? Maybe you were caught off guard. You thought you'd never see me again. Maybe you were just relieved I wasn't dead. I don't know, but I want to know what it means."

"It means," he said, dropping his eyes from mine as he fiddled with the blanket we were sitting on, rolling the hem between his thumb and pointer finger, before clearing his throat, his nervous gaze meeting mine again. "It means I want you to be my girl."

I tried not to smile, which I'm sure only made me look ridiculous. I was over the moon. But I didn't know if I wanted him to know it. Perhaps I should be demure, and hold back. It wasn't prudent to play your cards all at once, was it? I never had much experience in matters of love, and I wasn't confident in myself.

"I'm not sure what to say. I would like to hold back, be modest and not make any promises to you, because I guess that's what men like, a girl who is reserved and makes a man work for her love. But, I was never very good at being coy, Sam. And if you don't already know how I feel about you I would think you were a fool."

"Just for the sake of it, consider me a fool. For once and for all how *do* you feel about me, Serena?"

"Oh, I feel enough to leave everything I knew behind and chase you all over the country dressed as a boy. I feel enough for you to have endured army life, and it hasn't been an easy thing for me, Sam. I feel enough that, as you can see, I've gotten in well over my head just to be near you. Does that tell you anything?"

He smiled. "Then you always were my girl, and I just didn't know it."

"Yes. I always was your girl. How proud does it make you to have the affections of a girl named Frank?"

"Very proud," he assured me. He moved in closer to me, kissing me and holding me close. I felt so safe, so happy. I could hardly believe it was real. The thing I wanted most was really mine to have!

I spent the remainder of the day resting on and off, staying in my tent. Sam dug up some boots that had seen better days, and some other supplies such as a bedroll and haversack for me, then he doctored my feet up. The next day I ate my breakfast, and then I reported to the field for drills. And when I saw Old Whiskers he seemed to try to hide his astonishment at my being there.

I didn't take my eyes off of him. I wanted him to know I wasn't afraid of him. If he should chance to look at me, I was looking right back. I felt defiant. I wanted to show him he couldn't hurt me. So I set my jaw and gave him a hateful stare. It made me angrier still when he didn't seem affected by it at all. If anything, he seemed to be ignoring me. When drills were over Sam strode right up to him to confront him.

"I will have words with you!" he said. Jack was casual in his response to Sam's harsh words.

"What for?" he replied with a disinterested sneer. *What for?* How dare he? Boy that really riled me. He knew good and well what for.

"I heard what you done to Frank, and I won't stand for it," Sam informed him, getting in his face and poking his finger at him. Sam was growing heated and I feared he might engage him in a fight right there on the field.

"What has the little buzzard been saying 'bout me?"

"You know what's been said, and it's something I won't stand for!" Sam growled.

I tried to intercede. "Sam, please…Please do not do this. I don't want it. Why won't you listen to me?"

Sam ignored me. "I will have satisfaction," he said to Jack Monroe.

"Oh, and how do you aim on doing that?" Jack returned.

"We'll take care of it privately, you and me."

"No!" I yelled. "Sam, please! I don't want you to get in trouble because of me. Just walk away from this. You don't have to do it!" But Sam refused to listen to me. He was glaring sullen at Jack and if it were possible I believe he would have burned Jack up with his look.

Jack casually shrugged. "Suits me."

"This evening in the field out back of the old barn down the road," Sam continued.

"Just you and me?"

"Certainly," Sam agreed. "Just you and me."

"After supper. Wouldn't want you to get thrashed on an empty belly."

Sam smiled mirthlessly. "So be it. And we will see who gets thrashed!"

Chapter 25

Now there was nothing for me to do but beg and plead for Sam not to go. But he refused to acknowledge a word I said on it. In the privacy of our tent I shed tears; I tried to convince him with the most woeful imploring a person could have. But my solicitude did nothing to soften his heart. He would not hear of backing out.

"I want you to stay here, Serena. Do you understand? You must not be mixed up in any of this."

"I won't!" I told him. "You're up to no good, and I can't sit by and wait to see what becomes of you."

"I don't want you there! You stay put or I'll be very angry with you."

The moment he struck out for the field, on his own, I went to Mr. Haney. Mr. Haney was with some of the others, Darby and Felix and the Carroll brothers and Boss Tanner, playing a game of poker. I hesitated. How was I to get him away from the others tactfully without arousing the suspicion of everyone present?

"Mr. Haney, may I have a word?"

Mr. Haney seemed as though he didn't want to be bothered. "What is it?" he asked unwilling to put his cards down.

"Might I speak with you in private?" I requested a little more urgently. He looked at his hand and then to me, as if he were torn. Probably he held a good set of cards he wanted to play, but he reluctantly put the cards down and got up to follow me. We walked far enough away so the others couldn't hear.

"What's this about?"

"Sam. I…Well, he's gone out to fight Jack. And I have a bad feeling about it. I plan on going out there to make sure no harm comes to him and I need you to come with me."

"Why would Sam fight Jack?" Mr. Haney asked.

"On account of me," I told him.

He seemed confused. "On account of you?"

"It's difficult to explain," I said. I was growing more and more agitated because I wanted to go to Sam and make sure he was all right. Mr. Haney was wasting time.

"What is going on here, son?" Mr. Haney wanted to know.

"Sam found out Jack tried to kill me."

"What?"

"He was awful mad about it and he challenged Jack. Only I know Jack and I know he might do something low down, and I am afraid for Sam."

"Listen, Frank. Nothing you are saying right now is making any sense to me. How did Jack try to kill you?"

"That night at Rappahannock Station, when Jack said I was shot by a Reb, he was lying. I was trying to fish somebody out of the river and Jack pushed me in. He knew I couldn't swim. You were there when Vern told it to him. You and Sam and me and Vern and Jack. Remember? He pitched me into the river and left me for dead, then came back to camp with some made up story. Now Sam's set on teaching him a lesson."

"Why didn't you or Sam report this to Upton?" Mr. Haney wondered. I remained silent, torn between telling the truth and settling upon a lie.

"I didn't want anyone to know," I finally said.

"Why not?"

"Mr. Haney, it's personal," I said feebly.

"Something is not right here. You aren't telling me everything," he accused with his brow furrowed thoughtful. "If you've nothing to hide, we should go and see the Colonel about all of this."

"Please! Please!" I begged. Finally, I turned away from him and started off on my own. I was perhaps too weak to take Jack Monroe on my own, but I'd be darned if I let anything happen to Sam because of me. I was running, desperate to get to Sam. Mr. Haney must have felt some compassion for me, because he took up with me, the two of us hastening to the field where Sam and Jack were to meet.

Now, when we came upon the field it was good and dark, so we heard them fighting before we actually saw them. They were grunting and breathing heavily from the effort of it. In the murky night we could not tell who was who. They were like two cats engaged in a fight, growling with their hackles standing on end and then entangled and rolling erratically over the ground, one blending into the other until you couldn't tell which was which.

As tangled and tied up as they appeared, they finally fell away from each other, both exhausted, arms hanging at their sides to conserve strength in a short moment of truce. Their faces were already bloodied and bruised, their breaths ragged and distressed. While they were almost perfectly matched in height and weight, Sam had the advantage of youth. That small edge was now dissipating and falling away quickly as he grew fatigued.

It was clear in the following brief moments Sam was tired out and close to exhaustion. He was a mill worker, accustomed to throwing dead weight around, timbers and logs that didn't struggle against him. He would push, or pull and they would eventually yield to his power. Sam could box, no doubt about it, but he was not accustomed to the dirty fighting Jack was skilled in. No gentleman would fight in such a manner. It was clear Sam didn't have the experience the older man had with bar fights and violent quarrels. I assumed it was years of serving large working men who became sore at the thought of a tab coming due or being told they'd had enough liquor and must leave the bar which gave Jack his skills.

Sam wasted precious energy pacing and dodging back and forth, looking for an opening, and when one would open, he would lunge, only to have Jack, with a cool smile step quickly just to one side and redirect him, sometimes all the way to the ground. Sam looked enraged. I was sure much of his discontent was in having to see Jack smiling so smugly, that predatory smile I had before witnessed for myself.

It was obvious what the outcome must be, although Sam couldn't see it through his sweat filled eyes. He went for another feinted opening; Jack stepped to one side with little effort. Before Sam hit the ground Jack brought his knee up to his groin, and Sam's legs buckled. His body folded, his knees and then his face hitting the dirt, as his hands clutched between his legs.

"Mr. Haney," I cried. "Please, we must help him!"

"Jack, this has gone far enough!" Mr. Haney yelled.

Jack was defiant. "It's between him and me!" he grunted, pointing to Sam and then jerking his thumb back to his own chest. "We agreed upon it. You'd do best to get on out of here. Let us handle it."

Sam managed to pull himself from the ground despite his terrible pain, turning on Jack and throwing himself at the man with the full weight of his body. Jack tumbled backward, landing hard. Sam was winning for a brief moment. He beat on Jack with a fierce rage, pounding his fists over and over into his face and head with his full fury. His face was clenched, his body full of tension as he grunted with each blow.

Mr. Haney rushed over to intercede. He attempted to pull Sam off of Jack, tugging at his arm and then hooking his hands into the crook of Sam's armpits. Sam did his best to shrug Mr. Haney off, but was unsuccessful. Mr. Haney finally succeeded in pulling him away.

"You must stop this before someone gets killed!" Mr. Haney advised him as he ripped Sam from Jack. "Cool down, boy!"

Mr. Haney stood with his back to Jack, and Sam's attention was drawn away as well. The rascal saw his chance, reached down to his boot and brought up a hidden carving knife, only about three inches long, but lethal enough to do Sam in. While Mr. Haney was talking to Sam, they were oblivious to Jack's purpose. He must have intended upon playing dirty all along, the scoundrel, to have a knife hidden in his boot like that.

"Sam! Watch out!" I yelled.

Mr. Haney jumped clear. Sam sprang backward just in time to keep from being killed, as Jack came at him. Jack swiped across his belly with the blade, cutting deep enough to slice through his shirt and draw blood. When I saw what he did to Sam, I screamed. The scream was high pitched and desperate and I didn't even worry about the fact it sounded like a girl screaming. I sprang onto Jack wrapping my arms and legs around him, distracting him just enough to let Sam drop away. Jack staggered under my weight, but then got his bearings directly and brought the handle of the knife to my temple sending me sprawling and dazed. As I looked up Sam was bent over in pain and stumbling on his feet. The knife surprised him but my warning at least delayed his end. I tried to call out to him, and I might have but I couldn't hear anything for the deafening ringing in my ears.

When Sam saw my affliction, he was back in the fight again. Jack and Sam were struggling with one another, fighting for ownership of the knife. What would Jack do? Carve us all up? All three witnesses? He surely wouldn't leave it undone. A fear for my life and for Sam's and Mr. Haney's left me nearly paralyzed. I felt disoriented and crazed. Unable to get up of my own accord, I crawled desperately through the grass, trying to get away from him. In my haze, my hand came across something hard and cold. Sam and Jack had removed their coats and lay their pistols to the side before the fight, presumably so no weapons would be involved. I tried to concentrate my gaze, aware Sam and Jack were struggling over the knife which Jack gripped tightly in his fist. Sam was doing all he could to wretch it free from him. He might have come here to teach Jack a lesson, but the lesson was ours, Sam's and mine. In a life or death fight there is no fair, there is only the survivor. At that moment I didn't care for anything more than for our survival, for our future. I picked up Sam's Colt revolver and gripped it resolutely in my hand.

"Stop this now!" Mr. Haney was yelling. He stepped forward as if he might try to come between the two men, but Jack was not about to stop. He dived at Sam with the knife, and Mr. Haney, rather than come to harm, leaped out of the way again.

Through my still blurred vision I took the colt and placed a bead on Jack, just as he twirled the blade in his hand and readied to stab downward into Sam.

"Stop!" I shrieked.

I squeezed off a shot. The *boom* resonated loudly as the gun went off. Both men tumbled away from me. In my confusion I feared briefly I may've hit Sam, but he and Jack came up almost instantly, unharmed. The bullet went wide sparing them both. Sam briefly shouted toward me but was cut short by the flashing blade Jack wielded. He still had enough strength to stop Jack's upward strike through his belly and into his chest.

I squeezed the trigger again, again without any results. Jack was not looking at Sam now; he eyed me with a ferocity that made me quake in fear and with the same wicked smile upon his lips. Knowing Sam could wait and I was the greater threat, he kicked Sam down and then focused on me. I took another bead but he was coming at me in a half circle. Another round sounded, loud and jarring. Yet it didn't seem to affect the approaching man.

"Jack Monroe!" I shouted. "You put that knife down, or I will shoot you!"

Old Whiskers seemed to pause for a moment, perhaps judging whether I could find my target under such duress this time around.

My record was not very impressive thus far. Was I capable? I did my best to focus, aiming the gun at him while I tried to steady my trembling hand. I did not hear the shot, but saw the crazed look drain from his eyes, and the smile twisted and distorted in shock.

I kept pulling the trigger until the revolver stopped jumping in my hand. I shot him again and again. For a brief moment there was just Jack and me in this world, and the fear and hatred he inspired burst through me in a blistering rage I was incapable of controlling. The darkness hid what must have been a grizzly scene, but his ashen face, and those lifeless eyes were unmistakable. I knew he was dead, but I continued to try to fire the gun, only producing a clicking sound now that the cylinder was empty, until Mr. Haney put his hand upon mine and stopped me.

"Frank," he murmured, "put it down."

I did as he told me to, dropping the pistol to the ground. Both he and Sam were looking at me with troubled expressions. Without any warning I began to cry. I moaned loudly and then my body was overcome with great and terrible sobbing. Sam clutched his arm across his stomach, where Jack cut him open. He came to me with sympathy in his eyes, putting his other hand upon my shoulder.

"Are you all right?" he asked. I threw my arms around his neck, letting the tears come freely, without the strength to even attempt restraining them.

"I thought he would kill you, Sam," I whimpered. "He wouldn't stop."

"It's over now," he assured me. "All is well. It's all right."

"It's not all right! You're hurt!" I told him.

"I'm all right," he insisted, drawing me close.

"What would I have done without you?" I wept.

"It is over now. It is over," Sam assured.

"What would I have done without you?" I asked again. I pulled away feeling angry and relieved all at once. "You shouldn't have come here! Don't you ever do anything like this to me again!" I yelled at him, pointing my finger at him accusatory. I was shaking, my nerves stretched to a breaking point. But then I looked at Sam again and felt a collapse, as though everything inside of me that was holding me up had disintegrated all at once and there was nothing but massive rubble left. I began crying again and I clutched him to me, kissing him, burying my face in his neck.

We realized then, Mr. Haney was still with us, watching our interaction with a mix of confusion and horror. I pulled away from Sam, wiping my eyes in shame.

"What in the world is going on here?" he said incredulously. He was as I'd never seen him before, borderline infuriated. Mr. Haney who was so even tempered, so difficult to rile, was growing irate.

"It's not what you think," Sam replied with a pleading look on his face. He tucked me protectively behind him as he addressed Mr. Haney.

"Sam…" I began. The last thing I wanted was another person in on my secret. I thought to stop him from telling Mr. Haney, but I could see it was too late. It was far beyond being explainable. There was no going back. Mr. Haney would know it now too, and I must hope for compassion from him. Sam turned to me, looking from me to Mr. Haney as though he were torn as to what he should do. Without saying a word, I gave him my consent. He faced Mr. Haney resolutely.

"She is a *girl*, Reed. Frank is a *girl*," Sam blurted. He was watching Mr. Haney to see what he would do, waiting for his response.

"What?" he asked, his eyes searching me in disbelief. It was clear from his countenance he couldn't understand what was transpiring. When you are so thoroughly shocked by a revelation, it is difficult to recover your wits.

"Her name is Serena. She is the daughter of Matthew Stark," Sam continued.

"How did this happen?" Mr. Haney wondered. His befuddled reaction was only to be expected. He was looking at Sam and then back to me with what I can only describe as pure astonishment. It was incomprehensible to him. I didn't speak. I couldn't speak.

"She said she was a boy and went around in trousers. I suppose it should've been apparent to us all. Now that I know the truth, it's obvious; but I never saw no girl wearing trousers before. So I believed it, you see. We all did. But she is a girl. Do you understand?"

Reed Haney looked at Sam with his eyebrows raised, blinking rapidly. Again he studied me closely.

"You knew about this?" Reed inquired of Sam.

"He didn't know," I said, crying anew. "He didn't know until just a short time ago. And I swore him to secrecy. I begged him not to tell anyone else."

"Well, this is surely a revelation!" Mr. Haney exclaimed.

"I'm sorry for what I've done," I said. "Very sorry. But Sam is not to blame in any of it. I alone should be held responsible."

"I know what you must be thinking. I'm sure I had similar thoughts when I discovered what she did. It's just she had no ill intentions. The only thing she is really guilty of was not thinking things through before she made such a reckless decision."

"This will take some getting used to," Mr. Haney said. "I know your mother well. I cannot imagine she would approve of this."

"She doesn't know," I admitted. "Neither does my father. No one did. I kept it a secret. And when Sam found out, well, he kept it a secret too, although he was very much opposed to it."

"How long?" Mr. Haney asked, looking from Sam to me.

"Couple of months," Sam answered.

"Is this what your quarrel was over?" Mr. Haney wondered, a new understanding dawning on him when he realized why Sam and I had a falling out.

I nodded my head yes. "Sam was very cross with me for lying to him. And I deserved it! I know I did. Out of honor he wouldn't share the same tent with me, until he realized it was arousing suspicion. And now he tries to convince me to go home almost daily."

"Rightfully so. I can see you have feelings for one another, and it isn't suitable for you to be alone like you been."

"Yes, sir," Sam said.

"From here on out, you must share your tent with me, Sam," Mr. Haney advised. He was addressing us as a strict father might. "The two of you must avoid any impropriety. You are responsible for seeing to it her reputation remains intact," he told Sam sternly.

"Yes, sir," Sam said again.

"I hardly think that is a consideration at the moment," I said. "Not only will everyone know what I've done, but I may well go to the gallows for killing Jack," I pointed out. "I would say my reputation is very much nonexistent."

Chapter 26

The soil was cold and moist beneath my fingers as I tossed it into the shallow hole Mr. Haney dug. He snuck back to camp, found a shovel, and returned with it in record time. Sam and I took Old Whiskers by the feet and arms and dragged him to the trees beyond the pasture. Now Jack lay in his grave, and I was helping fill the hole in with dirt.

Sam, Mr. Haney, and I labored the better part of the night to get rid of his body. None of us spoke, and in the strange silence, we were united in purpose, although I cannot say what the others were thinking. My desire was to rid myself finally and completely of the hated man. I knew burying him wouldn't accomplish this objective, but it would go a way toward it. At least the physical evidence of his demise would be covered up forever. It would take much more to erase him from my memory.

When we put his body into the grave, and I swathed his face with his jacket, I could have sworn his dead eyes were looking at me just before I covered them. I got the eerie feeling they could see me; they were taunting me. I threw his pistol in with him, after which we worked to cover him up. Sam gathered several armfuls of decaying leaves and sprinkled them over the spot so it wouldn't be too obvious the ground was recently disturbed.

The three of us finished up and trudged back to camp mentally and physically exhausted. We were cautious as we returned, deciding it best if we each entered the camp perimeter separate and at intervals. If we were all seen together it might arouse suspicion. Then too, if one of us was caught, we wouldn't all be caught.

"I'll go to his tent and see nothing's left behind," Sam said. "He shares a tent with Vern, but if I'm careful, Vern will sleep through it. Once I've got his personal effects I'll dispose of them."

"Just leave them," I argued. "It's not worth the risk."

"I know what I'm doing," Sam insisted. "Besides, it'll definitely arouse suspicion if he's left all of his things behind. They'll know something's happened to him, and he didn't just leave on his own."

"But if you should get caught…"

"It will be all right," Sam assured me before he left me, giving my hand a squeeze. "Just do what we decided and there'll be no trouble."

Sam waited a few minutes after Reed Haney went to his tent and then drifted in and out of shadow as he navigated through camp to Jack's tent. I waited in the darkness, my ears straining to hear any movement or disturbance, waiting with dread to hear the sound of an alarm set off. Every muscle in my body was tense as I remained there waiting, until I'd waited some time and hadn't detected any sort of trouble. Sam must have not been caught.

I returned alone to the tent I shared with Sam, wishing desperately he was with me and I knew all was well. The last thing I wished for was to be alone. I was anxious for Sam, knowing he was going to Jack and Vern's tent, and I didn't have a certain knowledge of his well-being. I was terrified they would discover what happened to Jack Monroe and drag me off to prison for murder. I was equally frightened by the thought of his body moldering and decaying beneath the ground where we left him, picturing a web of fine black veins stretching across his translucent white skin and the dirt we'd used to cover him filling his mouth up. I wanted nothing more than to comfort and be comforted.

Sam promised me everything would be all right. I clung to that thought, assuring myself Sam wouldn't lie to me. I just needed to believe, to have faith.

At roll call the following morning, they called out names as they always did. When they came to Jack Monroe's name they repeated it several times with no answer. My knees trembled and I felt a wave of nausea come over me. I kept my eyes forward and my face blank, hoping no one was looking at me, scrutinizing me to see if I reacted to his absence. I supposed the guilt I was feeling was punishment in and of itself. If I didn't get caught, I would have to live with what I'd done for the remainder of my days.

Later we spotted the superiors in conversation with Vern Stapleton. Vern was shrugging and scratching his head. From his expression I could tell he was clueless. He didn't know anything. I thought it was a good thing. He obviously was unaware Sam visited his tent last night. When they finished with him, he came over to talk with us.

"What was that about?" Sam asked Vern.

"They was wanting to know about Jack," he answered.

"What about him?" Sam wondered.

"Well, he's gone. Didn't show up for roll call, seems he's took off."

"You don't say…Perhaps he's drunk somewhere sleeping it off," Sam suggested.

"Don't know. He said he had business to see to last night. Never come back. And oddly his things was gone this morning. He must've come and collected 'em last night 'fore he left."

"What kind of business?"

"He never said. Just said 'business.' How am I to know?"

"Seems very strange," Sam said.

"They'll string him up for sure, if they catch up to him," Vern said. "They was giving him a second chance anyhow, letting him join up instead of serve time. Now he's gone and deserted. Well, there won't be no getting out of that one."

This piqued my interest. Jack was a criminal? "What did he do?"

"Huh?" Vern asked.

"What did Jack do that he was in prison? Before he was forced to join up."

"Said he got into it with a whore up in Livingston and cut her up good, carved her face so nobody else would have her. Course he's full of stories. Who knows if it's true," Vern said with a shrug.

If what Vern was saying *was* true, I was horrified by it. I thought of Jack trying to force himself upon that poor woman at the farm, of him throwing me in the river and leaving me to drown, and then last night with his knife, and I didn't doubt it. As sorry as I felt about last night, I now felt very much vindicated for what I had done. The world was better off without Jack Monroe, that was a certainty. I had rid society of a man who abused and mishandled the weak. Perhaps God would pardon me after all.

"You think he deserted?" Sam pointedly asked Vern.

"Don't know. I wouldn't put it past him," Vern answered. "What do you care?"

"Well, I don't miss him any," I said, before Sam could respond. "Better off without him!"

Sam looked somewhat surprised by my admission. I suppose he was thinking I should say as little as possible about my feelings for Jack, seeing as how we were trying to keep the knowledge I killed him from getting out. We must be above suspicion. Lying low would be the smart thing to do. But I didn't care. I didn't enjoy killing a man. No, I didn't enjoy it, but I was beginning to believe I was justified. And when you believe you're justified, it becomes difficult to feel sorry.

"You never did like him, did you, Frank?" Vern asked.

"No, sir, I did not," I answered honestly.

When Vern was gone, I whispered to Sam, "What did you do with it?"

He needed no explanation as to what I was referring to. He knew I was asking what he'd done with Jack's things. "Wasn't much. Burned what I could in the fire, buried the rest," he said.

"That's all there is to getting rid of a man's existence?"

Sam shook his head. "Well, *that* man's existence anyway," he said vehemently.

Indeed, no one seemed to take note or care much he was gone. There was an ease about things, a calm which reigned in his absence. He was the instigator, the one who put nasty thoughts in people's heads, and encouraged contention among the ranks. There was something about his nature that had a negative effect on those around him. This was only further confirmed when it was discovered he'd filled out a false muster roll in order to get extra pay and extra rations. Everyone knew then what a low down dirty dog he really was. If there was any doubt before, there was none now. In the mind of everyone who knew him, he was a deserter.

Chapter 27

A week after the battle, we were put in charge of sweeping the river. This was a task I did not care for. From the river we pulled swords and firearms aplenty. It was the dead bodies that were hard to see. Sixty bloated corpses, all Confederate, came from the water. We gave them a proper burial. It was the right thing to do. I couldn't help but think one of them might've been me if I hadn't been so lucky.

Rappahannock Station was a raging success for us. It was difficult to describe the emotional thrill it left us with. One hundred and three officers were captured, as well as one thousand, three hundred enlisted men. Everyone in camp carried a trophy or two which they kept with them as a reminder of our triumph. Francis Morse had six Confederate officers surrender to him. He took every one of their swords and very pompously wore them all on his belt to show them off. He clanked about in a showy fashion for everyone to see, proud of his conquests and hoping he might be the envy of the lot of us.

In order to press our advantage, and before the winter became too much of a burden, we packed up our gear and headed out in pursuit of Lee and his armies. Our scouts reported seeing them, and told us we might find them near Mine Run on the other side of the river. Accordingly, we marched for two days in search.

This was no small task. Again we marched through wilderness treacherously dense with undergrowth and thick brush. It was terrible cold, and we all bundled up to keep the chill at bay. Our miserable conditions grew worse when the rain set in.

We navigated through the forest, doing our best to stay together as a whole. Sam did what he could to help me through it. I noted Reed Haney also seemed to stay close by. I felt some guilt over it. I thought I'd become the one thing I didn't wish to be. I was a burden to these men. Night was dark and heavy upon us when Upton finally ordered us to a stop.

"We'll stop for the night," Upton informed us. "No fires. We don't want the enemy to know what we're up to."

It was a miserable night for no fires. We could not cook our food, or warm ourselves. We ate hardtack and nothing more. Sam gathered a pile of leaves for me to lie on and I huddled beneath my blanket, trying to stay warm. It was no use. The cold penetrated every part of me. My hands and feet throbbed. I could not get comfortable, and I most certainly could not sleep.

When it grew light out, we moved on. Finally we drew near to the edge of the dense, thick trees, the end of our journey, and what we were met with was a sight which made us tremble in our boots. It wasn't the cold but fear that was responsible for it. We faced an utterly overwhelming prospect. The river ran wide before us, and held up on the other side was the enemy, dug in safe and sound.

On the opposite bank of the river, the Rebs had cut young trees, stripped them of branches and leaves, and hacked the ends to sharp points, before they anchored them into the soil at dangerous angles. They looked like the quills of a startled porcupine menacingly standing on end. Beyond the banks of the river, the landscape climbed upward to form tall ridges, where the Confederate forces set up their batteries. Their cannons all pointed down upon us, hot metal ready to shower down and obliterate us all.

I could hear the collective intake of sharp breathes as we took in the ominous sight. They'd planned their fortifications well. It seemed as though we didn't have a prayer in heaven for going up against them. Sam looked at me then dropped his eyes and shook his head. He seemed angry and I couldn't figure out why.

"What?" I asked.

"We're in a tight spot this time," he complained.

"No worse than Rappahannock Station."

"Much worse, Frank. Much worse. Fortune don't generally smile twice on fools who tempt fate over and over again," he replied, rubbing his fingers across his lips in an agitated manner before they came to rest at his temple. His expression was far off, haggard and worried. "How am I going to get you through it?"

"I will be fine, Sam. Stop worrying over me."

"How can I not?" he asked, his face skeptical.

I remained silent. I didn't know what to say to him. Whether I liked it or not, he would be troubled. There was no use talking about it. It would do no good. I figured if we must go to our slaughter at least we would do it together.

"I've been told skirmishing has already begun elsewhere," Upton informed us. "Now we wait for the order to move. The 121st will have the honor of being first line. Fix bayonets and prepare for a frontal assault," he ordered. Then he smiled rakishly as he told us his next bit of news.

"I've told General Torbert we will be there to welcome his men once they make it to the enemy's pits. And he has assured me it will be his men, not mine, that reach them first. We each were so sure of our own men's abilities we put a little wager upon it. Now you know me well, men. I do not like to lose a wager. See to it Torbert is sufficiently chastened, won't you?"

We waited most of the day, on edge, ready to be called in. I could see there was a lot of speculation among the uppers, as they consulted and passed spy glasses back and forth among one another. All of us regulars watched, jogging in place and rubbing our hands together to try to keep the cold at bay as we waited to hear what our fate would be. Eventually Meade himself, the general of generals, rode up.

"If he is smart he will give it up," Sam told me.

After much debate and conversing with others, Meade seemed agitated and left with a sullen look on his face. We all lingered still, wondering what our fortunes held. We got word Meade was still undecided. He wanted to wait to make any judgment on the matter until tomorrow, because he felt Sunday was not a good day for making decisions.

Perhaps it was divine intervention that saved us. Meade reconsidered his position and sent word he wouldn't wait until tomorrow after all. He decided it was too much of a risk, and we were ordered to withdraw. The men sent up a cheer the likes of which you've never heard.

"Thank the good Lord he's got a brain in that head of his," Sam said. "If he had attacked, he would have been without an army and you would have been without me."

"How do you know you wouldn't have been without me?" I asked defiantly.

"Because I'd have died before I'd let anything happen to you," he said.

It was now growing dark again, and the thought of having to endure another long cold night out in the open was a grim one. We headed out, taking the road instead of going back through the woods again. After regrouping, Upton asked Sam and I and several others to help with the wounded. We hadn't seen any fighting ourselves but there were some who did engage. We were put under the charge of Dr. Holt to do as he asked, serving as litter bearers for the men who needed medical attention.

"There is a house up a-ways," the doctor admonished. "We shall endeavor to find aid there."

The 121st followed after as we marched up the road to a home with a large property and many outbuildings behind it. We left the road and headed up to the house, while the others sought shelter in the slave quarters out back. Dr. Holt, who was from our regiment, and another doctor I didn't know, by the name of Dr. Bland, eyed one another as if they were undecided as to who should have the duty of knocking at the door. Finally Dr. Holt gave in and pounded his fist against the wood panel.

Shortly a group of three girls between the ages of sixteen and twenty-five answered. The oldest seemed to be representing the lot. She wore an unpleasant expression and seemed quite bold in her dislike for us. She threw the door open without ceremony and glared at us.

"What do you want?" she asked. Not even a hello or how do you do from her.

"Is the man of the house in?" Dr. Bland asked.

"He is not," the woman spat. "He heard you were coming and left. There is only my sisters and I."

"What a true gentlemen, running off and leaving the ladies to fend for themselves," Dr. Holt muttered.

"You are not welcome here. We don't care to have you on our property. It would be best if you would please leave."

"Whether you care or not, we are in need of this house. We have wounded. They need tending to, and we plan on using it as a hospital," he replied.

"You run our father out, and now you aim on running us out?" she fumed.

"You may stay as long as you are out of the way," he assured her.

"You can't just walk in and take over. This is our home and we should have a say. You can't go around taking what's not yours. It's downright uncivilized."

The two doctors were fed up with her. They pushed past the group of girls without further word and motioned for us to bring the gurneys with the injured right on in. We paraded past them into the front parlor where we unceremoniously laid the men out upon the hardwood floors.

"Have you got a pump in the kitchen or should we draw water from the well?" Dr. Holt asked one of the girls.

"If you think we will help you, you're mistaken," she replied coolly.

"Rest assured that we will only be here a short time. The sooner we finish, the sooner we'll be out of your way," Dr. Bland said. "Now we need water."

None of them answered, just kept their jaws clamped in defiant silence. They were clearly unwilling to accommodate us in any capacity. This did not bode well with the doctors.

"We have wounded men here. They are suffering," Dr. Holt said, as if he might appeal to their tender natures. He seemed to think that by saying this, they might come to their senses. They remained unmoved. I suppose in their minds, one less Yankee was something to celebrate.

"I was born in this house," the oldest said. "As was my father before me. And I will tell you I would rather see it burn to the ground with every one of you damn Yankees in it than have it used to your benefit."

This riled Dr. Blanding something terrible. He gave her a hateful smirk and bowed ever so slightly to her as though he were deferring to her. His lips were formed into a malicious smile, and he looked at Dr. Holt as if to prove a point. Then he looked her in the eyes with a casual shrug.

"I'm sure something can be arranged," he told her.

"Well, aren't you fair specimens of Southern hospitality?" Dr. Holt blurted. "Bunch of snuff-dipping, dilapidated, lantern jawed, bipeds of neuter gender…" he went on.

I was shocked, and so were they. Their eyes grew to the size of saucers, their mouths dropping open. One of them audibly gasped. Confederates or not, they were ladies. It disturbed me to hear him slander them so. A man should not be abusive toward a woman, no matter how disagreeable she might be. I was ashamed for him and the rest of us.

"How dare you!" The oldest huffed, her indignation mirrored in her sisters' faces. It was sore for them to be so insulted. "You surely are the vilest of men, sir, speaking to a lady that way! Rotten to the core!"

The doctor cocked his eyebrow and began to laugh at her in an amused chuckle, happy to see he'd affected them so.

"I have men here who require medical attention. If you will not assist us then get out of the way. I have no time or patience for a foul mouthed trollop such as you." He looked over at me and motioned by wagging his pointer and middle finger for me to come to him. I quickly did so, not wishing to further test him.

"I need you to fetch me some water, son," he said.

I took off at a trot determined to oblige him. There was a pump in the kitchen after all. I took up a bucket and filled it and brought it back. When I returned, everyone was working at something and the three girls were gone. For the next several hours I did as I was directed to do, assisting the doctors in whatever capacity they required of me.

After several hours, many of the men fell off to sleep, as did the doctors. They both were sitting in chairs with their heads leaning back, snoring softly. Sam caught my gaze and motioned with his head for me to follow him. He walked out of the room. I waited a short while and then I followed. I wandered down the hall, not sure where I was going, and then he startled me as he reached his hand out from a darkened doorway and pulled me in.

The study smelled stuffy, of cigar smoke and old leather. It was dark, with only the moonlight streaming through a window for light, but I could make out the shapes, two armchairs and a desk, and I could see the walls were lined with bookshelves filled with musty old books. Sam pulled me into his arms and held me close.

"What are you doing?" I whispered.

"I wanted to kiss you," he said. I felt my heart beat faster. I wasn't sure if it was the thrill of being in his arms or the threat of being caught, or maybe both.

"They might catch us," I replied.

"Yes, they might. But I thought I ought to take the chance. I might not get another like it, what with Mr. Haney always lurking about trying to keep you safe from me."

"Well, then, I suppose you're right. We really should make the best of it," I said.

He went to put his lips to mine, but our hats struck one another, fell from our heads and tumbled to the floor. We both laughed for a moment, then quickly forgot about them. He drew close to me again and put his mouth resolutely against mine. Everything about it was delicious, his smell, his taste. I thought it could go on endlessly and I would never grow tired of it.

I wrapped my leg around him, trying to draw nearer if it was possible. Sam responded by lifting my other foot from the floor, turning me around and sitting me firmly on the desk. He bent down over me with my head cradled in his hands, holding it with the pads of his fingers as if it was precious and fragile, as if it might break if he weren't gentle enough. Then he kissed me proper, his mouth settling on mine as my breathing came in fast, soft gulps and my pulse thrummed in my temples.

Although I felt lost in it, there was still a part of me completely aware of where I was, still listening for the sound of echoing feet upon the floors in the hallway just outside. And when I heard it, I pulled away quickly, rolled over the back side of the desk and disappeared into the shadows as I pressed myself to the floor. None too soon either. The door creaked open and Dr. Holt peeked his head in.

I could see most of the scene from the gap in the middle of the desk, where the owner must have sat with his chair tucked beneath, neatly writing out expenses in his ledger. Sam was left bleary eyed and in shock as he dropped his hands awkwardly to his sides and turned to face the doctor. I felt very badly for having left him in such a way, but it was better than the two of us caught together.

"What are you doing in here?" the doctor asked Sam.

Sam cleared his throat. He smoothed his jacket with his hand. He was on the spot and couldn't think of an answer.

"I…" He cleared his throat again, a long grumbling noise. It would have made me laugh, if I weren't so unnerved. "I was just looking at this impressive library. There are some volumes here that look quite interesting," he said. The doctor's brows furrowed and he frowned thoughtfully.

"In the dark?" he asked.

"I didn't want to wake anyone," Sam replied.

"I see. Well, we will be pulling out soon. Take what suits you so it shan't go to waste." He rubbed his face, as if he were trying to wake himself and then staggered back out the door and left Sam and I alone.

Sam took in a deep and shuddering sigh, relieved it was over. But I couldn't help myself; I burst out giggling, as quietly as I could manage under the circumstances. I couldn't see him, and he couldn't see me, as he leaned against the desk in the darkness, but I could sense he was smiling.

"Be quiet, you coward," he said in mocked annoyance.

I left before him, making an excuse of visiting the outhouse when I returned to the parlor. Several minutes later, Sam slipped in with a few books tucked beneath his arm to make it look good. He caught my eye and gave me a concealed wink when he thought no one else was paying attention. I felt a rush of excitement over him behaving so brazenly with a room full of witnesses who might have caught him.

The stars began to disappear from the sky, but it was not quite daybreak, still an inky shade of blue. I was nudged awake and told we would be leaving soon. We gathered up the wounded the doctors had worked so feverishly on a few hours before, carefully laying them out on the litters. We stuffed our gear into our haversacks, slung them over our shoulders and headed out. We carried the wounded out the front door, over the porch and down the stairs. In the hush of the lonely hour, Dr. Bland's voice rang clear and true. There was no mistaking his words.

"Burn it!"

Chapter 28

Before I knew what was happening, Dr. Bland tossed one of the kerosene lamps he'd carried from the house onto the front porch, just beneath one of the great windows facing out onto the lawn. The oil erupted in a small explosion, igniting the wooden boards on the porch. From there the fire spread rapidly, vivid orange flames licking the painted clapboard in quick order. I was in shock, the sickest sort of feeling running through my body.

It was all happening so fast, and I knew there was nothing I could do. I could only stand there with my mouth open, my lips quivering, in terrified awe. This couldn't be happening! It was all a big mistake. The thought *We are not the sort that would burn down the home of a bunch of defenseless women!* ran through my mind.

"What are you doing?" I gasped, turning on the doctor with a cry of outrage.

"Personally granting their wish," he said with a hard smile.

"The women are still in there!" Sam yelled.

For a moment the doctor looked chagrined, but only for a moment. Then he set his mouth in a defiant grimace and turned his back to the house, picking up his things and motioning for us to follow. No one did. We were all frozen in shock.

"We must go in and get those women out!" Sam insisted.

"They were plenty capable of taking care of themselves," Dr. Bland shot back.

In the back of the home more bright fires appeared, as the slave quarters were set ablaze. A flurry of activity ensued, people running and yelling and hustling to get buckets of water to try to put the flames out. It was a lost cause. There was no way they were going to save the property.

Relief washed over me when the front door burst open, and the three sisters, screaming frantically, came spilling out into the cold in their night dresses and shawls. They huddled together on the lawn, watching in horror as the house burned. They may have been out of a home, but at least they were alive. And I was ashamed to say while I was sincerely sorry for them, I was thinking about Sam. How glad I was he hadn't been forced to go in after them.

There was a tremendous heat burning my eyes and making me cough. I tucked my nose and mouth into my shirt as I watched helplessly. Sam dropped his head, as though he were unable to bring himself to witness it. The sky was as bright as noonday and ash began to rain down upon us in large sooty chunks, falling as soft as feathers.

The worst of it was the slaves. Everything they owned was in those huts, the only homes they'd ever known. They all milled about watching the flames eat up their lives, helpless to do anything to stop it. Their faces glowed from the light, faces that registered fear and despair. One small girl cried inconsolably with her arm stretched out, her hand, fingers open and clutching, toward the cabin she and her family lived in, as if she might be able to pluck it up in her hands and hold it safely there.

When I saw her, I could not stop myself, I began to cry too. The quiet seemed unbearable, the only sounds popping wood and sizzling rawhide from the tanner's barn where his stock was now nothing but ash. In the surreal aftermath, there was nothing but a hollow misery wrapping us all in its spell.

I heard Dr. Holt mutter, "They wanted their liberty and now they have it. They are free to go." As though what they'd done was a favor to those poor, dependent people. The only way of life they'd ever known was gone, just like that, and they were thrust into the cold world without even a coat to cover their backs. There was no satisfaction in it.

"We stayed here long enough. It is time to move on," Dr. Bland said. "Move out."

I knew there was nothing we could do for those poor people, but I felt an overwhelming guilt as I turned my back on the place. We picked up the litters with sick and wounded men, and we left. Yet, there remained in my heart a sore spot as tender as a bruise which aches when you put pressure on it. That place and those faces were forever seared into my memory.

War is a summer sport. When winter came we settled in for our annual hibernation, just a few short miles from Brandy Station. There was, upon the banks of the Hazel River, a thriving colony of us, over one hundred thousand in numbers, circled up like wagons. Like ants in an anthill, we went out and brought back all we needed to sustain us through the long months ahead.

At the center of our hub, General Sedgwick took up residence in the Welford Mansion, a grand and beautiful home. The mansion was brick, with two massive chimney stacks on each end of the home, two stories, and I counted eight windows on the first floor and nine on the second. No doubt he would be quite comfortable in such a majestic shelter. I wondered what it would be like to live in such a place.

At first, the 121st were assigned to a soggy and wretched location. But good Colonel Upton had Dr. Holt pronounce it unfit, telling the uppers we would be susceptible to disease and bad health if we were to stay there. Our regiment was lucky enough to be granted permission to move to the other side of the river where we became an island unto ourselves. The rest of the army camped together, and we watched them from across the Hazel in our own little city.

We began right off making preparations to hunker down for the cold months ahead. We were set up just like miniature city blocks, with wooden sidewalks connecting it all. The men built a number of dwellings for housing and other provisions. The cabins were large enough for a man to walk through the door standing upright, with fireplaces, and all that was required for comfortable living. We were not limited in what we could build, only as much as the imagination would allow. There was a roughly built post office, hospital, and of course the sutler's little place where you could go to buy whatever you might want, which was somewhat like a general store. I dared not go in there after my run in with our sutler last year. When I chanced to see him, I looked down and acted as though I was not aware he was there, and he thankfully did the same.

Upton and his staff took up residence in a local farmer's home, where we kept our horses in the barn there and viewed it as the headquarters and stables of the 121st campsite. Along with his aides, Upton would be more than comfortable in such a lovely home. It was nothing like the mansion but very fine nonetheless. The rest of us built around his living quarters.

Colonel Olcott didn't stay with Colonel Upton at the farmhouse. He decided he would have his own place, a fine lodging indeed. He asked for those who were experienced carpenters to assist in building his dwelling. Sam, being very qualified to do just that, was paid extra money to help in the construction of it. It turned out well for him because he was let out of other duties to work on it, a well-deserved break from the mundane tasks he would normally be assigned to. I envied him a little. While I was mucking out the stables, he was given the prestigious job of working on Olcott's cabin all day.

When it was finished you can't imagine what it looked like. Bigger and better than any of the others! There were carpets upon his floors, real furniture requisitioned from some of the farmhouses round about, such as a bed, a table, and two fat easy chairs by the fireplace. Sam secretly took me through it for a personal tour once it was completed. He showed me with pride his handiwork and we sat in the easy chairs to try them out and see how they felt.

In his spare time, when he was not working for Olcott, Sam helped me build a cabin too. He was still boarding with Mr. Haney, so it was to be all mine. We cut timber from the surrounding forest, notched the logs, and stacked them log cabin style. I spent hours filling the cracks in with mud from the river bank and papering the inside walls with old newspaper. Sam built up a straight and sturdy chimney for the fireplace. He also built a proper door that latched from the inside. We even took wood slats and covered the dirt floor with them, so there was a proper wood floor. It would be warm and cozy even in the bitterest cold.

One day, after working in the stables, I returned to my cabin and found the most wonderful surprise. I walked through the door and there was a small drop leaf table with two mismatched chairs, a single slat shelf on the wall behind the table where a worn out pot and assorted cracked dishes were stored, and a proper bed, the frame made by hand from logs with a mattress stuffed full of hay. It all fit just right. Any more would have been too much. I gasped out loud as I stood upon the threshold taking it all in. My own little house! It was more than I could have asked for.

I waited impatiently the remainder of the day to say my thank you. I managed to get a piece of calico which I covered the table with so it looked like a table cloth. I set the table with the dishes he got me, and I made the best meal I was capable of making under the circumstances. I wanted it to be just right. When Sam came around for dinner, he knocked on the door just as it began to get dark.

"May I come in?" he said, trying to suppress a smile.

"You may," I conceded. I stepped aside and ushered him in. "Won't you have a seat?" I asked, offering him one of the chairs at the table. He sat down as I scurried over to the fireplace and brought back the pot filled with stew meat and potatoes.

"Smells very good," he said. "Thank you for having me."

I dished a portion to him and then to myself, then sat down opposite him. I wondered if this was how it would be if we were back home, if he were coming to court me. The thought pleased me. I couldn't wait any longer to speak.

"How did you manage it?" I burst out. He knew exactly what I was referring to.

"I have my ways," he replied mysteriously.

"Not good enough. You must tell me!"

"Olcott. He told us to take some wagons around to commandeer furniture for his cabin. I just picked up a few things here and there while I was on his errand."

"Sam! It is all just so lovely! I am very pleased with it!" I squealed. "It was just so wonderful of you."

"I'm glad you liked it. Merry Christmas."

"It isn't Christmas yet," I pointed out.

"Everyone else has begun celebrating early. We may as well too."

"Now we will have a good meal together, you and me. Just as if we were properly courting."

"We *are* properly courting," he said.

I was delighted when he said that. It was like a soothing pat on the back. I don't know if other women are as insecure as myself, but I loved to be reassured I was his heart's desire. "Then tell me how your day went," I replied. "Like you would if you were at work and just come home to me."

"Oh, I was at work all right. We have finished Colonel Olcott's cabin. And it is fine. You will have to come and see it. Best of all I think he took a particular liking to me."

"Really? Well, it doesn't surprise me. But what did he say?"

"He said I done good work. Told me if I should ever need anything, I ought to come to him."

"You must feel very good about that," I said.

"I do. It was an honor."

"You may have gotten the furniture from round about here, but not the bed. You made the bed didn't you?"

"Yes."

"Just for me?" I said, attempting to flirt with him. I wouldn't go so far as to bat my eyelashes, for that would be downright silly with me in my soldier getup looking like a boy, but I enjoyed playing with him.

"For the time being anyway," he acknowledged, taking a bite. I thought it was a curious thing to say, but I ignored it and continued on, because it was borderline indecent to discuss such things.

"It will be such a treat to sleep in a real bed again. I think I may have forgotten what it's like."

"I hoped you would like it."

"Oh, I do. I feel so lucky."

"You ought to. Reed and me are still sleeping on our bedrolls." He chuckled.

"I'll feel bad when I'm comfortable and cozy in my bed, knowing you are on the cold, hard floor."

"It doesn't bother me," he said. "I wouldn't be able to sleep anyhow, with Reed's snoring. You were a much better bedfellow than he."

"You aren't sleeping well?"

He shrugged. "I've had a lot on my mind," he admitted.

"Yes, you've been very busy, I know."

"Listen, Serena, I have something I want to talk to you about."

Immediately the playful mood we had going on between us seemed to evaporate. I couldn't say why but it was instantly uncomfortable. I felt a nervous roiling ball spinning in my stomach. I set my spoon down, thinking I shouldn't eat any more, or I would get sick, and gave him my full attention.

"What is it?" I asked apprehensively.

"What would you say if I was to tell you I procured passes for the both of us?"

"What? Impossible. They're not giving out passes," I said skeptically.

"Not generally, no. Not to lowly soldiers like us anyway. But when Olcott wanted to know if there was anything he could do for me, I asked for furlough passes for you and me," he said.

"And?"

"Well, I tried for a ten-day furlough but could only just get five. Still, he got permission for it, and we can leave the start of next week if you choose. What do you say to that?" He looked triumphant.

"I don't understand. We are free to go for five days?"

"That is right."

"To do what?"

"Well, now, It's up to you, I expect," he answered. He fidgeted with the raw edge of the calico cloth, straightened his plate and spoon, anything to keep his hands busy. He was nervous. I'd rarely seen him so. It made me nervous too.

"Would we go home to visit Richfield?" I asked.

"I don't know if we would have time," he said. "By the time we got there, we'd have to turn around and come back. We could try to contact our families and see if they can meet us halfway maybe. I don't know if your father could travel with your mother? We would only have this week to get word to them and make arrangements. And with the mail as it is, they may get it in time, they may not…" I nodded to let him know I understood.

"It would be difficult, maybe impossible," I agreed.

"Or I have another idea." He reached into his coat and pulled a letter from his inner pocket. Sam studied me closely as he handed me the envelope with a folded bit of paper in it. I'm sure he could see I was confused. I turned the envelope over in my hands and began to draw the paper out. It was well read, I could see from the worn creases.

"What's this?" I wondered.

"I have written to your father," he told me.

"My father?" I became concerned.

"That letter is from him. And if you are willing, he has given his blessing so I might ask for your hand."

I could hardly believe what I was hearing. I stared hard at him, across the table from me, to discover if he was being truthful or if this was some elaborate joke. I wasn't sure if I should burst out laughing so I didn't look like a complete fool, or if I should take him seriously and keep my expression sober. But he was staring right back, as earnest as could be, his dark eyes intense and waiting.

"In marriage?" I asked him, completely taken aback. It wasn't so long ago Sam didn't even want to speak to me. He made no indication he was even considering such a thing. The thought of marrying him was too fantastic to believe. I thought I must be jumping to conclusions, reading into his words because that's what I wanted to hear but not really what he was saying at all. I didn't see it coming. To say I was his girl was one thing. He went with lots of girls back home. But to say he wanted me as his wife was something very different.

He laughed at me. "Well, yes in marriage."

"You are serious?" I gasped.

"Read it for yourself," he suggested.

I was in shock. For all of these years this was all I wanted, all I could dream of. Sam was the only man I'd ever loved. And now he wanted me in return. I felt the energy drain from me as I clutched the letter in my hand. I tried to skim through it as my hand trembled and the words tossed about before my eyes. It was addressed to Sam.

After having received your letter, and given it some thought, I can only say I am not only relieved but happy about this turn of events. Serena is my only living child, my heart and soul. She is all I've got left. Having her so far away has put a great strain on me, as I worry about her welfare on a daily basis. It pleases me to know she has someone close who will look out for her and take care of her in my absence.

I know you well enough to know you are a good boy, with a fine character, and you come from good stock. I believe a union between the two of you would be an excellent match. As her father, I most certainly give my permission for you to ask for her hand. I could never deny you that. However, I cannot speak for my daughter on her preferences. While I think it would be of great benefit to her, she must answer for herself. If Serena is of a like mind and wishes to have you, then I will gladly give my blessing.

Best of Luck,
Matthew Stark

I looked from the letter to him in disbelief.

"You want me for your wife?" I whispered. He leaned back in his chair with his eyes wide, as if he were exasperated.

"If you will have me, that is very much what I want," he replied, his lips curling into a mischievous grin.

"I don't want you to do this out of pity," I said, remembering back to the boy who rescued my bonnet for me. "You are a good man, this I know. But I don't need you to save me."

"No," he said thoughtfully, "I am proposing marriage, not salvation."

This brought tears to my eyes.

"Serena," he said, getting up from his chair and coming to kneel before me. He took me into his arms. "Don't cry. Why are you crying?"

"Do you mean it?" I wept. "Is this real?" I asked, holding the letter up as though it were the letter which was in question and not his intentions.

"You certainly know how to keep a man waiting," he pointed out.

"I'm sorry," I said.

"Well, will you be my wife?" he questioned.

"Yes, Sam. I would be ever so glad to," I admitted. I clutched him to me and kissed his beautiful face over and over again. I never wanted to let him go. I didn't want the moment to end.

Chapter 29

The week wore on tediously. It seemed as though days became years. And while I waited I did my best to prepare. I was set upon having a proper dress to wear for my wedding day. The best I could come up with was a bonnet embellished with trim and a fat, pale blue ribbon, a skirt, a plain white blouse, and a jacket trimmed in lace that I got trading with a local woman in town. I was lucky they parted with any of it. Things were scarce now, and many of the people there had worn out clothing and no cloth to replenish what needed to be replaced. One of the women looked as though she might cry when she gave up the jacket in return for a slab of bacon. It was not overly formal. Just everyday wear, but still nicer than a work dress. I was pleased to have it and I felt a little sorry I was taking it from her, even though the trade was fair.

I couldn't sleep nights for thinking of what was to come. I went over and over our plans in my head. I took the opportunity to write a letter, wanting my father to know I accepted Sam's proposal and we would be married soon. I didn't want him to wonder or worry. He likely wouldn't get the letter until after we were married, but it was news at least. Sam said he did the same. He wrote to his family telling them of his intentions.

Christmas day was a rowdy and boisterous event. Sam and I were assigned police duty in town that evening, along with Darby and Felix. Some of the officers had begun drinking days before and were now in a very sorry and drunken state. They went about looking for trouble to get into, which made for a difficult shift.

"'Tis strange to me the officers may indulge in drink, when us enlist-ed should suffer court martial if we was to do the same," Darby observed.

"Shameful, regardless of who it was that done it," Sam said.

This didn't appease Darby, who appeared put out by Sam saying anything against his complaint. I broke away from the group and went by the stables to see they were secure. As I walked around to the gate to let myself in, Felix came up behind. "I see less and less of you these days," he said.

For some reason, being alone with him made me nervous, al-though I had been alone with him before. I couldn't say exactly why, only I knew Sam did not much approve of Felix Newburn. I shrugged with a half-smile. "Been busy," I replied. "I've been work-ing on my cabin."

"Your cabin, huh?"

"Yes. It's a right nice one."

"If you say so."

"I do," I said. "There's a lot to be done with winter upon us. I'm sure you've been up to the same, haven't you?"

"You aren't any fun anymore," Felix accused.

"How's that?"

"You used to be up for some sport every now and then. Not anymore. Seems you'll talk only to Sam now. You follow him around like a pup."

"Sam and I have been together from the beginning," I said. "He is like a brother to me."

"You don't get tired of him bossing you around and telling you what to do?"

"He doesn't boss me around," I told him. I found it comical he thought so. Sam was not the type to tell others what to do. In general he minded his own business and didn't stray too far from his own affairs unless he needed to. I wondered what would make Felix think such a thing. Perhaps it was Sam's promotion that irked Felix. I wasn't sure.

"Has he told you not to speak to me?"

"No. He's never said a thing about you."

"If it's on account of what happened with Jack, well, now you know I didn't have anything to do with that," he told me. I felt the familiar twinge whenever Jack Monroe's name was mentioned, a moment of panic and paranoia wondering if someone found out what really happened to him. Had Felix Newburn found out?

"What do you mean?" I asked.

"The farm that day. I'll have you know, I'm not like him. You were there, and you saw I had no part in it."

I wondered what his point was in telling me this. It was water under the bridge. Jack was good and gone, and what happened on the farm was many months ago. I continued to check each stall in the barn and then moved for the door.

"I never said you did," I pointed out.

"No, but I figure that's why you aren't as friendly anymore. And I just want you to know, I don't condone what he did. If you hadn't stopped him, I would have."

I thought it was easy to say what you would have done, much easier than actually having to do it. I didn't think Felix was a bad sort, but he was the sort swayed by the popular voice. Who knows how he would've reacted if I hadn't been there that day. It dawned on me he was saying all of this because he couldn't stand the thought of me not liking him, or anyone else for that matter. He was the kind who needed to be liked. And, for whatever reason, he was worried about what I thought of him.

"We remain friends. I have no hard feelings toward you."

"Good. And I hope you won't go around telling tales."

"Since when was I ever the sort to do that?" I asked, truly perplexed by the direction the conversation was taking.

"Well, good. Just so we are clear on it."

"We are clear on it," I assured him.

We walked back to the street where there was a commotion going on. Sam and Darby, and a group of soldiers surrounded Colonel Olcott, who was drunk as a skunk and shouting. He was staggering about with a bottle in his hand and waving it in the air as he yelled.

"I asked you to have a drink with me. As your superior you insult me by refusing!"

To his credit, the fellow in question stood his ground and remained calm. "As much of an honor as it is, I must decline, Colonel."

"Do you think you are too good for it?" Olcott railed. "Is that what you think?"

"No, sir. I simply don't wish to drink."

At this point Olcott launched himself at the other man, knocking him to the ground. He pinned the man's arms to the ground with his knees, and then he took his bottle of liquor and pressed it to the man's lips. The drink spilling out all over his face as Olcott screamed at him, "Drink it! Drink it!"

The crowd formed a circle, and the soldiers pressed in and began cheering Olcott on. The poor fellow who was being assaulted began to cough and splutter as the liquid from the bottle poured out onto his face, in his nose and mouth. He fought desperately to get up, but Olcott had pinned him good. In all of the commotion I watched transfixed, wondering what I should do. Finally, Sam managed to push past the crowed, stepped up and pulled Colonel Olcott up and away from his hapless victim.

The poor man crawled away from the crowd, and once he was clear he sprang up from the ground and took off at a run. When Olcott saw this he became indignant. He staggered slightly, doing his best to steady himself, and then turned on Sam. "I command you to go arrest that man!" he yelled, pointing his finger into the air emphatically.

"Yes, absolutely! We'll see to it, sir," Sam replied calmly. "In the meantime, let's get you back to your cabin." He took Olcott by the arm and gently steered him toward his dwelling. I trailed along behind, careful not to get too close for fear of what he might do.

"You may have ten men to round him up," he hollered, "and if it isn't enough you have my permission to get a company of men to round him up!"

"Yes, sir," Sam agreed, as he continued to lead him along.

"And if it's still not enough, I will call out the whole regiment to round him up!" he blustered.

As they approached his cabin Sam told him, "Yes, sir. Of course, sir."

"You're a good man Second-Lieutenant Barlow," he babbled on. "You bring him back to me and I will promote you. You hear?"

"Thank you, Colonel."

"Orderly Sergeant. That's what I shall promote you to. And you know I am a man of my word."

Sam now opened the door and showed him into the cabin. Darby and Felix stayed behind to try to get the rest of the crowd under control and I waited alone for Sam to come out. He was gone for a few minutes before he reappeared looking somewhat relieved.

"Did you get him to bed?"

Sam nodded his head yes. "Thankfully he didn't fight me on it. I took his boots off and tucked him in, just like a child."

"I don't care for him," I admitted. I was very unimpressed by his behavior.

"I can understand why. But don't forget he managed to pull the strings that got us our passes," Sam pointed out.

"I don't have to like someone to be grateful."

"Smart girl." He smiled approvingly. "And what was Felix following you around for?"

"Not sure what to make of it. He was worried I didn't like him anymore."

"Mark my words, he will be a politician. Someday we will read about him in the papers."

"Perhaps." I was done talking about Felix. "But we have better things to talk about, you and I."

"What would that be?"

I dropped my voice. "I've gotten a dress put together."

"Excellent," he said. But I could tell he wasn't as excited about it as I was.

"I suppose it isn't the kind of thing you get a thrill over, but I am very pleased."

"No, that's good news."

"It is silly, but it means a lot to me."

"I'm thinking we should head for Pennsylvania. Get as far away from here as we can."

"I have something for you," I said. I reached into my haversack and pulled out an orange, tossing it to him. He quickly caught it. "Merry Christmas."

He grinned at me. "Haven't seen one of these in a very long while." He began to peel it. "Here, we will share it." He separated a wedge and handed it to me.

"Thank you," I said, taking a bite and sucking the juice from it.

"And I have a gift for you as well."

I perked up, smiling expectantly, eager to see what he'd gotten me. "What is it?" I asked.

"News."

I was confused. "News?"

"Yes. A letter from home."

"What is it?"

"When I thought to ask for your hand, I wrote my father to make arrangements on my behalf. I sent some money to him and asked him to put it down on a little farm there in Richfield," he said.

"You did?" I was surprised. He'd mentioned before he was intent upon getting a place of his own long ago, before he knew the truth about me. But he hadn't spoken of it since.

"It isn't much," he said. "Eighty acres. Not far from town. I took all I've been saving and my father threw in a small share. He says it was owed to me for working at the mill for him. Well, anyway, it was enough. Do you remember the old Derringer place?"

"No," I answered.

"Sure you do," he insisted. "The little brick house with the sagging porch and shudders. It's going to need a good coat of paint. Widow Derringer lived there up to five or so years ago. It's been empty since she died, with nobody to claim it. It was probably on your way home from school."

"The one with the great oak that was struck by lightning?"

"The very one. Anyhow, the house will need work and the barn will probably have to be torn down and rebuilt, it's pretty shabby, but my father said he could get it for a good price, it's been sitting empty for so long, and it will be a fine place to start out with, don't you think?"

"Yes, Sam," I agreed enthusiastically. "We can put our own touch to it, and make what we want of it."

"Every time I passed the place, the house looked sad. And I always thought a house like that needed a family, needed some hard work and a family to make it look cheerful again. Before I signed up, I would think maybe it would be mine someday, and I would buy it and move in and fix it up, but then I put it out of mind when I decided to enlist. You aren't displeased I went ahead and put money down on it, are you?"

"Not at all. I'm just very surprised. I didn't know you were thinking of it."

"You must have a home to go back to," he reasoned. "A place of your own you can be comfortable in."

"You mean a place of *our* own," I corrected.

"That's what I meant. A place of our own…"

"Because I'm not leaving without you," I said with a smile. But I didn't feel the smile. I only did this to keep the mood light. I could feel him ready to bring up his old conversation about sending me home, and I wouldn't have any of it. I stopped him before he got the chance to bring it up again.

We spent the rest of the evening making plans and talking about what we would do with the house and the property. I told Sam I was not afraid of hard work. He told me he would be close enough to town that he could continue to work for his father at the mill, and in his spare time he could work on making repairs and improvements.

In my head I could picture it all. I could see it. I realized I still hoped it could actually happen. That he and I would be there together some day, and the war would finally come to an end.

"I've been thinking about re-enlisting," he told me.

I grew still. "Why?"

"They have offered a three hundred dollar bonus and a thirty day furlough for anyone who will sign up for another three years."

"Three years?" I shuddered.

"It would give me time to go home and help you fix the house up, and the money to do it with."

"It's not worth it, Sam."

"Three hundred dollars is a lot of money," he reasoned.

"No one could put a price on your life and what it is worth to me," I told him. "I think we should finish our time and get out if we can."

"It was just a thought…" he said.

Chapter 30

When the day finally came for us to leave, Mr. Haney bid us have a safe trip and a pleasant rest. He was the only one to see us off, and the only one who knew what our intent was. We left camp with our secret between us, eager to get away from the place. Several miles down the road we paused in a grove of trees just outside of the depot. I took the clothing I acquired and went deeper into the woods where I would have some privacy, and there I changed from my blue uniform into my women's wear while Sam kept a look out.

It was cold out, so I dressed quickly. I combed my hair as best I might and put on the bonnet. With the bonnet on it was near impossible to tell I had no hair. I wished I had a mirror with which to take a look at myself, but I knew this would have to do.

When I emerged once again, Sam looked me over long and hard, really studying me. I realized it was the first time he'd seen me dressed as a woman in a very long time, and now here I was wearing a gathered and flounced skirt with a dart-fitted bodice, full pagoda sleeves, an under sleeve peeking out white and lacy beneath, as close to delicate and refinement as I could be. I wasn't sure if it was surprise or pleasure or concern I read in his expression. Then he smiled and nodded. He took my hand in his and without a word we headed for the train, where we undertook the remainder of our journey.

Curiously I felt bashful, even as a stranger might, as we sat side by side on the train headed toward our nuptials. It was not a particularly long journey, but it felt like one. There were others on the train, mostly men in uniform. There were some wounded, most likely being shipped home or to a bigger and better hospital farther north. One of them recently had his arm amputated, the bandages upon his stump humanely hiding the mangled flesh, but still wet with the bright red blood seeping from his wound.

It occurred to me each of these individuals had a story, had a life, just as Sam and I did. They had wives or sweethearts or mothers all eager to hear of their safety, worrying over their bodies and souls. Instead of bringing me comfort, it made me all the more agitated. Were they too looking at us and wondering what we were doing here, trying to guess at our purpose, at our secret errand? It seemed as if they might be watching us. Was it only my imagination?

"Are they staring at us?" I whispered to Sam, my discomfort growing worse by the minute.

"Possibly. Many of them haven't seen a woman in a long time," he said. "Or at least not one as handsome as you."

I laughed, knowing what he said was rubbish, but still liking the way it made me feel. He was able to ease my apprehension, making the stress ebb away from me. I was so wrapped up in hiding the fact that I was a girl that I'd learned to be always on guard. I realized for once, I didn't have to be on guard. I could relax.

"I nearly forgot I was a woman," I admitted. I looked down at the skirts I wore and realized they weren't pants. Maybe Sam was right. Even if I wasn't the most beautiful girl in the world, I had to look pretty good to them, after not having seen a woman in many months.

"I haven't," he said, with a grin.

We pulled into our intended depot after having spent the night in travel. I rested my head against Sam's shoulder but was unable to sleep at all. It was our plan to travel until we were upon friendly soil for our honeymoon and so we went as far north as we must in order to be out of Virginia. Some out of the way place, far from the south and Washington too, where we wouldn't be constantly reminded of the war. It was a small town just across the border in Pennsylvania, one of the towns we passed by on our march from Gettysburg, although forgettable because we'd never had the luxury of stopping there.

There was a general flurry of activity as some got off and some got on to the train. This was our stop. My nerves surged within me. The thing I desired more than all else was soon to be mine. Sam politely held my hand as I descended the steps, which made me feel like a lady indeed.

The town had but one hotel, two general stores, a church, two eateries, a few small businesses nestled between, with some very fine houses along the main street. I admired the place, glad to be somewhere other than camp.

"Our first order of business, I think, should be securing a room. Drop our things off, and then we can look around and see what they have to offer," Sam suggested.

"That sounds fine."

"I reckon you must be tired," he said.

"I don't feel at all tired," I replied quickly. To which he chuckled. I was entirely too full of nervous energy to be tired.

The only inn in the small town was once a grand and spacious home. The front desk was next to the fireplace where a fire burned warm and welcoming. A middle-aged gentleman who hobbled about on a crutch greeted us. I liked how confident Sam seemed to be as he walked right up to the desk. I wished I could act as self-assured as he did.

"Hello, sir. We've come looking for a room. Do you have any available?"

"Certainly I do," said the man. "Several, as a matter of fact." He took in Sam's uniform and asked, "You seen some fighting?"

"Yes, sir. Seen Antietam, Fredericksburg, and Rappahannock Station. Was at Gettysburg too, but never was in the fighting there."

"I never made it that long," he said. He lifted the stump of what was left of his leg onto the desk before him. "Bull Run done me in. First piece of fighting I saw. And the last…"

"I am sorry to hear it," Sam answered. "I heard tell it was a terrible day indeed."

"You on furlough?" he asked.

"I am. I come to meet my girl here and we plan on marrying," Sam informed him.

"You don't say," he retorted with a broad smile. He craned his neck to look past Sam, and openly inspected me. I felt foolish and dropped my gaze, unable to meet his. "And she's a pretty little filly. Well, then we'll have to see to it you get the best room in the house!"

"It would be greatly appreciated, sir."

"Think nothing of it. If there's anything at all we can do for you, why you just let us know. How many nights you staying?"

"Three nights, if we might."

"We can do that. Awful quiet around here of late. Not too many customers. So three nights, two dollars a night. That's gonna be six dollars."

Sam pulled his money purse from his haversack and put the money down upon the desk. "We have some things here that need laundered. Will that be a problem?"

"No problem at all. You lay it out on the bed and I'll send Rose or Della on up to collect it shortly."

"I will, thank you," Sam said again.

"I'm called Daniel Garth. If you need anything at all I'd be more than happy to help."

"Thank you, Mr. Garth."

The man gave Sam a pen and ink pot. "Think nothing of it. Think nothing of it. Just sign your name here," he said pointing to an empty line. Then he got up with his crutch and went over to retrieve a key dangling from a ribbon on a hook. "The room to the top of the stairs, all the way down the hallway on the right," he told us.

"Are there any good places to eat around here?" Sam inquired as he took the key from Mr. Garth.

"My daughter makes breakfast every morning, and you are welcome to it. Served between seven and eight o'clock each morning. Besides that we got two places here in town. Now there is Mrs. Norbert's place, there across the road. She makes a good spread. Fine woman, too. And then there's the Herring House Tavern, fancier and pricier. They have good eating, but now Mrs. Norbert's just as good. She knows how to cook a meal, she does. Only she does it all herself, you see. So it takes a bit longer, but just as good nonetheless. Herring House is just fancier is all. Just fancier."

"I'll keep it in mind," Sam said. "One more thing, Mr. Garth, and then we will be out of your way. Might you know where we could find a Justice of the Peace?" Sam wondered.

"No Justice of the Peace here. He joined up and we got no one to fill his place. We have a right nice preacher man who will fit the bill. Now you follow the road outside to the center of town and there be the church, plain as the nose on your face. He lives in the back there, and I am certain he will be more than glad to help you folks out."

"We appreciate your help, sir." Sam accepted the key from him after he finished signing his name. I followed Sam into the hallway and up the staircase. We turned right and passed two doors before we came to the third and last door at the end. Sam opened the door with the key and held it open, waiting for me to walk through first.

The room was very spacious and quite nice. To the right of the door was a small desk, stocked with pen and quill and paper in the event you might wish to write someone. On the adjacent wall was the bed, a four-poster with a thick feather mattress and a pile of warm quilts making it look like a giant pincushion. On the other side of the bed was a washstand with a small mirror. And then on the wall with the window was a dainty lady's vanity. Directly across from the bed was a vast and impressive fireplace with a hand-carved wooden mantel painted white. In the corner to the left of the door sat an overstuffed, upholstered armchair with a footrest at its base, which looked most comfortable.

There was a home-like quality about it, although it was much grander than my home. The thick carpet, the draperies, and the floral wallpaper were charming. I was certain when the fire was put upon the hearth it would lend just the right feel to it. I surveyed the room for a moment and then looked for something to do rather than stand idle.

I wandered over to the window, parting the curtains to look out over the main street below. A wagon ambled along, passed beneath the inn and then disappeared down the lane. Sam went over to the bed and laid out my uniform along with his extra so they would be laundered, and then he came and stood next to me by the window with his hand on my shoulder. He kissed me softly upon the cheek. I leaned into him, resting my face against his shoulder.

"What do you think of it?" he asked.

I looked up at him with an earnest expression. "It is very nice."

He smiled at me, and I attempted to smile back. He was studying me, perhaps trying to discern my thoughts. There was a strange awkwardness between us I didn't understand, but it was as if the two of us were now strangers to one another. I searched my brain for something to say, but could think of nothing. The air grew stale and I wanted to open the window and stick my head out and take a deep breath.

"Perhaps we should go look around, see what there is to see," Sam suggested.

I nodded my agreement.

"Yes, that sounds like a good idea." We left our room, went back through the hall and down the stairs.

"Just one moment, I need to speak with Mr. Garth," Sam told me, leaving me to wait by the door. He went over and spoke to Mr. Garth for a short while in whispered tones and then returned to me. "Shall we go?"

"What was that about?" I asked.

"Nothing, just making arrangements for our stay."

Sam led me along the street, where we spotted the restaurant Mr. Garth mentioned, some town homes, and a few other businesses. The bell above the door gave a pleasant little jingle when Sam opened the door for me at one of the two mercantiles. I thanked him and slipped in to see what they offered.

There were several people perusing the goods stocking the shelves, and I trailed along behind Sam as he too began inspecting things here and there. I ran my fingers along bolts of fabrics and looked over barrels and glass jars with interest, savoring the pleasant smells and enjoying the feel of being in the cool dimness of the place. Eventually an older man, dressed in an apron with garters upon his sleeves approached and kindly asked if he might assist us. He'd only just finished aiding a lady who was trading in her eggs for credit before he moved toward us. Sam nodded cordially to him, with an air of maturity which made me proud to be on his arm.

"You might," he said. "We have need of a few items for the lady," he told the man, gesturing to me.

His smile broadened. "What can I help you with?"

"I had my eye on this," Sam said, motioning toward a nightdress that was lovelier than I could have imagined. It was made of a white, soft cotton flannel with hand tatted lace at the hem and sleeves and neckline. Thankfully the clerk didn't react, only nodded his head and respectfully kept his eyes off of me. I blushed a deep red from the roots of my hair down to my toes. The man went to get it and put it at the front desk and then came back.

"Will that be all, or were you looking for something more?" he asked.

"What about perfume?" Sam asked me. "Would you fancy some perfume, Serena?" I shook my head with a quick jerking motion.

"Oh, Sam, it's too much," I protested.

"Some perfume, sir," he said. The man ushered us over to a display of ornate glass bottles, filled with amber liquids smelling marvelously exotic. I could detect their sweet scent before I unstopped a single one.

"This is the fine selection we carry," the man told us, selecting one of the perfumes and proffering it to me with the bottom of the bottle nestled the palm of one hand and the neck grasped between thumb and finger with his other hand. "All the way from Paris, France," he informed me.

I accepted the perfume and took a whiff, sneezing as the fragrance tickled my nose. Who was I to say I didn't care for perfume all the way from Paris, France?

"That is nice," I said with and ambiguous shrug. "What do you think, Sam?" I asked, holding the bottle up for him to smell.

"Very sweet," he observed.

"Yes. Perhaps something not as strong?" I put the stopper back in the bottle and tried another. After several samplings I discovered the one I liked best, orange blossom and vanilla in an intricately cut glass bottle.

"I like this one. Do you like it?" Sam sniffed it and then nodded his approval.

"Sure. I like it." He took the bottle and handed it to the clerk. "This one, please. And perhaps some lady's hand cream."

"Really, Sam, what we've already chosen is more than enough," I protested. "I don't need hand cream."

"But you shall have it anyhow," he said. The clerk crossed the room to find a jar of lady's hand cream. When he was out of hearing range, Sam turned to me and said, "What good is pay if you don't enjoy it?"

"What about you wanting to fix up the farm, build a new barn?" I wondered.

He took my hand in his and patted it. "There will be time for that."

We continued to walk around the store, looking at all of the lovely things. Now and again Sam picked something up to inspect. We didn't need to be anywhere, and took our leisure with it. My eyes fell upon a silver comb and brush set, with a beautifully etched intricate pattern. Sam looked from me to the brush set and picked them up, taking them to the front with the other things we were purchasing. I didn't say anything this time, for I surely did want them.

"You haven't gotten anything for yourself, Sam. Isn't there something you might like?" I asked.

"How's about a few of them lemon drops?" he asked the clerk. I looked at his meager lemon drops next to my substantial pile and the smile faded from my face.

"This seems very unfair," I pointed out.

"Nonsense." Sam pulled his purse out. "What do I owe you?" he asked the clerk. The clerk gave him the amount, which Sam paid. The clerk packaged the items in a paper sack and then we left the store with our sack in hand.

"It was more than I expected," I said apologetically.

"You remember what I said about buying the cow when you could get the milk for free?" He whispered to me. I nodded. "Well, I'm intent upon buying the cow," he said, holding up the bag and dangling it in front of me.

This made me laugh. It wasn't really a laugh, more like a very unflattering snort.

"What now?" I asked.

"I think we should find the good reverend, don't you?"

I walked along next to him, feeling downright giddy at the prospect.

"And then perhaps a wedding dinner to follow?" he suggested.

Chapter 31

It didn't take much to find what we were looking for. The church was a white weatherboard structure with a gabled front entrance at the heart of the town. The little rectangular building with long narrow windows was grounded in gray brick. Between two massive columns, a wide staircase with a wrought iron handrail led up to the solid wood front doors. While it was a very proper church, it still possessed a folksy sort of feel to it.

Sam opened the door for me. My eyes took time to refocus, as the vestibule was dim and cave-like compared to the sunlight outside. There were pegs to hang coats along the walls and, on either side, stairs leading to the balcony. It being a small town, I was sure there wasn't much use for a balcony, but it made the little church seem somehow much bigger.

Through the next set of double doors was the main room where worship took place. On either side of the aisle were pews, and at the front a pulpit. Behind the pulpit, velvet drapes hung against the wall, and a large crucifix which looked as if it had been carved by hand was mounted from the ceiling. It was a beautiful church, though modest in its content. It was over a year since I'd last attended devotions in a proper church and yet the reverence for it came back to me instinctively.

Our feet echoed unnaturally in the stillness as we walked down the aisle in search of the reverend. Suddenly the velvet curtain parted and, as if by miracle, a man appeared. His living quarters must have been somewhere beyond the curtain in a little room off of the back of the church. He seemed surprisingly young, possibly in his mid to late thirties. Most of the men his age were enlisted. I was sure he must've remained here to lead his flock.

He had a kind but unenthusiastic smile, as he asked, "May I help you?"

I let Sam do the talking. "Yes, sir. We are looking to get married. We were told you could perform a wedding ceremony for us?"

"You were not led astray," he said with a chuckle at his own jest. A sense of humor in a holy man is surely hard to find. I caught on to his silly pun and began to laugh in the most annoying nervous twitter. His attention focused on me.

"Sorry," I said, quickly growing sober.

"Just the two of you?" he questioned.

"That's right. I am on furlough and we only have a short time. We couldn't manage to get our families together for it."

"I see it more and more," he said. "First things first, do you have rings?"

"No," Sam answered. "That will have to wait."

"All right. A ring isn't necessary. You will need a witness, though."

I panicked. "But, we don't have one!"

Sam sought to calm my nerves. He smiled reassuringly, giving my hand a squeeze. "That shouldn't be too difficult. You know of anyone who would stand in for us?" he asked the reverend.

"Anyone here in town will do for the purpose," the reverend informed Sam. "Doesn't matter who, just someone to say they were here for the ceremony and who will sign their name to attest to it."

"Well, then give us a moment, and we will be back," Sam promised.

Taking my hand he tugged me back down the aisle, and out the door, back onto the street. One of the first shops we came to was a barber shop. We went in together. The proprietor was sitting idle, reading a newspaper in one of his own barber chairs. He dropped the paper to his lap and looked the two of us over with mild interest. His gaze rested upon me, somewhat confused by the fact I, a woman, was there too in a men's barber shop.

"What can I do for you?"

"We have just come from the church up yonder and the reverend has told us we must have a witness in order to be married."

"All right…" the man prodded, unable to see how this affected him.

"We were hoping you might be willing to do the honors?" Sam finished.

The man's eyes narrowed shrewdly. "You wish to marry, huh?"

"Yes, sir."

"Oughtn't a groom look nice on his wedding day? A quality shave and cut perhaps?" he asked. Sam lost the smile, pursing his lips instead as he studied the other man.

"You're trying to fleece me on my wedding day?" Sam accused. The man was beyond reproach. He grinned broadly, clapping his hands together and then rubbing them briskly.

"I have no such intentions. I am doing you a favor by offering you the best cut and shave you'll ever have, young man. I guarantee it."

Finally Sam shrugged. "I suppose that would be customary," he said dryly.

"Just so happens I can get you right in," the man said.

"How fortunate," Sam said, resigned to the fact he must do as the man wanted or look for a witness elsewhere.

The man heaved himself from the chair and offered it to Sam. Sam sat down and the barber went to work. He wrapped a cloth around his neck and began cutting Sam's hair. He was meticulous in his work, his brow furrowed in concentration as he labored. Once he finished with the cut, he took a small brush and dusted all of the small loose hairs from Sam's neck and ears.

He leaned Sam back in the chair, humming softly as he worked. He carefully coiled a hot and steaming towel onto Sam's face, waiting for a few moments before removing it. When he took the towel off, Sam was red faced and irritable.

"Could we speed it up a little?" He asked.

"You get what you pay for here," the man replied. He took his mug and brush and lathered Sam's face up with shaving cream. Then the barber took his straight edged razor and tested it with his thumb, before he went to work shaving. "No need to rush a good shave, even for a woman, my friend. She'll still be there when it is done. An' you shall have her forever after. But a shave…a good one anyway…is rare."

When it was all said and done and Sam had paid for his cut and shave, the barber agreed to follow us up the road to the church. The three of us filed back down the aisle where the reverend waited. The reverend nodded to the barber.

"Marvin," he said by way of a greeting.

The barber nodded back. "Reverend Brandie."

"Haven't seen you in a while," the reverend said, lowering his face so his chin disappeared into his neck, and his eyes, nearly obscured by his bushy brows, were looking up toward the barber.

"Well, now, Reverend, I don't aim on hurting your feelings none, and surely I hope you don't take it too personal, but I spend my Sundays in worship with a different sort of brandy."

"God certainly cannot strike you down for lying," the reverend countered, snorting contemptuously.

Sam grew impatient and cleared his throat. "Reverend Brandie? We don't wish to take up too much of your time…"

"Moving along then," the reverend said. He grew solemn, puckering his lips, wrinkling his brow, as he took a deep breath and plunged in. "This is a most serious commitment, not to be entered into lightly," he began. "Just so we're clear, you both wish to continue?" He looked from Sam to me, where his gaze rested an unnatural lengthy time.

I hesitated, thrown off by his attention. "Yes, Reverend," I said haltingly.

Sam nodded his head decisively. "Yes."

"That said, let's dispense with the formalities and just get into it, then. Repeat after me," he commanded. "I, and then fill in your christened name, take you, and fill in her christened name, to be my wife."

Sam sat our paper bag of things from the mercantile on the ground, at his feet. He took my hand in his and said, "I, Sampson John Barlow, take you Serena —" then he looked at me blankly, for he didn't know my whole name.

"Elizabeth Ann," I whispered.

"Take you, Serena Elizabeth Ann Stark, to be my wife."

"To have and to hold from this day on," the reverend continued on.

"To have and to hold from this day on," Sam repeated.

"For better or for worse, for richer, for poorer, in sickness and in health."

"For better or for worse, for richer, for poorer, in sickness and in health."

"To love and to cherish; until death do us part," Reverend Brandie finished. Sam's expression was serious, as he looked from our hands to my face and gave me a small smile.

"To love and to cherish; until death do us part."

Reverend Brandie turned to me. "Are you ready?"

"Yes," I replied. It was difficult to get the yes out. I felt a great lump in my throat and a strange sort of feeling as if I might be sick, but I didn't feel sick.

"I, and then fill in your name, take you, and fill in his name, to be my husband," he said.

"I, Serena Elizabeth Ann Stark, take you, Sampson John Barlow, to be my husband," I echoed.

"To have and to hold from this day on."

"To have and to hold from this day on," I said. I chanced a glance at Sam and he was smiling at me encouragingly. He could perhaps tell I was nervous and was trying to put me at ease.

"For better or for worse, for richer, for poorer, in sickness and in health," Reverend Brandie gave me the words.

"For better or for worse, for richer, for poorer, in sickness and in health," I said.

"To love and to obey and to cherish; until death do us part," Reverend Brandie closed.

"To love and to obey and to cherish; until death do us part."

Reverend Brandie ended by putting a hand on my shoulder and a hand on Sam's. "What God has joined together, let no man put asunder."

We stood there dumbly looking at one another not sure if it was the end of the formalities or not. The silence was comforting. I wished we could sit in this cool darkness and just say nothing, but hold hands as we were and be near one another. But then the barber broke in.

"I have a business to run. Are we done?"

The reverend said, "Well, that's the short of it. You are now husband and wife. Before you leave, I'll need you to sign the registry, along with your witness here."

He showed us to the back of the chapel where there was a pedestal on which rested a ledger. We each took our turn signing and then the barber left, and Sam and I were alone out on the street. The only word I can think to describe it was surreal. It felt as if my head were not attached to my body.

"Are you all right?" Sam asked.

"Yes," I replied.

"Shall we go have ourselves a wedding dinner?" Sam suggested. "It *is* customary."

"That would be very nice," I agreed.

"There is the tavern over there, the one Mr. Garth mentioned. Should we try the place?" he asked, pointing to a two story stone house with shutters. The sign dangling above the door read *Herring House Tavern* in elaborate black scrolling script.

"It looks very nice," I said.

"Or we could go to the other place he mentioned," Sam offered.

"No need, this looks fine."

"You're sure?" he said.

"Yes. I'm sure."

"All right then."

We went down the street to the *Herring House* and entered. The room was spacious, with a fire burning in the immense, red brick fireplace. We selected a small table spread with a linen cloth situated near the window and waited for someone to notice us. A man came out shortly and took our requests. Sam ordered the roast beef and potatoes, while I got the fried chicken and peas. They were both served with homemade biscuits and brown butter.

"Well, this certainly is good eating," Sam said enthusiastically.

"It is," I agreed. After a lengthy pause Sam spoke to me with concern.

"Tell me, is there something wrong? You seem as if you're ruminating over something."

I dropped my eyes from his, feeling very much put on the spot, and sighed deeply. "No, Sam, there's nothing the matter."

"But you are being very quiet. It is your general disposition to speak more," Sam observed.

"We are really married?"

"Yes, very much so."

"It hardly seems real, does it?"

"I'm sure it will take some getting used to," he said.

"Yes, I suppose it will."

"How is your fried chicken?" he asked.

"Very good, thank you. And your roast beef?"

"I am enjoying it," he replied.

"Do you suppose it would seem more real if our families were there? Or if I'd worn a proper gown?" I asked.

"Would you like to wait until our families can be here? Would it have been better if you had a proper gown?" he asked.

I felt horribly guilty. How could I make him understand what I was feeling? I didn't care about the dress. I was sorry our families weren't with us, but not so much that I regretted what we'd done. There were no words to describe my emotions.

"No! I am…I am very, very glad we were married," I insisted. "I just meant…I mean, I don't need those things. I really am very happy. It's just very strange, is all." I paused. "We are really married."

"You are Serena Barlow now," he informed me with a faint grin.

"It seemed like the waiting went on forever, and then it was over just like that. I mean, it took moments and then he tells us we are man and wife, you know?"

"And you are all right?"

I hesitated. I didn't want to sound as if I were complaining. After all I was thrilled to be Sam's wife. It was beyond words how I felt, to finally have what I wanted so desperately. And perhaps that is why I was feeling the way I was. To be given the very thing I yearned for for so long was too much for me to take in all at once. It felt overwhelming.

Along with being in shock, I was worried too. I had a general idea of what was coming next, and I was on the verge of being terri-fied. I was sixteen when Dancy Garrety, married only four months, spoke in hushed whispers to Carry Rollings and me outside of church one Sunday. I went to school with Dancy, and although we weren't terribly close, she must have felt I was safe to talk to, as she looked around apprehensively trying to make sure no one else was listening to our conversation.

She didn't go into a great deal of detail, she didn't have time to, but she did tell us enough to leave both Carry and I wide eyed and dismayed. My father had called for me to come and I hastily made my farewells and left. All the way home I couldn't rid my mind of Dancy's words. I experienced the strangest feeling in my gut, close to excitement, but something like being sick too. I knew the natu-ral order of things. I had seen animals on the farm mate and have offspring, but it was a great stretch to imagine a man and a woman coming together in the same manner. The idea of it was fascinating but frightening at the same time.

Living among men for so long may have had its effects on me too. They spoke about all sorts of things a lady shouldn't hear. I did my best to steer clear of that sort of talk, but there was no way of avoiding it all together. And now that I was alone with Sam I felt uncomfortable, self-conscious, and spooked even thinking about it.

"Yes, I'm very happy. I am." I attempted a smile, but my nerves were getting the best of me and the smile faded before it fully materialized. "It just doesn't seem real!"

"I was there. It is very real," he assured me with a boyish grin.

When the man came around to clear our plates away, Sam asked him, "Have you any fruit cake? It is our wedding dinner and we ought to have a fruit cake."

"We have fruit cake," the man replied.

"Then we'll have some," Sam said jovially. The man came back with the fruit cake and sat it between us. We leisurely helped ourselves to the cake until it was gone.

"Well, now you don't eat like this every day," I said. "I am full up. How are you, Sam?"

"I am very good, wife."

"It seems peculiar for you to call me wife. I am very pleased by it," I confessed. I sat my fork down, wiped my mouth with my napkin, and laid it upon the table. "I am finished. I couldn't eat another bite."

"I am too," Sam informed me. He got up from the table and pulled my chair out for me. "Should we go?"

"Yes, thank you." I liked how formally polite he was treating me. This is what I imagined it should be like. I took his arm and let him lead on.

Chapter 32

We headed back down the street to the inn, walking slowly arm in arm. The anticipation of what was to happen next had me feeling shaky and apprehensive. When we got back to our room and opened the door, the fire on the hearth was started and a tin tub with steam rising from it was sitting next to it. I was taken aback because I didn't expect it. Sam must have planned it without telling me.

"What is this?" I asked Sam.

"I requested they start the fire and prepare a bath for you," he admitted. "I thought I might go for a walk, let you have a moment to yourself to relax."

I was speechless, my jaw ajar as I looked for something to say. "That was very thoughtful, Sam."

"You go ahead and have your bath, and I will return shortly," he said, handing me the parcel of things we purchased from the mercantile. He shut the door as he left.

I was taken off guard by this turn of events. I didn't expect the bath, and I certainly didn't expect him to leave. I stood for a moment, looking at the fire and the bath, and then at the door he'd just shut. I shook my head to clear it and then moved to the bed where I opened my bag and laid everything out, putting the cream and perfume and comb and brush set on the vanity and draping the nightgown across the coverlet. I undressed, slinging my skirt and blouse and jacket over the chair before I slipped into the tin tub and soaked restlessly in the warm water. I simply couldn't get comfortable. I was in a strange place and what would happen next was an unknown for me. I didn't want to admit to myself just how frightened I really was. Yet, there were so many reasons for my terrible anxiety.

A lady would like to think she is desirable. She would like to think she has the ability to inspire emotions in her lover that will make him feel she is indispensable to him. I yearned to possess the requisite traits of an attractive mate, so Sam would think he got himself a good deal, so he might be proud I was his wife. Being alone did little for my anxieties because it gave me pause to contemplate my current situation. My emotions were a tangled mess of conflicting extremes.

I bounded between curiosity and desire, feeling the immediate need to have Sam there with me, then to apprehension and dread and hoping he would stay away for good. It wasn't that I didn't want him. It was just that I was afraid of him, afraid of Sam. How could it be? I scolded myself for being such a goose. I was Sam's wife. We were married. We belonged to one another now. Surely it would be all right?

I took my time in the bath before the fire because I hadn't had a bath in so long, but I fretted every moment of it. I used the bar of soap smelling of pine, and I ran it over every square inch of me. This was something I missed very much in my travels—the chance to be clean. The water was clouded milky white and cold when I finally, shivering and deeply wrinkled, emerged. I let the water on my skin evaporate from the heat at the hearth and slipped the nightdress Sam gave me over my head. Padding barefoot across the floor I chanced a look in the mirror.

There was something so unfamiliar about the girl looking back at me. I was thin and pale. Short hair, still damp and slightly untamed, made me feel unattractive as I tried to comb it down with my fingers. I thought perhaps a ribbon might help, so I took the ribbon from the dressing table and tied it in my hair. It looked ridiculous. I looked like a boy with a bow. I ripped it out and threw it to the floor.

The nightdress was beautiful with its ivory cotton lace and soft gauzy fabric. I'd never owned something so delicate. A farmer's daughter couldn't find the money for such frills. Still, on my body, the way it molded to my figure, well, I didn't exactly fill it out well. I caught sight of my eyes, large and frightened, dominating my oval face, and I must admit to myself I looked skittish, reminiscent of a wild animal backed into a corner. The moment when they realize they are caught, when their brain registers they may not make it out of the encounter a whole and living thing, and their instinct is to run.

I felt ridiculous. No matter how beautiful the nightdress, it could not disguise the real me. I was plain, and I was funny looking, with my boy's haircut and my woman's nightgown. I was on the verge of making a complete and total fool of myself, that's what I was doing. I hastened to the chair where the maid had laid out my uniform, all freshly laundered, and I frantically tossed the nightdress aside, pulling on my shirt, buttoning the buttons all crooked in my haste, with shaking and unwilling fingers. I yanked the hat onto my head, and was in the midst of pulling on my wool stockings, managing to get only one on, when Sam came through the door. I froze, caught in the act of dressing, painfully aware I was basically naked!

His expression was one of amusement and confusion and interest. I was mortified, my bare legs the object of his curious gaze. I wondered fleetingly if he'd ever seen a pair of girl's legs before mine. He acted as though he hadn't, hardly able to tear his eyes away from my nakedness. He cleared his throat, shutting the door behind him, and then crossed his arms waiting patiently for me to explain myself. I grabbed hold of my britches and tried to cover my lower half with them.

"Sam, you're back," I said, as casually as if we were meeting at supper or after drills or cleaning the latrine for that matter.

He raised an eyebrow, his eyes soft and inquisitive. "Yes, wife, I am back," he agreed. "Are you well?"

"Very well, thank you," I answered with an absurdly nervous sort of twitter. What was the matter with my laugh today? As I feared, I was now making a total fool of myself. I was aware of this and yet could not seem to stop myself as it all unfolded.

"Were you going somewhere?" Sam wondered, taking in my semi-dressed state.

"I…uh, was just going to look for you," I lied.

"In your pants and not your skirt?"

"I did it without thinking," I said. "Habit I suppose."

"Well, I am here now, so no need."

"Yes. Yes, you are."

"The hat is a nice touch, though," he said.

My hand went up to the hat on my head, and I took it off and fiddled with it at my side, while my other hand still held firm to those britches. Sam walked over to me and wrestled the hat from my fingers, laying it aside. Then he worked on getting me to relinquish the britches.

"Sam—" I began. With my hands freed, I worked on tugging at the bottom of my shirt, doing my best to make it longer, if it was at all possible.

"What's the matter, Serena?" he asked me gently. I suppose he could sense I was ready to bolt for the door, britches or no britches. His tone was patient, as he did his best to soothe me. "Did the nightdress not fit?"

"No," I said. "No, it isn't that. It fit right enough. I just, I don't know…I just saw myself in it and…"

"What?" He put his hand to my face, his eyes searching mine.

"I looked like a complete goose in it!" I burst out. "Something as beautiful as that, well, I just looked ridiculous!"

"You look very nice from where I'm standing," he said, his gaze wandering over me and lingering upon my exposed legs. "As a matter of fact, the shirt is quite fetching."

I could feel my face turning several shades of red. If I could have willed it, the earth would have split in two and swallowed me whole. For all of my casual airs, I felt any composure I might have forced in my attempts at seeming calm fly right out the window. It was difficult to swallow, and then my lips began to quiver, and then the tears spilled in great drops down my face even though I tried hard to keep them back. Why was I constantly crying in his presence of late? I couldn't figure it, because I didn't count myself the weepy type.

Sam pulled me to him, and I buried my face into his jacket, burrowing my head so forcefully against him that I could feel the buttons digging into my forehead.

"What's this about?" he whispered into my ear, as his hand stroked my back.

"I don't know," I sobbed. "I'm very sorry for it."

"You don't have to wear the nightdress," he told me. "You don't have to do anything you don't want to."

I'd made a fine mess of things this time. I broke into tears anew.

"Oh, I've ruined it all," I lamented.

"Nothing is ruined," he lightly scolded. "I hoped the bath would calm your nerves. Perhaps I left you too long? In any case, maybe you could just use a good night's sleep in a proper bed is all."

He walked me over to the bed and pulled back the covers. "You take the bed, and I will rest in this chair over here," he offered. He dropped his head and moved toward the chair where my clothing was laid out.

I was outraged. I grabbed hold of his arm to stop him. "You cannot spend your wedding night sleeping upright in a chair," I said, running my hand down his sleeve and clutching his hand so he wouldn't go anywhere.

He chuckled. "I'm fairly certain I wouldn't be the first man to do so," he informed me. "Besides, it looks to be a comfortable, well cushioned chair. A fine piece of furniture," he reasoned. I could see a hint of disappointment in his expression, but he was too much of a gentleman to voice any displeasure with the situation. The fact that he was so willing to give up his own comforts on my behalf made me feel a good measure of remorse. I wanted so badly to make up my shortcomings to him but was powerless now to know what to do.

"Well, I won't have it," I said stubbornly, wiping my face abrasively with the back of my hands. "You will not sleep in a chair!"

"There is no hurry," he assured. Then his expression grew serious, and he ran his fingers through my hair, doing his best, in my estimation, to tame the mess too, as I'd done earlier. He kissed me tritely upon my lips. I looked at him, really looked at him, and nearly began crying again.

"I am such a fool!" I groaned.

"No," he said, shaking his head back and forth with the glimpse of smile. "Crazy maybe, but you're no fool."

I laughed out loud. "I love you," I said helplessly.

"I love you, too."

"Come to bed with me," I ordered.

He hesitated, looking vulnerable, which confused me. What did he have to be self-conscious about?

"You're sure?"

I looked at him long and hard, confused and scared by what I saw. Could he really want me?

"Whatever made you see anything in me?" I choked. "I have nothing to offer you."

"*You* are the only thing I want you to offer me. Just Serena. That is all I want," he said.

"I want to be beautiful, really beautiful, for you."

"But you are beautiful," he said.

"I'm not. I know I'm not."

"How can I look upon this face but to love it?" he asked, cupping my cheeks within his two hands, where his palms met. Then he traced his fingers along my brow, down the ridge of my nose, across my lips with a pleasant tickle. "You are a rare woman, Serena, not only endowed with physical allure, but you possess a beauty within, a rare quality to be found in anyone."

"You make me sound as if I were something special, Sam, when I know I'm not."

"Then you know nothing," he said in a slightly stern voice.

I was speechless. What could I say?

He gently put his lips to mine and murmured, "But I hope soon I will help you to understand. I will have you see what I see."

"I'm afraid. I don't have any idea what I'm doing," I admitted in a timid whisper, my breath coming out in a shuddering sigh.

"Well you're in good company. I don't know what I'm doing either, but we'll work it out together, you and me."

This was why I fell in love with Sam to begin with. He was a good and decent man, someone who wouldn't let me down. I was safe with him.

I felt such gratitude for his courtesy and compassion, such overwhelming love for him. And so I gave him the only thing I had to give, the only thing really and truly mine to offer him. And he took it with such tenderness and affection it was a joy to give it. We had the pleasure of experiencing a happiness only known between a husband and his wife, lying in an embrace of adoring arms, exchanging sweetly passionate kisses, his hands strong and tender on my flesh, drifting to sleep and awakening as if to a dream to have him there beside me.

I thought back, several times, on the long ago day when I only wanted nothing more than to be near him, without the hope of believing he could ever be mine. And it seemed impossible that here and now we were linked together in a bond of love. Perhaps I had begun by idolizing him. But I had gotten to know Sam as he truly was, with all of his faults and frailties, as well as the qualities I valued the most about him and his quiet heroics. I loved him for all of it. I loved him for everything he was, the good and the bad. Even his flaws made him seem fragile and yet beautiful to me. What good would he be to me if he were unblemished, perfectly complete and did not need me?

"Is this real?" I chanced to murmur against his hair in the darkness of the night. His head rested against my shoulder. He stirred, drawing nearer.

"I hope so," he replied in a drowsy voice. "But if it is only a dream, don't wake me. Let me have this sleep."

Chapter 33

I t was mid-morning before I got up in my nightdress and staggered
to the washstand. I felt just fine, up to the point where I actually
moved. I was aware immediately of a vague ache that spread through
me and made me hesitate to walk the short distance. Pouring the
water from the pitcher into the basin, I splashed the coolness onto
my face and neck and chanced a quick look into the mirror hanging
against the wall. If I thought I looked bad last night it was nothing
compared to how I now looked. Was it just my imagination? Did I
look different? Or was it just that I looked so haggard, and the dark
circles beneath my eyes made me look older?

Sam was in nothing but his short underwear, looking like the
sun, radiating his strength and beauty, looking rested and fine. How
could I look so wretched and he be so fetching? It wasn't fair. He
stretched out, his hands above his head as he yawned loudly. Then
he rolled onto his side, propping himself up on his elbow. He was
watching me, frowning slightly.

"Are you all right?" he asked.

"I am," I answered.

"Does it hurt?" he asked. I could see the concern in his eyes.

"Just a little uncomfortable," I said, unwilling to disclose the
whole truth to him. "It will pass."

"Come and rest for a bit," he told me, patting the empty space
next to him. I was slow and graceless as I made my way back to the
bed and lay down. He grimaced a little, wrapping his arm around
me and pulling me close to his side.

"I'm sorry," he said. "But it's to be expected I think."

"I did not know," I admitted. "I wish my mother had told me something more about it."

"Would you like me to have them make another bath for you?" he offered, brushing the hair away from my forehead. The thought of a warm bath was appealing, but I didn't want to be a bother.

"It's too much trouble," I said.

"It isn't too much trouble," Sam insisted. He took the room divider and brought it over to arrange it so it would hide the bed. He finished dressing himself and then went to make arrangements downstairs. I dozed for a moment, until I heard the door open again as the hotel employees switched out the bath water for me.

Sam came and sat next to me on the edge of the bed once they'd left, kissing the tips of each of my fingers.

"It's all ready for you," he said. "Do you want me to help you?"

I shuddered at the thought of it. "You're staying?"

"I don't have to," he said. "I can leave and come back."

"You don't need to do that," I said weakly, hoping he would insist so I wouldn't be the one requesting it. All of these years I was told to be modest, to guard myself against impropriety, and in one day all of it flew out the window. All of a sudden it was all right, and *expected* as a matter of fact. I couldn't help but feel shy in the light of day before him. Sam got up and moved the room divider again so it was between the tin tub and the rest of the room.

"Is that better?" he asked.

"Yes, thank you, Sam," I said, relieved. I slipped out of the night-dress, tossing it over the divider, and then slid into the warm water, feeling relief flood through me. I leaned back and soaked with my eyes shut, moving as little as possible.

"Do you feel up to getting something to eat?" Sam asked me from beyond the partition.

"That sounds nice," I agreed.

When I finished, I dressed in my blouse and skirt. Sam watched me as I sat before the dressing table and brushed my hair, rubbed the sweet smelling cream into my hands, and dabbed the perfume to my neck. It was as if he were infinitely amused by my preparations.

"Are you enjoying yourself?" I teased, looking at his reflection through the mirror.

"Very much," he replied. "I have never seen a lady at her dressing table before."

"Nor have I," I confessed. "I've never had a dressing table." I smiled. "Do you remember the house in Fredericksburg, where we found that woman?"

"Yes," Sam said, his eyebrows drawn together as he tried to piece together the correlation between the occasion and our current situation.

"She had a beautiful bedroom, something like this one, with lovely things and a vanity too. I thought, wouldn't it be nice? And look at me now. Here I am sitting before one, getting myself ready for an outing with my husband," I said.

"You shall have a dressing table all your own soon," he replied. "I promise." He took my hand and pressed it to his lips. "You shall have whatever you ask for, if it is in my power."

I put my bonnet on my head and tied the bow carefully, arranging it so it settled to the side of my face, away from my chin, at a flattering angle.

"I am ready," I said.

"Let's get you something to eat."

Mr. Garth in the hotel lobby nodded politely, suppressing a grin and enthusiastically bidding us have a good morning as we left. Sam took my hand and tucked it into the crook of his arm after he opened the door for me. On our way down the street we saw the Reverend who'd married us along the other side of the walk. He tipped his hat to us when he spotted us, showing us all of his teeth as he beamed broadly. We gave him a little wave as we went on.

We got to the restaurant and allowed the woman, presumably Mrs. Norbert, to show us a place to sit. She was slightly overweight but still pleasant to look at, although she wore a grim expression. Her hands were cracked and dry, her eyes tired, her shoulders slightly stooped. I could see she had worked hard for many years, probably barely making ends meet.

"We don't get much business these days," she told us. It was reminiscent of what the barber said yesterday. Apparently the town had seen better days. "It's good to have you."

"Thank you," we said.

"Are you all from around here?"

"I am on furlough," Sam told her. "We only just got married."

"Felicitations," she said, her face brightening with a smile.

I sat at the table with a cloth spread over my lap, drinking strong, hot coffee and eating steak and eggs. I don't know if it was because we were half-starved, or if it was because I felt the food restoring my energy, but we ate it greedily all down to the last crumb. When I finished, I dabbed the cloth to my lips, laid it upon the table, and leaned back in my chair.

"It's a good thing I'm not corseted," I said. "Or I could not have eaten it all." We sat staring at one another, smiling all the while. He reached across and entwined his fingers with mine. My, it felt good to be his wife. Sitting across from the man I loved made me feel proud, made me feel worth something. It occurred to me we must look very peculiar to everyone else, acting all moony-eyed and silly. Was it just my imagination that they were giving us strange glances?

"I feel like I am being fattened for slaughter," I confessed. "There is so much to eat, and I just keep eating it."

"Better than hardtack, ain't it?" Sam observed.

"I won't argue with that." I rubbed my tummy with a sigh. "Just look at the two of us, like a bunch of idiots grinning at each other. We must be the only ones to have a reason to smile so," I told him. "Everyone probably thinks we are escaped from an asylum. Notice how oddly they are behaving? How they look at us?"

He laughed. "I'm sure they understand it," he said with a wink. "After all, we have reason."

I felt the color drain from my face. "What do you mean by that?" I asked.

"Well, we've hardly made it a secret we are just newlywed," he explained, and his words had implications I struggled to understand. When it dawned on me, what he meant, I grabbed my napkin back up and pressed it to the side of my face, ducking behind it so only Sam could see me.

"You mean they *know?*" I hissed.

He studied it out before he said reluctantly, "I didn't mean to upset you."

"But they *know*," I squeaked, feeling mortified. "That's why they're all behaving so oddly around us?"

"Serena, the woman who brought you your meal is wearing a wedding band. They know because they are all doing it too," he reasoned.

"No!" I said, completely scandalized.

"Well, yes," he replied. "It is part of the rights and privileges of entering into matrimony, isn't it?" he rationalized. It took a moment for this all to sink in.

"You're right!" I whispered. "Everyone knows and they're all doing it too." I looked at him with wide eyes, a new understanding dawning on me. "This is so strange. As a matter of fact it's downright scandalous."

"Why?"

"I just had no idea. All of those people doing such a sinful thing."

"Why is it sinful?"

"You don't think it is?"

"No. God made men and women to fit together to make a whole. If it was so bad why did he put Adam and Eve jointly in the garden? It's how it was meant to be. There's nothing wrong with it. We are married. We belong together, you and me."

"I guess it's true." Although what he said seemed to have merit, it was difficult for me to comprehend all at once. It would take some getting used to. "But this is all too new to me."

Sam helped me from my chair. "You've obviously never read the Bible," he said with a hint of mischief.

I was somewhat offended. "Yes, I have," I said adamantly.

"It says *they two shall be one*."

"That's what it's talking about?" I gasped.

"What did you think it meant?"

"I don't know. Certainly not that." I was feeling overwhelmed, as though my brain couldn't comprehend it all. It was like trying to keep up with a bolting horse. Sam was enjoying my shocked expression. He was wearing the most mischievous grin on his lips.

"That's not all. Perhaps you should look over Song of Solomon again." He laughed.

"What's in it?" I asked, racking my brain to try to recall what he might be talking about.

"Oh, all sorts of wicked things arranged in the most beautiful poetry. And I've discovered all have their merits, now that I've had the privilege of having you."

"I don't know what you're talking about," I said. "But I know enough to know I should be embarrassed."

"You should never be embarrassed with me," he chided. "Never with me."

I leaned my head against his shoulder with an ill-repressed smile, content to just be near him.

"I think we should take it easy today," he proposed. "Let you rest."

"I don't want to waste our precious time doing nothing." Really I was not feeling up to much, but we only had a short leave, and I imagined he didn't want to fill it up with empty hours. It would be selfish of me to ask it of him.

"It is not a waste of time if we spend it together," he insisted.

Sam took me back to the mercantile, and together we selected a book called *Lady Audley's Secret*. We spent the rest of the day idle and resting in our room. We lay on the bed together beneath a pile of cozy, warm blankets, taking turns reading out loud from our novel. Now and again Sam would get up and stir the fire or put another log on to keep it going. We read until my eyes were blurry from it.

"What a strange and thrilling plot," I commented.

"I certainly hope there is no George hiding in your past somewhere," Sam joked, referring to the fact Mrs. Audley's secret was that she already had a husband before marrying again to poor Mr. Audley.

"No George," I assured. "Only Sam. That is all there has ever been for me."

"I know it." He took me in his arms and kissed me softly. I felt a familiar excitement rush through me. "And you are the only girl for me, too."

I laughed, shaking my head and rolling my eyes at him.

"What are you laughing at? What?"

"I was just thinking of the yellow haired girl from Albany."

"I think you remember her better than I do," he complained.

"How could you not remember her? She was exquisite. And she had her eyes on you. I was all ate up with jealousy."

"Yes, well, I thought it was strange you were being so outrageously rude."

"When she offered me a piece of pie, I thought I might take it up and throw it in her face," I admitted.

"I got a sassy one, didn't I?" he teased.

"What were you saying to her?"

"When?"

"When? When the two of you were over in the corner whispering. Right before we left there. Seemed very intimate from where I was standing," I complained.

"Oh, yes…" he said, as if he suddenly remembered. "It was completely innocent."

"I'm sure," I said sarcastically.

"Really, it was. I was only asking her for the recipe for her pie."

I burst out laughing and bludgeoned him on the head with a pillow. He was laughing too and wrestled the pillow from my hands. Then he looked into my eyes and grew serious as he kissed me.

"It was flour…" And he kissed me. "Lard…" Another sweet kiss.

"Sugar?" I offered.

"Yes, of course, sugar…" He never got around to finishing the recipe.

Chapter 34

The following day was our last in town. We would spend the night at the inn, and the next morning we would leave for camp again. Sam and I decided to go to the *Herring House Tavern* for supper because we liked it so well on our wedding day. We were strolling down the street, his hand resting upon mine as I held to his arm. The touch of his skin against my own was giving me a pleasant tingle, when we chanced upon a storefront advertising tin types. I pulled Sam to a stop before it.

"Should we have a daguerreotype done? It would be so nice to have a memento to carry."

He agreed and we went into the establishment, our arms linked. The man was pleasant to the point of annoyance. He chirped about what a handsome couple we were and how he had never seen a more charming pair. I knew he was outdoing himself when he said he'd never had the honor of taking the likeness of such a fair and pretty lady as me. I looked at Sam with what I was sure was subtle exasperation.

The man seated me on a plump velvet chair with a thickly draped curtain, heavy with fringe along the edges, hanging behind. I thought it looked ever so elegant. Sam stood next to me, his hand resting on my shoulder. Then the man arranged my skirts just so, fussing over every detail. He took my chin in his hand and tilted my head. Then he straightened Sam's coat before he stepped back to look at us.

"Maybe you ought to show off that pistol of yours, son." He took Sam's other hand and rested it gently on the handle of his pistol. "Show off your girl and your weapon," he joked.

"Now keep as still as you can," he directed us. "If you move it won't come out right." He was backing up to position himself behind his camera. "That's it. Just relax your faces and try not to blink your eyes."

He slipped beneath a dark cloth covering the back of the camera, pausing to look at us. "You must stop smiling, ma'am. It will ruin the picture."

I tried to relax the muscles of my face, working to expunge the smile from my lips. That was proving difficult, because I felt such pride and joy in the moment. Here we were, husband and wife, getting our likeness taken so I might carry it as a reminder of our devoted love. When he finished, Sam asked to do another, wanting one for each of us. The man was more than accommodating. It was another penny in his pocket. So we posed for a second picture.

"I will carry it always," I told Sam, admiring it as we left.

"And now to supper," he said.

We ate a fine meal and Sam pointedly ordered pie for dessert. The two of us got a good laugh over it. We cleaned our plates before heading back to the inn.

When morning broke, I burrowed myself deeper into the covers and covered my face with the pillow. I felt a sense of dread overcome me at the thought of having to leave this place. I wished our time together in this town would go on indefinitely. Sam stirred and moved to get out of bed, but I latched on to him and wouldn't let him.

"Time to get moving," he whispered sleepily. I groaned.

"Must we?" I protested.

"If we don't go back, some other poor fellow won't get his furlough," Sam reasoned.

"Let's just stay here in this bed forever," I replied.

"I don't think that is at all realistic, Serena. Beds are only good for so many things. The remainder requires a moving body."

After some coaxing and cajoling he managed to talk me out of bed. Once I dressed, he drifted over to me, caressed my cheek with the palm of his hand, and kissed me tenderly. I reveled in the intimacy of it.

"We will still be together," he said.

"Yes," I replied, suppressing my tears. "We've got each other. That's all that matters, as long as I can be with you."

We packed what little we had and went down to breakfast. Mr. Garth's daughter made biscuits and ham and eggs. I felt sorely troubled that this was our last breakfast before we returned to camp, and although it was good, I found it difficult to eat.

"I wish it didn't have to end," I told Sam as we walked toward the depot.

"Yes, I know. It has been a good few days for us," he said. "But we have our little cabin waiting for us. We can play house together, you and me. It is a much better place than where we were last winter. Remember?"

"That is true," I agreed. "I shudder to think of the wretched cold and discomfort we endured then. Doesn't it seem so long ago? I wonder where we will be in the coming year."

"God willing, together before our own hearth," Sam said. "And the old Derringer place will be called the Barlow place."

We trudged down the walk nearly to the depot now, a light snow descending down upon us, marking our footprints as we walked. We climbed the steps to the train and sat near a window, looking out over the town as we pulled away. The place was so dear to me. I mourned the loss of it as we left it behind. I leaned my head on Sam's shoulder and watched it go by in the blink of an eye.

Chapter 35

When we got back from the depot, I stopped in the same stand of trees to change back into my uniform, stuffing my skirt and blouse and jacket into my haversack. Winter was setting in, and the cold penetrated me all the way through. I found the vigorous walk back to camp kept my circulation going. Our cabin was just as we left it. Sam started a fire in the fireplace, and we waited for the room to warm up.

Mr. Haney came around dinner time with a jug of cider, wishing to know how the trip went. We recounted to him our journey and how we had gotten married. As he left, we gave him *Mrs. Audley's Secret* to read. He leafed through the pages, tucked it under his arm, and then headed out into the cold evening with the sounds of men talking and a banjo playing filtering through the door as he left.

The next morning was business as usual, only now I carried two secrets which I kept close to my heart. I was a woman, and I was Sam's wife. Winter camp was evolving into a grand diversion from the war. Everyone was safe and comfortable in the diminutive town we'd built up on the river bank. And they managed to come up with many exciting activities to keep themselves busy.

In the evenings there were musical numbers, sometimes instrumental, sometimes vocal. Some of the companies formed their own choral groups and took turns putting on performances. On some nights there were dramatic presentations, and a number of men participated in putting on plays. Growing up in Richfield there was no playhouse, no productions, and no such entertainment that I could remember. We sang in church. We read in school. There was a dance or two throughout the year. The arts were sorely lacking.

The poetry readings and play productions were particular favorites of mine. Sam and I attended, sitting apart and aloof from one another, our gazes carefully trained on the performances, barely acknowledging the other who was just a stone's throw away. We watched with rapt attention, and then returned home to discuss them while we intimately lounged in one another's arms, warm and comfortable by the fire.

There were also grand dinners sponsored by General Sedgwick at the mansion, with elaborate menus and dripping in champagne. Sam was invited to one and said it was a rollicking good time. He snuck home some food so I could sample it. I'd never tasted such rich fare. It was better than anything I'd ever eaten. It was not as difficult to get things we liked or needed now that we were so close to the depot. There were numerous vendors who set up temporary shops, making a pretty penny with supply and demand from all of the troops. Sam and I kept our purse strings tied tight. We didn't want to spend on things we didn't need now that we were paying for a house.

Sam and I were not the only ones with love and courtship on our minds. Wives and sweethearts felt safe enough to visit our winter camp, desperate to see the men who'd left them behind. Without a woman in sight for so very long, some of the men forgot themselves. They would hoot and holler as a lady walked by, or say outrageously forward things, making inappropriate and unwanted advances. They targeted respectable women who were already committed to other men, not the camp trollops who were used to and welcomed such attention. It was no way to treat a lady.

Ugly or beautiful, short or tall, thin or round, married or single, they all received the same adoring glances and flirtatious attentions. The men's pandering and wanton advances caused many problems.

"That behavior is very rude and unsuitable. I'm glad you aren't getting their interest," Sam said. "Because I might have to knock a few heads off."

I laughed at him. "We agree. I don't think I would feel safe as a woman in this camp."

Being a boy had its merits, but it was not such a good thing when I wanted something I could only have as a woman. I got wind there was to be a ball, and I could think of nothing else but going. I'd never been to a ball before. And it nearly ate me alive to think I would actually have an escort if only I could go with Sam. Everyone would be there. Everyone.

"I want to go to the ball, Sam," I told him one night when we were warm in bed beneath our blankets.

"Well, of course we will go."

"No, I mean I want to go as me. I want to dance with you, Sam," I explained.

"That's not possible," Sam said.

"Why not?" I complained.

"Someone would recognize you."

"How do you know? Maybe they wouldn't notice me at all."

"Oh, they would notice," he said. "They take note of anyone in a skirt. It's not worth the risk."

"What fun would it be to go as a boy?" I reasoned. "We couldn't dance together."

"I'm sorry. That is true. But it will still be something to see," he consoled.

"If you say so." I couldn't help but sound bitter.

"It isn't my fault," he pointed out.

This only further irritated me. He didn't need to remind me it was my sorry self who put me into my current predicament. If it hadn't been for my deception, I might freely go to the ball and be Serena.

"I'll figure something out," I insisted, unwilling to give it up.

"I'm sure you will," Sam agreed. "So long as no one sees that pretty face in a dress, I am all for it."

He gave me a kiss and then rolled over and fell asleep. I knew he didn't think I would find a way. I was determined he would be sorely mistaken. I figured I would say nothing else on the matter for several different reasons. First of all, I didn't want to ruin the surprise, and second of all, I didn't want to have Sam tell me no. So I went ahead and made my arrangements without him. I told him, as innocently as possible, he should go on ahead of me, and I would meet him there.

On a chilly February night, I got myself dressed up and headed down to the Fifth Corps headquarters. It was just after nine o'clock when I arrived. The doors were open with bright light spilling out and reflecting from the packed snow on the ground. The music could be heard from within, a rollicking tune suitable for a reel. A row of ambulance wagons was lined up in front, and several officers were assisting ladies, dressed in their finest, as they stepped down from the wagons and floated into the dance hall.

This was certainly a sore spot for the head surgeon at division headquarters. He insisted it was not at all ethical to use ambulances to transport women to a dance. He was bypassed, and Sedgwick himself gave his permission for it. It was to be a grand, over the top sort of affair, and nothing was off limits for such a worthy cause, not even the ambulance wagons.

I wandered in and stood at the edge of the crowd, taking the scene in, with my heart skipping nervously in my breast. There were hundreds of men and women crammed into the small space, laughing, drinking champagne, dancing, or in conversation. I scanned the room, looking for Sam's familiar face. When I didn't see him right off, I ventured further into the room.

I was immediately grabbed up by a soldier in parade uniform, who swooped in and spun me out onto the dance floor before I even knew what was happening. I was taken off guard and felt a rush of alarm and confusion. I tried to pull away but he held me fast. He was smiling with a look of determination telling me he was not giving up without a fight.

"What are you doing?" I asked.

"Dancing."

"I know that. I can see that," I replied. "But I don't remember you asking, and I don't recall me agreeing to it."

"Oh, now, let me have some fun, won't you?" he said as though he were a small child, petulant and pleading.

"I shouldn't be dancing with you," I protested.

"Would you rather I dance by myself? Just think of it as your patriotic duty."

I could see he wasn't going to take no for an answer, and so I gave up and finished the set with him. When the next tune started up, he held tight again, as if he might compel me to dance with him the next round, but I put my foot down. I forcefully pulled away from him and put my hand up to stop him when he moved in closer to me and acted as though he wasn't going to let me go.

"You had your dance," I pointed out.

"It wasn't a full dance," he protested.

"It will have to do," I insisted. He acted as though he might argue with me further. I didn't linger to see what he was going to say. I quickly plunged into the crowd and tried to lose myself in it. It took some doing, but I finally discovered Sam near one of the windows, standing with a cup of punch in his hand and looking rather unamused by all of it.

I managed to sidle up next to him and stood silently observing what he was watching. Eventually he turned to me and gave a polite smile and nod. The fact he didn't know it was me gave me a great deal of satisfaction. I gave a nod back, then slipped my gloved hand into his idle one. This certainly surprised him, and he hastily drew his fingers away from mine, jerking so violently he spilled the punch on the front of his coat. He fumbled to wipe it away.

"Pardon me," he said, his face red. I found it humorous he was asking for the pardon of a strange woman he thought was making a pass at him, as though he were somehow the one at fault.

"Sam, it's me," I whispered.

He stopped what he was doing and turned to stare at me. After a moment of his scrutinizing, he grudgingly smiled. I'm sure he wasn't happy I had indeed gotten my way, but what could he do?

"I should make you leave," he told me good naturedly. "But if your own husband don't recognize you, I don't guess anybody else will either."

"I'm glad I have your permission," I teased, because we both knew I didn't need his blessing.

"Where'd you get that get up?"

I looked down at my black dress and black gloves through the gauzy veil attached to the crepe bonnet I wore. The veil was drawn over my face as it would be if I were in deep mourning. I'd borrowed it from an older woman in town, in exchange for some flour and coffee with the promise it would be returned to her tomorrow. Although she'd fallen on hard times, I assumed due to the war, I could tell she was once someone with money, because the dress was of excellent quality made by a worthy seamstress. It was the sort of garment that would cost a pretty penny to have made. Why tell all of the particulars to Sam? I wasn't there to bore him to death; I was there to have fun, like everyone else.

"I have my ways," I said trying to sound mysterious.

"Yes, you have," he agreed with narrowed eyes and a half smile.

"What does a lady have to do to get a dance partner?" I asked.

"It doesn't take much around here," he said. "If you haven't noticed, these men are clamoring for any lady's attentions. I doubt being a widow would deter any of them."

"I have noticed. It took some doing to get away from the short fellow over there," I admitted, calling to his attention the man who grabbed me on my way in.

"You ought to tell them your dance card is filled up. Mark every line with Sampson Barlow's name so everyone knows you belong to me."

A waltz began, and I stretched my hand out for him to take. He accepted it and navigated us through the crowd and to the dance floor. He clasped my hand and fitted his other to the small of my back, and we began to dance. It was as I always thought it would be—heaven. We glided about the floor as if we were floating. He was excellent at leading, and I was not the least bit hampered by my veil.

"What an excellent pair we make," I observed.

"I thought you said you'd never been to a dance before," he accused.

"I haven't. It didn't stop me from learning to dance. I have to say it is much more enjoyable to have a male partner though."

"I'm glad you approve."

"Oh, I do."

When we finished the dance, another gentleman swooped in and tried to take me away. Sam would not let go of me. He smiled charmingly but was shaking his head no. I felt wanted. There was something inside of me which thrilled at the notion of another man desiring me. I was glad Sam knew how I felt when I saw him getting the attention of other women. I realized, with a hint of remorse, I wanted him to be jealous.

"I'm afraid she can't dance with you, sir. She is, after all, a widow. And that would be unseemly," Sam told him.

"Well, you've just had a dance with her," the man protested.

"That is true, I suppose, but she did it against her will. I've managed to single-handedly ruin her reputation, something I feel truly awful for. I will tell you it's not the sort of thing you want on your conscience."

Without waiting a beat, Sam led me back into another dance, leaving the poor man to look somewhat stunned at the edge of the crowd. Beneath my veil I was laughing. This was a side I had never seen of Sam. He was downright possessive and I loved it.

"I think I like being so desired," I told Sam. "I've never had men fighting over me. But the veil perhaps gives me an advantage."

"You're lucky you have that on. They might be a little more insistent if they knew what you actually looked like."

"How terribly sweet of you."

The next set was a reel. I was twirled down the line and back, until I cycled through partners several times and ended up back in Sam's arms again. Throughout the night I danced with him, watching as he fended off other men who approached for a dance. At one point a superior officer requested my hand. You did not say no to a superior. It was just not done! The repercussions could be severe. I grudgingly took my hand from Sam's and thought to allow him the dance. I didn't want any trouble. Now, Sam had no right to refuse him, but he did anyhow. I was not only astonished but a little frightened too.

"I'm sorry, sir. I cannot allow it," Sam said with a determinedly grim frown.

"Excuse me?" Oh, the superior officer was good and mad at Sam's impertinence. It was apparent he wasn't used to being told no.

Sam managed to seem sufficiently chastened. "I'm sorry, sir. I do not mean any disrespect, but I feel it would be unsuitable for my sister to dance with anyone but me. She is after all a widow, and I promised my parents I would look after her and see she is well cared for."

For a moment I thought it might come to blows. The tension between the two men was palpable, and I could sense we had become the center of attention. Many of the other men were watching us, waiting for a show. The officer was greatly put out, but how could he argue with Sam's gallant gesture? After all, who could fault Sam for looking out for his sister's interests? With veins bulging, eyes narrowed, and jaw set firmly, the officer reluctantly conceded. He bowed to me before he turned and stalked off. I was relieved it hadn't escalated any further, thinking not only that he and Sam might have gotten into a fight, but also that my true identity could have been revealed because of my stupidity in coming to the dance.

"I would have felt terrible if you'd gotten into trouble because of me. This may've been a very selfish thing for me to do, insisting on coming to this dance. I'm sorry."

"It would've been worth a court martial to dance with you all night."

"I am being serious," I insisted. "I don't want to cause trouble for you."

"I think it's probably far too late for that," he said with a smile.

The remainder of the night Sam and I danced together, until it was dinner time. The clock chimed one o'clock in the morning, and the crowd that had grown boisterous and loud with the champagne now ceased dancing. The lot of them filed into the dining area, laughing and fighting good-naturedly over who should sit next to the ladies. Sam led me over to the door.

"Wait here a moment," he spoke softly to me. I could feel the energy between us, the playful banter with more behind it. There was a subtle draw connecting the two of us. I felt the need to be touched, to draw closer to him just as he was pulling away. I could sense his reluctance to leave me too. Our parting was prolonged and sweetly drawn out as he disentangled his hand from mine and backed away. I was hoping that the officer Sam slighted wasn't watching, because it must be completely apparent to everyone in the room we were not sister and brother, we were lovers.

I lingered idle as he disappeared for a time. He returned with a plate loaded with roasted potatoes and carrots, beef covered in gravy, and two fat dinner rolls. I stood at attention when I saw him approaching, pushing myself away from the wall I was reclined against to welcome him back.

"What a night," he said with a mischievous grin when he returned.

"Yes, some night."

"Why don't we slip off to someplace more private," he suggested.

"I'm all for it," I agreed. He took the plate of food in one hand and my arm in his other and slipped out into the night, leaving the dance behind.

Chapter 36

Several weeks later, the 121st was called in as support for a raid on Charlottesville. The raid was led by General George Custer's cavalry, the objective being to burn the bridge which spanned the Rivanna River. This assault was in connection with another raid upon Richmond taking place concurrently.

"We are just the diversion again," Vern Stapleton complained.

"It serves its purpose," Reed Haney pointed out.

"What purpose? Put all of us in harm's way to free a few men from prison," Darby said.

"It would be a better thing to die free, than to die slow and terrible, rotting away in one of their prisons," Sam said.

"We may do just that," Darby replied. "I do believe this cursed weather has it out for us."

It was true that the weather was terrible. It rained and then snowed, and while we were cold to the bone from the rain and snow, the wind would not let up on us. With no tents for protection, we took to huddling in groups with our faces turned in to the circle and our backs to the storm, like a bunch of cows. We slept in the open, none really able to rest because of the discomfort of it.

"I heard tell five from our regiment have died in those hellhole prisons in one month's time," Felix informed us. "Read it in the *Courier*."

"The name Andersonville strikes fear into the heart of anyone who knows anything about it. Those Rebs treat animals better than they do men," Sam said contemptuously.

"Oh, it is bitter cold," Darby grumbled, blowing into his fists.

"This is what it means to be out in the field." Sam chuckled.

"God willing it is a short excursion," I added. "I am missing the warmth of our cabin something terrible."

There was little to console us. The warmth of our cooking fires was not more than a breath of heat to temporarily warm our hands with. I tried to keep my complaints to myself, because I knew Sam was troubled by my discomfort. Not that he hadn't been sympathetic before, but now that he knew I was a woman, he took my deprivations very personal.

Two days into the march, our goal was achieved. Our regiment hung back near a small town called Madison, ready to support Custer and his men if they should have need of us. As it turned out, we again were not involved in any of the fighting. General Custer's Calvary attacked a camp in Carrsbrook, and a scuffle ensued.

They set fire to the camp and took what they could get their hands on. In a comical twist, one of the small cannons, heated in the fire our men had set, blew up. Custer and his Calvary mistook it for artillery fire from the enemy. Confusion set in and the Union troops began firing on one another. In the panic and mayhem, General Custer called retreat.

Luckily there were only a few wounded, but it was an embarrassment to Custer who called retreat when there was no enemy resistance at all. That was the end of our brief foray into Charlottesville. With relief we collectively headed back to winter camp.

We struggled through the snow, worn out and bitter cold. It took a great deal of effort to lift our feet above the drifts to walk. Our food was frozen, so we ate very little. The wind beat against our faces and stole the breath from our lungs. Men began to fall out along the way, unable to continue. Sam would not let me do the same. He pulled me along. At times our progress was painfully slow, but we didn't stop.

Sam said, "We're that much closer. If you keep going we'll be in a warm bed with a fire on the hearth in no time."

Soon we were safe and sound in our small village at Hazel River again. The whole outing lasted a matter of four days total, yet it seemed much longer. Due to the cold and exposure to the elements, a great number of us fell ill upon our return.

Chapter 37

Some things are too perfect to share. Sometimes it is the sharing that makes them commonplace and ordinary. There are moments that grow more marvelous in the secret places of your mind. With each recollection, the details become more meaningful, more significant, until it becomes a treasure which sustains you through the worst of times, the thing that keeps you going with the promise of better times to come.

That is what that winter was for me.

When you put your eye to a kaleidoscope and twist, you see the brilliant colors and patterns cycle themselves through, never remaining the same for very long. A flash of beauty lasts for a heartbeat and then is gone, transforming to another scene entirely. You are left to wonder over the metamorphosis and how it is possible it could happen so quickly, so absolutely.

Our existence upon this Earth is much the same. As a youth, you spend your days longing to be grown up, to have a trade, and a lover, and then children, and a will of your own. You long to be taken seriously, to say important things and do great deeds. You wish to make your mark upon this place. You want to skip over the painful learning moments and move past them to miraculously already possess the knowledge and self-awareness gleaned from such experiences. You have a deep desire, a sincere longing to speed time up, to make it work to your advantage.

Perhaps we are granted our wish. Because it seems days and weeks and months do indeed accelerate as you become older. The spinning wheel of time picks up velocity until you scarcely know where it has gone, and you seek to slow it, but there is no stopping a downhill descent. Suddenly you are old and used and all in the twist of the kaleidoscope. Then pain becomes desirable, because it means that you are still alive, and the desire to have the innocence of youth once again is a longing that leaves you aching and wanting and hollow inside.

There is remorse too, for what could have been. I should have been a painter or poet or doctor. I should have married another. I should have been a better husband or wife to the one I did marry. I should have held my babies tighter, for they weren't babies very long. I never said anything important or did great deeds as I thought I would. It is over and I have nothing to show for it. Give me more time! Slow the clock!

Sam and I had those four months as husband and wife to relish and indulge in. We had those few months in the cabin we built at winter camp on the banks of the Hazel River before the spring came, and the army could not stay put. During the warm months, the Union and the Confederates sized one another up, and then began a wrestling match which wore one another down and made each so tired they left the match in a truce, until they could rest for a time and recuperate. And then it was to the wrestling match once more to see whose will was greater, to fight to exhaustion all over again.

As the weather grew warmer near the end of April, I could sense the change, but did my best to disregard it. I didn't want to admit the fighting season was coming around again. We would be on the move, and with the constant threat of an impending battle. Still, I felt Sam was mine, and if we were together I could endure anything! Anything!

One morning Sam woke early and stoked the fire and made coffee. I could hear him moving about, but I wasn't ready to get up myself just yet. I was tired, a weariness that seemed to penetrate my whole body, making my arms and legs feel heavy and weak. He tapped my shoulder and held a mug out for me to take. I moaned as I rolled over and took the coffee from him.

"What's gotten in to you?" he asked.

I pulled myself up and took a sip. "I don't know," I answered. "My head aches, and I just want to sleep and sleep."

"I wish you could," he sympathized.

I finished the coffee before I got up and dressed. We headed out together for drill, but I didn't get very far before I suddenly felt sick, my stomach clenched and then unclenched and my knees went liquid. I knew I would vomit. I ran haphazardly to a bush and heaved my breakfast into it. I was ashamed as I wiped my mouth, my eyes watering, my nose dripping.

"Are you all right?" Sam asked.

"I knew I didn't feel well. I should've stayed in bed," I said weakly.

"There are a lot of men coming down with the shakes," he said.

"I don't want to be sick," I lamented.

"You should go back to the cabin and rest. I'll tell them you are unwell."

I stumbled back to the cabin and threw myself across the bed, falling into a deep sleep. When I was roused again it was nearly noon. I heard Sam come through the door and managed to force my eyes open.

"How are you?" he asked.

"I can scarce lift my head. All of my energy has left me," I told him.

"I brought you something to eat," he said.

I pulled myself up to a sitting position and took the biscuit and jerky from him. He sat in one of the chairs at the table and pulled his boots off, stretching himself out. I ate what he gave me and then lay down again, watching him as he watched me.

"Reed Haney says there are seventeen men out sick."

"Well, I can't go to the hospital, so I must endure it," I told him. "You should go away. I don't want you to see me this way, and I don't want you to get what I've got."

"I've already seen you this way," he pointed out.

"What do you mean?"

"Antietam."

"That's right. I completely humiliated myself didn't I? Well, I'm glad you remembered."

"I was just trying to say there's nothing you could do that would make me like you less."

"Oh, dear!" I rolled off of the bed and made for the door, vomiting all of my lunch onto the ground just past our doorstep.

Sam pulled his boots back on. "Come lay down. I'll get some water and wash it away."

"I'm sorry," I apologized feebly. But I was too weak to do much more than obey him.

The sickness persisted, to the point I could not keep anything down, not even water. My head ached with an intense throbbing that made me think my brain might be ready to explode. Several days into it, I felt as though I were on death's door. I could do nothing but lie in misery. I felt as though I might cry but there were no tears for it. Sam rarely left my side, eagerly bringing me a drink, or rubbing my back to bring me comfort. He hovered over me, tucking the blankets in close, wanting to meet my every need, with an intensely concerned expression on his face.

"I think you may need to have a doctor look at you," Sam said. He wouldn't suggest such a thing unless he was truly worried.

"No," I insisted. "That is out of the question."

"You haven't eaten in days and days."

"I've eaten," I told him.

"What have you eaten?" he asked skeptically.

"Remember the pastries."

"What pastries?" he asked.

"The pastries…"

"You haven't had pastries in at least two years, Serena. What are you talking about?"

"I don't know." My mind was cloudy. I couldn't think. Everything seemed to go round and round in my head. I tried to lick my parched lips, but my tongue felt dry and fuzzy. He was ruminating in the corner, watching me closely. He began to rub his fingers over his jaw and chin gruffly, and then he sprang from his chair and came to sit on the edge of the bed.

"I don't care what happens, I am taking you to the hospital," he said. He was trying to sound determined but his voice shook slightly. "Can you get yourself dressed?"

"Yes, yes I can do that," I said. I tried to move, but had no strength to do so. I just lay there.

"It's all right, I've got you." Sam wrapped me in a blanket and picked me up, holding me in his arms pressed against his chest. "I've got you."

"Wait. Please wait. Evelyn…Evelyn Rogers," I croaked.

"What is it?" Sam asked tenderly.

"She…she is a nurse. She will help me," I said. "Send for Evelyn Rogers."

Chapter 38

The light from the candle seemed harsh, and I blinked rapidly, trying to grow accustomed to it. I was vaguely aware of the two of them whispering urgently. Mr. Haney and Sam wore the same expression, their brows furrowed, their mouths drawn down in a frown. Their concern was evident.

"I can't leave her," Sam said. His arms were straight with his fists buried deep in his pockets. "If you can go to the hospital and try to find this Evelyn Rogers…"

"Certainly, certainly," Mr. Haney agreed.

"If you can bring her back here, Serena says she will help."

I heard Reed leave sometime thereafter, closing the door softly behind him. I stirred, trying to reach my hand out.

"Sam," I called. My voice sounded strange even to my own ears, as if my tongue were too large for the hollow space of my mouth.

Sam rushed to my side and bent down next to me. "I'm here," he said. "What do you need, dearest?"

"It must be very bad. You've never called me dearest before," I said, trying to laugh. But it didn't come out as I planned. It was more like a dry wheeze. "Was that Mr. Haney?"

"Yes. How are you feeling?"

"Fine. I'm fine."

"Would you like a drink?"

"I don't think I can keep it down," I confessed. I didn't want to waste time talking to him about how I felt. "My father…" I began.

"Yes."

"I don't want him to ever know. You must see to it, Sam."

"Reed is going to get Miss Rogers. She will know what to do," he said confidently. Was it a little too confident? Did I detect a moment of self-doubt in his overly certain words?

"I'm dying, aren't I?"

"I won't let that happen," he replied, stroking my hair. "Everything will be all right."

"I am in such misery, I don't think it would be so bad to die," I said.

"You're talking nonsense," Sam scolded.

"If I die, please, Sam, please do not let my father know the truth. Please promise."

"Shhh. It will be all right."

I feebly raised my hand and rested it on his cheek. "Promise me."

His eyes reluctantly met mine. "I promise."

There was a knock at the door, and Sam got up to open it. Mr. Haney returned with Evelyn Rogers in tow. He ushered both of them in to the small space, pressing himself against the wall to make room for them. I could hear them whispering again.

Mr. Haney said, "If you need anything, you'll let me know?"

"Yes, Reed. I thank you for your help," Sam said.

Mr. Haney left again. Sam shut the door behind him and then turned and approached Evelyn Rogers. She was just as I remembered her. Her dark hair was done in a long braid. She looked more rested than the last time I saw her, and her apron was clean and freshly starched now. Evelyn knelt next to the bed and smiled kindly at me.

"You again," she said.

"She didn't want to risk going to the hospital," Sam told her. "She told me to send for you. She said you knew her secret and would help."

"What seems to be the trouble?" she asked, her voice offhand and casual.

"She is very ill. I've heard some of the other men have fallen sick too."

Evelyn turned toward Sam and nodded her head up and down. "Yes, we've had quite a few. It's kept us busy." She turned back to me and asked, "Can you tell me what your symptoms are?"

"My head aches." I put my hand over my forehead and then let it slide away. "And I can't keep anything down," I croaked.

Evelyn touched the back of her hand to my brow. "She doesn't seem to have a fever," she remarked. "What are her other symptoms?"

"She is complaining of feeling weak and tired. She can't seem to keep even water down," Sam told her. "And she was talking nonsense."

"The other men who are sick," Evelyn said, "they all seem to be suffering from the ague, the chills, and fever. I don't know if this is the same."

"Can you help her?" Sam asked a little too desperately.

"I think you are dehydrated," she told me. "Your lips are dry, and if you can't keep anything down, you're probably in need of fluids." She turned to Sam. "Could you get her some water?"

"Certainly, but she throws it up when I give it to her," Sam said. He took the tin mug from the table and handed it to her.

"Don't take a big drink, just a small sip, no more than a spoonful. Can you do that for me?" Evelyn coaxed.

She held my head up and put the cup to my mouth. I took a sip, and then she pulled the cup away before I could take any more. I lay back on the pillow, rolling the small bit of water over my tongue and around my mouth before I swallowed. Evelyn reached over and handed the cup back to Sam.

"We will wait a short while, see if she keeps it down and then try another sip." She told him. Sam nodded, dutifully holding the cup in his hands.

"Thank you," I murmured.

"How long have you been sick like this?"

"At least a week," I told her. "Although it feels longer. I have never been so sick before. My stomach feels as though it were bruised." She was shaking her head sympathetically, patting my hand as if to console me. She waited a moment before she spoke.

"Now I must ask something," she said. I sensed her reluctance to broach the subject, although I was sure she'd seen much and must be used to uncomfortable situations in her work as a nurse. "I don't want to pry, so please don't take offense, but I must know what your arrangement is here."

"What do you mean?" Sam asked.

"Your living arrangement," she specified.

"This is our cabin," Sam replied as if it should be evident enough without him saying it. But I understood right away what she was getting at.

"We are husband and wife," I answered.

"I see," Evelyn said. "How long have you been married?"

"Three and a half months," Sam informed her.

"I don't mean to be indelicate," Evelyn said. "You must understand I only want to help. Please take no offense. But it seems to me, well, it may not be something communicable." She laughed nervously. "At least not in the sense that it is contagious, I mean. What I'm trying to say, what I'm wondering is, if it's possible you're with child?"

The question lingered in the silence that followed. Sam's and my eyes, wide and in shock, instantly fastened on one another. I considered it for a moment and then shook my head no.

"I don't think so."

"Are you certain?" she asked. "Because I believe you may have the morning sickness."

"It's not in the mornings," Sam piped up. "She's sick all the day long."

"Well, that's more often the case than not," she replied. "Many women aren't sick only in the mornings. Some of the worst cases, a woman can become very sick and it lasts all day," she explained.

"Maybe it's something I ate," I offered.

"If it was something you ate, you'd likely be over it by now. Food illnesses usually clear themselves up within a day or two," she said.

"How would we know for sure?" Sam asked.

"There is no way of knowing right away." She cleared her throat as though she were uncomfortable with the topic of conversation with Sam there. "First off, you miss your term. The sickness is another way. Your breasts may hurt. Then, of course, your belly will begin to grow big and you will feel a stirring. It's difficult to say. It is different for everyone."

Evelyn busied herself by giving me another swallow of water. I didn't say anything and neither did Sam. It was awkward with Evelyn there. This was not something you spoke of in mixed company. I shifted uncomfortably. Sam sat down heavily in a chair. He lowered his eyes, his expression thoughtful. What must he be thinking? How awkward for him to be talking about all of this with some strange woman present. I was not too sick to feel sorry for him.

"I will get some ginger root. If you boil it in water and then drink it like tea, it should help settle your stomach. If it is the morning sickness, the best thing to do is eat just a little throughout the day, keep something in your stomach so it's never empty."

"Thank you," I said.

Evelyn looked to Sam again. "Just keep giving her a little sip, until she seems to be keeping it down. Then give her a few bites of bread or biscuit until she can keep it down. Once you've got that mastered, she should be all right. If she vomits you'll have to start all over again, giving her little sips and working her up to drinking a full cup."

"I will," Sam promised.

Evelyn got up as if she might leave. I grabbed her hand to stop her. "This is between us?" My voice sounded pathetically desperate.

She nodded her head up and down. "I won't tell anyone," she assured me. "But you won't be able to hide it for long if that's what it is. I will bring the ginger root around. It ought to help."

"Thank you," I said again.

Sam stood up and walked her to the door. He stepped outside with her for a minute, pushing the door nearly shut behind him so I couldn't hear what was being said. When he came back he was intensely quiet. He sat down again with the tin cup in his hand, leaning forward in the chair with his arms resting on his legs, his head slightly bowed. He was looking at me as though I were some strange new novelty. I grew uncomfortable.

"What are you thinking?" I spoke in a low voice because it seemed somehow wrong to break the silence.

"Do you think it's true?"

"How should I know?" I said in frustration.

"Well, how do you feel?"

"Like hell."

"You know what I mean," he replied plaintively.

"I don't know. I feel sick. I feel tired. I feel terrified," I said. "I feel terrified…"

He sat the mug down on the table and came to me, lay down next to me on the bed, and held me close in his arms, his chin resting on the top of my head.

Chapter 39

It seemed strange to think there was possibly a life growing within me, a life I could not yet even detect. Evelyn's ginger tea soothed my sickness, as did keeping something in my stomach and never letting it be empty. Sam was very sober all the time now. He followed me around feeding me a steady supply of hardtack, whether I wanted it or not. I could not look at the stuff before I ate it, because if I saw the maggots it made me immediately nauseous. There were still moments when I was ill, but my discomfort greatly improved when I followed Evelyn's recommendations.

"You must stop coddling me. They will suspect something if you keep acting this way," I complained again and again. "I am not some pet project. I can take care of myself." But it did no good. He was too careful with me, too considerate, and it set my nerves on edge.

His particularly thoughtful manner made me wonder what he was thinking, what he wanted to say but wouldn't. I wished I had the courage to ask him. But there are times when you know what needs to be said is something you aren't strong enough to hear, and so you don't ask, and hope they won't tell.

At night he would prop himself up on his elbow with his other hand on my belly, his fingers splayed, his palm cupping my abdomen while he studied me as though he might see some physical change that would give him a clue as to what was happening within. This great mystery kept us both enthralled, but he more so than me.

"What is it like?" he asked.

"I don't feel any different, other than the sickness part of it," I answered. "I wonder if it isn't true. Shouldn't I feel *something?*" I wished there was some significant and profound thing to say about it, but I couldn't think of any.

"I think I would like a son," he declared one night.

"What if it is a daughter?"

He smiled with a little laugh. "I think I would like that too."

"I can't go wrong then, because if there is a child, it is positively one of the two."

"If it's a girl you can call it whatever you'd like," he said. "So long as I can name a boy Luke. I have always liked the name Luke. I have always thought someday I should have a son with the name."

"That is a good name—Luke. And if it is a girl, I may name it?"

"Yes," he agreed.

"I like the name Augusta."

"What?" He was unpleasantly surprised by my choice.

"You don't like it?"

"I picture a large old woman with a number of hairy moles on her face and a set of substantial wooden teeth." He bundled his fingers and tapped his thumb to them. "Chomp, chomp."

"You don't like it?" I was offended.

"Not one bit," he said with a sour face.

"But I liked Luke," I complained, as if my liking his name should automatically ensure his liking mine as well.

"Well, yes of course you did, because Luke is a good solid name. A very fine name."

"And Augusta is not?"

"It won't work unless we have a very ugly girl. And you know as well as I do you and I could not produce a very ugly girl."

"Well, I am outraged!" I cried. "You just got through telling me I could pick the name, and now you are telling me I can't?"

"Be true with me, were you completely serious about that name?"

"*Yes!*" I said, shoving his elbow out from under him so he collapsed onto the bed.

"I'm sorry," he apologized through laughter. "Really I am. But I must intercede on behalf of the child."

"Maybe I don't like Luke then," I said in a huff.

"Yes, you do," he said with a self-assured grin.

"You really are insufferable," I grumbled.

"In a charming sort of way."

I shrugged. "In a charming sort of way," I agreed. "Although I am reluctant to admit it, because I don't believe your ego needs any stroking."

"You are, as always, very perceptive."

"Yes, well, women's intuition and all that sort of thing," I said with a roll of my eyes. I waited a moment before I said, "You realize I may not be having a baby at all. It may just be some strange stomach disorder."

He gave me a winning smile, with a look to tell me he thought I was completely wrong. He didn't argue, though. He just shrugged. "Time will tell," he said knowingly. Then he put his hand back to my belly and resumed staring at my flat stomach. "In the meantime, be careful what you say. He may hear you."

Chapter 40

The end of April was a time of great changes, not only for Sam and I, who were apparently to become proud parents in the near future, but also for General Grant, who was now the proud parent of the whole Union army. The shift in management was not to end there. Upton was given a new command of the 2nd Brigade, and Olcott was now to command the 121st. We also received good news when Olcott gave Sam another promotion, this time to First Lieutenant. He received an increase in pay effective immediately.

"What do you think of your husband now?" he asked with child-like glee when he informed me of it.

We drilled and exercised on a daily basis for much of the day now with the warmer weather. We were very envied for our abilities, the pride of our superiors. All of this was in preparation for the summer months and the battles to come. They had us in fighting condition, ready at a moment's notice. We need only receive word.

Our first indication things would be happening soon was when one of the Carroll brothers told us all about the news he just heard circulating among uppers, after he came back from Brandy Station with a fish for his dinner.

"General Grant has given directions that all visitors, particularly women, should leave camp," he said in an excited fluster. I still never could figure which brother was which, if he was the elder or the younger. Then I thought perhaps he was the younger because it seemed to me older siblings were always the more sober. He must be Alden.

"When?" Sam asked.

"Right away, without delay," he replied eagerly.

I saw Sam and Reed Haney exchange a significant glance. This did not escape my attention, nor did it make me happy. I knew the two of them were probably plotting behind my back. The next day the depot was flooded with departing friends and relatives. The scene was mostly one of controlled chaos. Women wept openly and held their men close, whether it be son or brother or more often than not, lover. The lingering good-byes lasted until just moments before the train pulled away from Brandy Station.

The camp was eerily silent in the days to follow. The grand party was over. The mood which was once festive and cheerful was now somber and sedated. Our visitors took all that was merry with them, and in their absence, the grim months ahead loomed dark and foreboding. I did my best not to think too much on it because I didn't like to speculate about what was to come.

Then in the late night hours of the third of May word came down. I hardly saw my husband that day. He was indisposed from early in the morning until very late at night. Sam came home after a meeting with Upton, Olcott, Sedgewick and others looking not only tired, as was to be expected, but downright wretched. I imagine they had been discussing dissolving winter camp and striking out to look for Lee. I knew time was running out for us. He always did his best not to disturb me if I was sleeping when he came home, but that night he shook my shoulder gently until I was roused. I sat up in the bed, knowing from the troubled look on his face something was the matter.

"Serena..." he began in a hushed tone.

He drew me close as he sat on the edge of the bed, resting his lips upon my forehead. And then he did something that alarmed me. His body shuddered and he let out a sob. I pulled away so I could look at him. Sam was grappling with his emotions, doing his best to get control of himself, but his eyes betrayed his torment.

"What's the matter, Sam?" I asked softly. I'd rarely seen a man cry, and not only did I feel uncomfortable but almost panicked by it. Sam wasn't an overly emotional person. It took a great deal to rile him to any extreme. So I knew he was very troubled.

He swallowed a few times, paused to try to get himself under control, and then he took my face in his hands and kissed my forehead again. "I can't do this anymore," he told me.

Now this could have been taken in several ways. My initial interpretation was to believe he had decided he didn't want me, that he'd discovered being married wasn't for him, and having me and a soon-to-be baby was too much responsibility. Playing house was not fun for him anymore. My stomach plummeted, my eyes widened, and I thought I might become hysterical.

"What do you mean?" I choked out.

"I can't go on like this. You must go home," he said.

Although I was somewhat relieved he was not remorseful he had taken me as a wife, I was sick anew over his revelation. He was going to try to convince me to go home again. After all of my refusals he would still not give it up. I dropped my eyes and tried to pull away from his hands.

"Why do you make this so difficult for me?" I complained.

He held my face firmly in his hands. "I can't stand the thought of something happening to you. Can't you understand?"

"Nothing will happen," I insisted.

"We both know you can't say that with any certainty. You are deceiving yourself if you think otherwise, Serena. You will do as you want, you always have, but I wish you would listen to me for once."

"I do listen to you, Sam," I cried.

"I can't bear the thought of you getting hurt, or worse, getting killed. I think of nothing but you, and it makes me weak. It makes me vulnerable. I can't do what I need to do when I'm sick with worry over you. Do you understand? Do you care nothing for what this is doing to me?"

I didn't have anything to say. What could I say? How could I argue with him? He had my best interests at heart, and it may not be what I wanted, but I couldn't simply dismiss his wish when I knew his point was valid. Even though I knew this, knew what he was saying was true, I couldn't bring myself to say it aloud. I couldn't say, *You're right, Sam. I should go home. I should let you wash your hands of me. I should burden you no more.*

"You want to get rid of me," I accused, doing my best not to cry.

"No."

"You think I am a burden and you want to get rid of me," I wailed.

He was shaking his head. "No!" he insisted. "You know that's not true. You know it isn't."

"You don't want me anymore," I said, pushing him away. He drew me into his arms and held me fast as I fought against him.

"You've grown tired of me."

"Serena, stop saying such things. I love you—"

"You want to send me away!"

"—adore you," he continued.

I burst out into tears, throwing my hands up and covering my eyes. He tried to pull them away, but I pressed them harder against my eyeballs, until they ached under the pressure.

"Serena…"

"Why do you want to hurt me?" I asked. "Why do you want to *hurt* me?"

He waited until I cried myself out, holding me tight the entire time. Finally after a long quiet moment he said, "I don't want to hurt you."

"It would kill me to have to leave you," I whispered.

"It would kill me if something happened to you or our baby," he replied. "Call it my foolish pride if you'd like, but I would like to think I'm a man who can take care of his wife, protect her, keep her safe, and provide for her. I want you to have a good life, Serena. And this is not a good life."

I shook my head vehemently.

"It is time," he said. "It is time…"

"I never would have done any of this if it wasn't for you, Sam, because I loved you, because I wanted to be near you. I would endure any manner of affliction to be with you."

"Well, I can't do it anymore. I can't be in constant fear of something happening to you. It is a painful distraction. I am eaten up with worry over your welfare. Why can't you understand?"

"Please…" I began to beg. "Please don't send me away."

"There's more to it than just you and me now," he said. "It's not just my love for you, Serena. It's my love for the child, too. There's that to think about. If anything happens to you it happens to him too. Do you want such a thing on your conscience?" He paused for a moment. "We already made our choices. Now there is nothing left to do but live with them."

How could I argue? With nothing to say, I remained silent. I began to cry again, and he continued to hold me. My world was crumbling to pieces, and I knew inevitably I would have to go home. He was right, no matter how I fought it. He was right, and I would have to leave. But in the moment I hated him for being right. I hated him for being the voice of reason.

Chapter 41

The depot was teaming with last minute travelers, eager to abandon the place before the army pulled out. I packed hastily before leaving our cabin, waiting until the last possible minute out of dread. I donned my wedding dress and put on my shoes before reluctantly shutting the door behind me for good. I clutched my bag to me in nervous dread for the journey ahead, trying to keep pace with Sam. He held my arm firmly as we navigated past the throngs of people, picking his way toward the front of the car, where I would board. Finally he pulled me aside so he might say his farewell.

"I want you to take this," he said, pulling all of the cash from his pocket.

"I have my pay, Sam. Keep it in case you need it."

He thrust it forward again. "I kept a little for myself. You take this," he persisted. I knew he wouldn't take no for an answer. I reluctantly accepted it and tucked it into my bag. "You will need it to get started back home."

I nodded gravely.

"I know you can handle yourself," he continued, "But you have the pistol in case. If there should be any trouble, you don't hesitate to use it, hear?"

"I won't," I assured him in an empty voice.

"When you get back to Richfield, you have the farm. I know your father will help, and so will mine. My father, my brothers, they can get you on your feet, help with the work."

"It will be fine, Sam," I said.

"I hate to have you go without a chaperone, but you'll be careful won't you?" Again I nodded my head yes. "You'll take care?"

"Yes, Sam."

"I don't have much time now. They will be leaving soon."

"I know. You must go."

"I love you. Oh, how I love you. It is so hard to say good-bye. But we must pray we will be reunited soon. You must pray for your husband, that God will preserve him. Pray he will see to it that we may be together again," Sam said emotionally.

I told myself I wouldn't cry, but his words touched me so. I felt my chest constrict and the tears warm and wet upon my cheeks. "Sam," I howled.

"You mustn't cry," he said, wiping the tears away with his thumbs. "You have always been a brave girl. And you must be one now too."

"When I think of leaving you…when I think I will not have you with me, I feel so desperate, so empty. How will I endure without you?"

"What a silly question. You are a survivor, Serena. No matter what happens to me, you will go on. And you listen — now, you see to it you take good care of our child. You see to it he's well until I should see him for myself. Do you hear?"

"I will," I cried.

"It can't last forever. And I will be coming home to you."

I wrapped myself around his waist, determined I would never let him go. He returned my embrace for a time and then he kissed me before he pulled away. "I must go now," he said.

I knew we were being indecent, but the thought that I might never see him again made me frantic. I drew near and kissed him again, long and lingering.

"I love you so," I told him, and then put my lips to his in desperation, thinking I must memorize the way he smelled, the way he tasted, how it felt to be held in his arms. "You are everything to me. Swear you will come back to me! Swear it, Sampson Barlow!"

"I will do all I can," he pledged.

"Swear it!" I begged.

He put his hand over his heart. "I swear it."

One last kiss. "I love you," I sobbed.

"I love you," he vowed. He backed away from me with a look of longing, and then he turned around and was swallowed up in the crowd. I stood there on the platform unable to hide my despair. It occurred to me others around me witnessed us kissing, and were now watching me cry. It was shameful, and yet, I could not control it.

Finally I drew myself up, resolved to be strong. I clutched my bag to my chest and climbed up the stairs. Sitting next to a window, I watched the other people scurrying to and fro upon the platform. The train whistle blew, and a short while later it pulled away from the station. I began to cry anew, knowing I was leaving Sam behind and I didn't know when or if I would see him again. I felt the loss penetrate my heart and was sure it was broken into a million pieces. I wondered if I would ever be whole again.

THE END

Teaser for Upcoming Sequel: The Emancipator

...He acted as though he might get up to leave, but paused with his case in his hand, leaning forward in his chair as though he wanted to share something with me, some juicy bit of gossip that required delicacy.

"Was there something else?" I inquired.

"I am just curious," he admitted. "I must know—what happened? I mean after you left Sam, what became of him? Of you?"

"I went home and Sam went to Libby Prison."

He was astonished. His eyes grew wide, and his mouth fell open as though he were in shock.

"Libby Prison?" he gasped.

Who had not heard of the infamous Libby Prison? The name was said as a hiss, an expletive. It was a dirty, foul place where men went to waste away and die terrible, agonizing deaths.

"Please," he implored, "tell me what happened."

Acknowledgments

Thank you to CJ Creel, my amazing editor; Michelle Glad, my sounding board and greatest support; the staff at Omnific Publishing; and my beloved family, who make it all possible.

About the Author

Tracy Winegar enjoys cooking and gardening in her free time. She loves all things vintage and considers several family heirlooms to be her prized possessions. She's also always on the lookout to score pieces to add to her growing Jadeite collection.

Tracy lives with her husband Benjamin and four beautiful children in the Treasure Valley area of Idaho. Born and raised in the Midwest, her philosophies of life, love, and family are deeply anchored in those small town Indiana roots.

www.ingramcontent.com/pod-product-compliance
Lightning Source LLC
Chambersburg PA
CBHW020511120726
47904CB00003B/786